An Uninvited Visitor ...

As she approached the old house, she looked at it dispassionately. In the winter dark, it was still lovely, strong and square. The few lights that she had left on were glowing gold. Meg pulled around to the side near the barn, turned off the engine, and slumped in her seat, unable to move. She was tired. No, worse, she was tired and depressed. She had tried to do the right thing, had talked to the state police, had told the truth, but no one had wanted to listen. So she had stood up in public and made her case, but it still looked like no one wanted to believe her. She was the outsider, and the community would close ranks against her. *All right, Meg. You can't sit here all night.* She smiled wryly at the image of someone coming by and finding her frozen corpse still sitting in the car.

She hauled herself out of the car and walked toward the kitchen door, jiggling her keys in her hand. Then she stopped: even in the dim light, it was clear that the storm door hung slightly askew, the lock splintered in the jamb. Someone had broken into her house; someone might still be there. She fumbled in her bag for her cell phone and punched in 911.

One Bad Apple

Sheila Connolly

BERKLEY PRIME CRIME, NEW YORK

THE BERKLEY PUBLISHING GROUP
Published by the Penguin Group
Penguin Group (USA) Inc.
375 Hudson Street, New York, New York 10014, USA

Penguin Group (Canada), 90 Eglinton Avenue East, Suite 700, Toronto, Ontario M4P 2Y3, Canada
(a division of Pearson Penguin Canada Inc.)
Penguin Books Ltd., 80 Strand, London WC2R 0RL, England
Penguin Group Ireland, 25 St. Stephen's Green, Dublin 2, Ireland (a division of Penguin Books Ltd.)
Penguin Group (Australia), 250 Camberwell Road, Camberwell, Victoria 3124, Australia
(a division of Pearson Australia Group Pty. Ltd.)
Penguin Books India Pvt. Ltd., 11 Community Centre, Panchsheel Park, New Delhi—110 017, India
Penguin Group (NZ), 67 Apollo Drive, Rosedale, North Shore 0632, New Zealand
(a division of Pearson New Zealand Ltd.)
Penguin Books (South Africa) (Pty.) Ltd., 24 Sturdee Avenue, Rosebank, Johannesburg 2196,
South Africa

Penguin Books Ltd., Registered Offices: 80 Strand, London WC2R 0RL, England

This is a work of fiction. Names, characters, places, and incidents either are the product of the author's imagination or are used fictitiously, and any resemblance to actual persons, living or dead, business establishments, events, or locales is entirely coincidental. The publisher does not have any control over and does not assume any responsibility for author or third-party websites or their content.

PUBLISHER'S NOTE: The recipes contained in this book are to be followed exactly as written. The publisher is not responsible for your specific health or allergy needs that may require medical supervision. The publisher is not responsible for any adverse reactions to the recipes contained in this book.

ONE BAD APPLE

A Berkley Prime Crime Book / published by arrangement with the author

PRINTING HISTORY
Berkley Prime Crime mass-market edition / August 2008

ISBN: 978-0-425-22304-8

BERKLEY® PRIME CRIME
Berkley Prime Crime Books are published by The Berkley Publishing Group,
a division of Penguin Group (USA) Inc.,
375 Hudson Street, New York, New York 10014.
The name BERKLEY PRIME CRIME and the BERKLEY PRIME CRIME design are trademarks
belonging to Penguin Group (USA) Inc.

PRINTED IN THE UNITED STATES OF AMERICA

10 9 8 7 6 5

To Eleazer Warner
and
John Chapman.

Acknowledgments

Like an orchard, it takes a lot of people to nurture a book to fruition. First thanks go to my agent, Jacky Sach, who took the seed of an idea and brought it to life, and my editor, Shannon Jamieson Vazquez, who polished the draft until it shone. And as always, Sisters in Crime and the wonderful Guppies (especially Lorraine Bartlett) provided bushels of encouragement.

Since I am not an orchardist, I relied on many people to help me get the details right: Duane W. Greene, Department of Plant, Soil and Insect Sciences at the University of Massachusetts, and Director of the University's Cold Spring Orchard, who provided much useful information about orchard management; Richard Pelletier of the Nashoba Valley Winery in Bolton, Massachusetts, who shared his orchard's wealth of antique apple varieties; May Peters of Peters Family Orchard and Cider Mill in Acushnet, Massachusetts, who provides a wonderful example of managing a local orchard; and Joyce Manzello, who educated me about the realities of making an orchard work—and pay.

On the genealogy side, I have to thank many generations of ancestors who left such a wonderful history for me to find—all the Chapins, Downings, Montagues, Seldens, Sheldons, Shumways, Taylors, Townes, Wakemans, Warners, and Woodfords who settled in western Massachusetts and whose spirits drew me there. Among the living, I'm grateful for the help provided by the Granby Historical Society, the Granby Public Library, and the Granby Town Clerk's Office.

And of course I have to thank Marvina and Jon Brook of Muddy Brook Farm in Granby, without whom this book could not have happened. They are the current owners of the house built by my ancestor Stephen Warner, and they let me spend time getting to know the property and the house—including the very interesting basement!

I should also thank Mother Nature, who made this past season's apple crop absolutely spectacular.

Finally, I need to thank my entomologist husband, who has served as my consultant on aspects of integrated pest management, and my daughter, who tramped through a lot of orchards with me and carried a lot of bags of apples.

1

"Orchard? What orchard?" Meg Corey stared in confusion at the man standing on her doorstep. He reminded her of a hobbit: shorter than she was, his silvery hair combed forward in an endearing bang now rumpled by the wind, his cheeks rosy, his blue eyes twinkling. "I'm sorry—who did you say you were?"

"Oh, forgive me. I'm Christopher Ramsdell, with the Integrated Pest Management Department, the Small Fruit Management Project, at the university." When Meg looked blankly at him, he went on. "Of Massachusetts, at Amherst. We've been using the apple orchard as an experimental site for, oh, decades now. But I was looking for the Tuckers. Are they no longer here?"

"The Tuckers were only renting. My mother owns this place, and I'm fixing it up to sell." *Or trying to*, Meg amended to herself. Every time she tried to "fix" something, it seemed to generate more problems. Usually expensive ones.

"Well, then, you're the person I should be talking to!" Christopher beamed at her, and Meg couldn't refuse the delightful man a return smile. At least he wasn't some crazy person, as she had wondered when she first opened the door.

Which was letting in the freezing January wind. "Uh, come in, I guess. Will this take long? Because I'm expecting a plumber any minute." She hoped.

"I'd be delighted. And I won't keep you, but I'd like to explain exactly what it is I'm doing." He stepped into Meg's hallway, and she slammed the door shut behind him—the slamming part was necessary if she wanted the warped, if authentic, four-panel door to close at all.

"Take a seat." Meg gestured vaguely toward her front parlor on the right. The lumpy furniture was draped with drop cloths, old sheets, and anything else Meg could find, since she had been scraping, spackling, and sanding for a couple of weeks now. "I'd offer you some coffee, but my sink is stopped up and I don't want to run any water until I know what the problem is."

Christopher was still standing in the middle of the room looking around with clear admiration. "Grand old house, isn't it? My sympathies on the plumbing problem. Drains are a constant torment." He rubbed his hands briskly. "Well, I don't want to take much of your time, so let me get right down to it. I can't believe you don't know about the orchard. You haven't seen it?"

"I don't know where to look," Meg said. "Where is it?"

"To your west." When Meg looked bewildered, Christopher waved toward one side of the house. "Up that way. It runs from the top of that rise down to the highway, Route 202. Surely you're familiar with that. Roughly fifteen acres, and you have perhaps a hundred and fifty trees, primarily apple. And we—by that I mean the research group at the university—and the Tuckers, and the ... let me see ... I think it was the Lothrops before them, have been managing it for more than twenty years."

Meg nodded. "I guess that explains it. My mother inherited this place back in the eighties, and I don't think she's been here since. She just sticks the rent checks in the bank. But I found myself at loose ends recently"—no reason why this nice stranger needed to know she'd been downsized out of her job—"and she thought it might be a good time to finally fix up the place and sell it, so here I am. So, what is it you want from me?"

Christopher cocked his head at her, like a friendly sparrow. "Well, my dear, first and foremost I'd like to introduce you to the treasure that you own."

"Now?" Meg's voice rose in disbelief. It couldn't be more than twenty degrees outside.

"Why not? It's far easier to distinguish trunk and branch configurations when the trees aren't in leaf."

"What about my plumber?" Meg sputtered.

Christopher smiled. "When did you call?"

"About half an hour ago."

"Then I'm sure he'll be along in an hour or two. Plenty of time!"

Meg considered. The less-than-appealing odor of whatever was seeping out of her sink was beginning to filter through the house, even though she had shut the doors to the kitchen. Just like the front door, the kitchen doors of the two-hundred-year-old house didn't fit very well. Moreover, she hadn't been out of the house for—she stopped to count—three days, and some bracing fresh air wouldn't hurt. She could watch for the plumber from outside. And she had to admit she was curious. It had never occurred to her to check out what lay on the far reaches of the property. Since she had arrived she had been focused on the house, and that was more than enough to keep her busy.

"Okay, I'm game." Obviously the right answer, if Christopher's delight was any indication. "Let me get my coat." And gloves. And scarf. And hat. Taking a walk in western Massachusetts in winter involved a lot of preparation. She slipped her cell phone into her pocket along with her house keys, and returned to the waiting Christopher, who was bouncing like an eager spaniel. "Ready."

Outside, Meg pulled her balky door shut and followed Christopher as he set off at a brisk pace, up the low rise toward what he had informed her was west. When he noticed her lagging behind, he slowed and waited for her to catch up. "Forgive me. I spend so much time outside like this, I forget that some people aren't as accustomed as I. You've been here how long?"

"About three weeks. Since just after the New Year, when the lease on my apartment ran out." Meg was happy to note that she wasn't panting—much. Maybe vigorous home renovation was good exercise. "I figured I'd just camp out here and get to work. There's plenty to be done." More than she could have imagined.

Christopher continued to pepper her with questions, not even slightly out of breath. "So you're telling me that you've never walked your property?" His tone implied that such an omission was inconceivable.

Meg smiled into her coat collar. "No. I've had plenty to work on inside. The house is in rather bad shape, but I was hoping to list it for sale before summer."

"Then at the very least you'll be here to witness full bloom—that's the middle of May around here, weather permitting. It's truly lovely, you know. Of course, I may be a bit biased, but I think an orchard in bloom is one of nature's wonders, all the more precious because it's so brief a phenomenon. Not that an orchard in fruit isn't equally lovely in its own way."

"Christopher, you're not from around here, are you?"

"Ah, you've caught the accent. No, my dear—I was born in England, but I've been here for most of my life now. And yourself?"

"I grew up in New Jersey, but I've been living in Boston since college." She paused to catch her breath. "What is it you're doing to the trees? You're not spraying them with anything nasty, are you?"

"Oh, no, no. In fact, we spray as little as possible, or preferably not at all, although I'm afraid some spraying is unavoidable in apple management. I'm in integrated pest management: working with nature and natural enemies, and spraying only when we have no alternative. You're not familiar with the process?"

"No—I'm a city girl, through and through."

"Ah, well, you can learn. Here we are!"

They had reached the crest of the rise, and the land sloped down before them. Meg could see sparse traffic moving along the highway maybe five hundred feet distant. Between where she stood and the highway, neatly spaced rows of trees spread out in a long, narrow strip parallel to the highway. The trees were uniform in height, although they varied from slender young trees to craggy gnarled ones whose age she could only guess at. She could see a few lingering, shriveled apples on nearby branches.

"So this is it?" she said.

"It is indeed. Isn't she grand?" Christopher spoke with a paternal pride.

"Grand" would not have been Meg's first choice of word. "I guess. Sorry, but it looks kind of dead." Now that she was here, she realized she'd been driving right by it for weeks, and it had never even registered on her radar. An orchard. *Her* orchard. It had taken her a while to even get used to the idea of owning the barn behind the house (although from the way it was leaning, she wasn't sure when it would stop being a barn and start being a pile of rubble). But an orchard was a living thing, with a past and a future. It needed care and attention, as Christopher seemed to be telling her. She wasn't sure she wanted to know what that meant—dealing with the house was more than enough for her at the moment. But still ... her own apple orchard. It was an appealing idea. *Oops, Meg, bad pun.* She tuned back in to what Christopher was saying.

"Oh, not dead at all. Just dormant. Wait a month or two and you'll see."

"How much land does this take up?" she asked.

"As I said, about fifteen acres. It's about a quarter mile to the next property there, to your north."

Meg could feel Christopher's eyes on her, anxious. It was obvious that he really did care about this field of scraggly trees. "Well, then, tell me about it. What am I looking at? What's so special about this orchard?" Meg asked, her breath forming clouds in front of her face.

"Ah, my dear, where to begin?" Christopher all but rubbed his hands in glee. "This orchard has been here nearly as long as the house. No, the individual trees aren't two hundred years old, but some of the species have been planted and replanted over time. You've got some real treasures here. Tell me, what do you see?"

Meg, bewildered, turned to survey the trees before her. "They're, uh, trees."

"Yes, but look closely. You see that one there?" He pointed, and Meg followed his finger obediently. "Stayman Winesap— see the thick trunk, the slightly purplish cast to the bark? And over there, Rome Beauty—you can tell by those drooping limbs. What do you know about apples?"

"Only what I see in the supermarket—Delicious, McIntosh. Aren't there some new ones with funny names? Mutsu, or something like that?"

Christopher snorted. "Dreck. Commercial pap. Bred for their ability to withstand shipping across country, only to sit in warehouses for months on end. By the time they reach a store, they all taste like packing peanuts. You, my dear, are in for a treat come harvest time. There's such an array of flavors—subtle but delightful. I envy you the experience of encountering these for the first time. Ah, hold on!" He swung a small pack from his shoulder and rummaged through the contents. He emerged with an apple about the size of a baseball and shaded from red to a speckled yellow. Christopher polished it on his pant leg and offered it to her with a flourish. "Try this."

Meg took it from him. "Do I eat it?"

"Of course you do."

"What is it?" Meg thought it was a good idea not to eat things she couldn't identify, especially when they had been given to her by someone she'd met only an hour earlier.

"Baldwin. Originated not far from here, in Massachusetts, in the eighteenth century. Very popular in the early twentieth century, until it got squeezed out by the McIntosh. Harvested that one myself, right here, in early November—it's a keeper. Try it."

Holding the apple in her gloved hand, Meg took a bite. The skin was thick and resistant at first, but the flesh inside was coarse and juicy, with a spicy tang. It bore no resemblance to any apple she had ever bought in a supermarket. "Wow. It's good."

"Of course it is. It hasn't spent six months in a shipping container or a warehouse."

"I have these in the orchard here?"

"These and many other varieties. As part of my job, I seek out and preserve old varieties that are in danger of disappearing forever. There are still many old stocks, lurking around the countryside here. Now that technology is improving, we need these forgotten varieties for genetic crossbreeding, to try and put the flavor back into this country's apples. And I fear it is nearly too late. I've seen far too many trees or even whole orchards fall before the bulldozers of progress. But there is much we can learn from the old orchards, and it's a shame to lose them. Why, you even have a quince, over there toward the road."

A quince? Meg wouldn't know one if it bit her, or if she bit it. Her fingers were getting numb. "I'm sorry, but I really should go back and wait for the plumber. Is there something you want me to do?"

"I'm hoping you'll allow me and my staff to maintain our study program here. We won't be in your way."

"Sure. Of course. Do I need to give you official permission or something?" It wouldn't bother her if there were people wandering through her apple trees—she couldn't even see them from the house. And she needed some time to think about whether having an orchard on the property was good or bad, in terms of selling the house. And how she felt about it.

"That's grand! We did negotiate a formal agreement, oh, years ago, when we first started using this orchard. I believe it was the Warren sisters who agreed to it? It might be wise to draft a new one for you to sign, if you don't mind."

"That shouldn't be a problem." Meg couldn't bring herself to worry about giving away rights she hadn't known she had.

Christopher beamed happily. "Wonderful! I'll let our department chair know, and we'll set the wheels in motion. Thank you so much! I've been a bit concerned because we need to start pruning soon. I'll send you some reading material so you can familiarize yourself with what you have. Ah, I can tell you're chilled. Let me walk you back to the house."

As they made the easier downhill trip, Meg asked, "What about the apples? What happens to them when they're harvested?"

"The Tuckers sold them to a local cooperative."

Meg laughed. "Funny—they never mentioned *that* to my mother. And she thought she was doing them a favor, keeping the rent low." They reached her front door. "I'm glad you stopped by, Christopher. I'll look forward to seeing what happens in the spring."

"It's been my pleasure, dear lady. And you're in for a treat!"

2

Meg hoped that the next knock on the door would produce the plumber, but when she opened it she found a middle-aged woman with fashionably styled blonde hair, wearing a smartly cut wool jacket and tailored pants, and clutching a clipboard. "Meg Corey?"

Shoot. The Realtor she had called—before her plumbing had gone funny on her. She had forgotten that they had scheduled a walk-through today. "Yes, that's me. And you're Frances?" Meg drew a blank on the last name.

"I am. Frances Clark, Valley Realty, biggest firm in the Pioneer Valley. You going to let me in?"

"Oh, sorry, of course." She stepped back to let Frances in, then went through her wrestling routine with the door.

She turned to find Frances's petite nose wrinkled, and sighed. "Sorry. The plumbing's acting up. I called a plumber, but he isn't here yet."

"Who'd you get?" Frances asked.

"Chapin Brothers."

Frances nodded. "They're good—at least, Seth is. Can't say as much for his brother Stephen. Stephen's heart's not really in plumbing, if you get my drift."

Meg tried to imagine the intersection of hearts and pipes and gave up. "Well, someone should be here soon. You want to go ahead with the walk-through now, or come back some other time?"

Frances checked her watch. "I'm already here, so why don't we just get it over with? This is only preliminary anyway." She scanned the room with a professional eye. "So, what've we got here—looks like your basic colonial, four up, four down. Bathrooms?"

"Um, yes? One and a half."

"Come on, show me." Frances led the way to the hall and then up the central stairs, Meg trailing helplessly behind. Frances continued to fire questions, and Meg answered as well as she could. Which wasn't very well, since she didn't really know the house, and certainly not its history, old or recent. She followed Frances the real estate agent, feeling more and more depressed. The woman had arrived armed with not only her clipboard but also a screwdriver, and she alternated between jotting an alarming number of notes and using the screwdriver to poke at things—plaster, woodwork, bricks. If she kept it up much longer, Meg was going to have to take the screwdriver and poke *her* with it.

After a very long hour, they arrived back where they had started. "What do you think?" she finally asked Frances.

"Meg—I can call you Meg, right?—Meg, you've got a real gem here. Authentic colonial, probably 1760s, nice piece of land—I checked the tax records. All good. But there are a few teeny, weeny problems that you should take care of before you even think about putting this place on the market."

Meg sighed. Even her unskilled eye could pick out problems, and she shuddered to think what she hadn't yet discovered. "Tell me."

"Maybe we should sit down—this could take a little time."

"All right." Meg led the way to the dining room, which looked deceptively sunny and cheerful. "Hit me with it, Frances."

Frances consulted her notes, flipping through the pages. "Let's start with the structural stuff. From the top"—Frances giggled at her own joke—"your roof is shot—has to be at least fifty years old. Replace it. Your windows are single pane, no storms—big heating bills. The exterior needs to be scraped and painted, especially the trim. Your foundation seriously needs repointing. Haven't you noticed a bit of a breeze in the basement?"

"I try to avoid going into the basement. And the attic. And what's repointing?"

"Oh, well, that's why you didn't see the water stains on the roof boards where the leaks are—which are pretty obvious, since you don't have any insulation up there. Repointing means replacing the mortar between the stones of your foundation. In case you haven't noticed, most of your mortar is gone. Moving right along. Your gutters are nonexistent. Your driveway is mainly dirt with a sprinkling of gravel. Your barn out back is about to fall over, not that that counts in the formal inspection—which, by the way, this is not."

Frances sat back and cocked her head at Meg. "You know, it might not be a bad idea for you to get an official inspection done. Oh, not until you've taken care of a few of the problems. But it might make a good selling point. Reassure nervous buyers, you know? They'd probably want an inspection of their own, but it's a good-faith gesture coming from you."

And it would cost her more money. "I assume you're not done?"

"Oh, Lordy me, no. Let's see, did I cover all of the outside? Roof, paint, foundation, grounds." Frances consulted her list. "Okay, let's move inside. Systems. Your electric is half knob-and-tube, which makes modern buyers very nervous. It should be upgraded, and I'd put in a two-hundred-amp box while you're at it. Your piping is mostly copper, which is good, but it's old, and you've got a few leaks. And you could really use another bath. Your hot-water heater, forget it. Your furnace? Not good. It's got to be at least thirty years old, and it's definitely creaky. How you holding up?"

"I guess it's nothing I didn't expect." Meg stifled another sigh. "Is that it, or do you have more?"

"Sure do," Frances said crisply. "Okay, we've covered the basics. Oh, and your kitchen appliances are pathetic. You'll have to do something about those. Now, cosmetics. Looks like the last time this place had a makeover was maybe 1980?"

"Could be." Meg shrugged. "It's been rented out since about then."

"That explains why none of the big stuff has been done, right? Absentee landlord?"

"My mother."

"Gotcha. Anyway. Interior: wallpaper's got to go—most of it

makes me gag. Ditto the carpet. Floor in the kitchen, too. Haven't seen that vinyl pattern in years. The bathrooms need upgrading. A lot of the woodwork could stand to be stripped."

Meg fought despair. This was worse than she expected; she'd had no idea that things were in such bad shape. "Look, Frances, can you tell me anything good?"

Frances gave her a look of sympathy. "Sure. It's a beautiful house, or would be if it were fixed up. Good-size rooms, good layout. Some original features, if you can dig them out from under the crap. Like I said, nice lot, pretty views. Close, but not too close, to town. This is a great area—all those colleges within a few miles. Amherst, Smith, Mount Holyoke. It just needs a little work."

A little work? Was Frances being sarcastic, or was she just naturally simpleminded? Meg wasn't sure. "And there's the orchard," Meg blurted, surprising herself.

Frances stared blankly at her for a moment, then nodded. "Oh, right, up toward the highway. That's right—that's part of this parcel, too. Pretty, in the spring."

Meg allowed herself another sigh. "So tell me, if I do everything you ask to the house, will I get a better price? Will it sell faster?"

"Honey, that's a hard one. I think the short answer is 'yes,' but I can't give you a formula. You said on the phone you're a banker, right?"

"I am—was." Meg wasn't sure herself anymore. "But I specialized in municipal finance, not residential."

"Well, in any case, you know that sometimes it takes money to make money, right? I can tell you what buyers are going to want to see, and that might give you an idea of where to spend your money. You do have some money to put into it, right?" A look of anxiety flashed across Frances's face as she saw her commission evaporating.

"Some, yes. But from what you've been saying, we're talking about a lot of expensive items." Meg's severance check was dwindling fast. Would she recoup all these outlays when the place sold? Or should she cut and run right now, before things got any worse?

"I know. But it should be worth it, in the long run. Why don't you get some estimates, see what it would cost you? And, to be honest, it never hurts to leave a few things undone—buyers like to feel there's something left for them to do, gives them a sense of ownership. But that usually doesn't apply to the behind-the-scenes stuff like furnaces. They like to do the pretty things, the ones that show."

Meg wondered, not for the first time, just why she had agreed to help her mother sell the house. It had seemed like a good idea at the time. She hadn't had anything else to do with herself after her job had vaporized, and there was nothing holding her in Boston. At least she had been careful to work out a formal arrangement with her mother—much as she loved her, Meg knew her mother didn't have a head for business. Meg made sure that her mother had named her joint owner of the property, which would entitle her to a share of the proceeds from the sale. With the stipulation that Meg had to oversee repairs. When Meg had signed the documents, she had had no idea of the extent of those repairs, and now she was kicking herself. She had foolishly agreed to use her severance money to fund them (maybe her mother was more savvy than she had thought), to be reimbursed from the profits. Those hypothetical profits were diminishing daily.

She squared her shoulders. "Okay, give me a time line. When would be the best time to put it on the market?"

"Certainly not right away, if you were thinking of it. Market's kind of slow right now, all across the state, and mortgage lenders are pretty wary. In any case, spring and summer are always best—places just look prettier, you know? I mean, unless you're in a real hurry to unload the place. You could do it, but it would cost you. You'd have to lowball your price." Frances wrinkled her nose at the idea.

"So I'd have maybe four months to get it into shape?" Meg asked.

Frances looked relieved. "Right. I really think it would be worth it. Oh, tell me—you have anything like a history on this place? I mean, it's been here for a while, since before the Revolution. If you could come up with a good story, that might be a nice selling point."

Meg shook her head. "I have no idea. It belonged to a couple of my mother's unmarried great-aunts, Nettie and Lula Warren, and I think they'd lived here all their lives. As far as I know, it's always been in that family, and they were the last of that line. I'm amazed they left a will at all, but I gather they were into genealogy, so they knew that their closest relative was my mother. They did want the place to stay in the family. Anyway, I have been thinking about looking into the house's history." Whenever she had anything like spare time, which at this rate might be never.

Frances beamed. "Well, there you go! You can look up some old maps, maybe some deeds—get copies of them, frame them, and hang 'em in the hallway. Lookers love that kind of thing. They think they're buying a little history." Frances checked her watch. "Well, I've gotta run. Look, Meg, I know this seems like a lot to think about, but if you put some effort and some money into the place, you won't regret it. And if you need some names to do the work, give me a call."

Meg escorted her to the door. "Thanks, Frances. At least you've been honest with me. I'll be in touch." After she watched Frances pick her way along the icy path to her car, Meg turned to contemplate the interior of "her" house. Freaking white elephant, that's what it was. History indeed. It was old, period. And it was suffering from all the ailments of old age—creaky joints, failing internal organs. It would take an unthinkable amount of work to do even half of what Frances had suggested, not to mention money.

Once Frances had driven off, Meg cautiously opened the door to her kitchen—and closed it quickly: the smell seemed to be getting worse. This problem was not going to just go away. Where was the plumber? She was trying to do as much of the work as she could herself, but plumbing was outside her pitifully small area of home-repair expertise. She needed a professional, even if she had to pay him.

Why had she ever thought she could rehab an old house in the rolling hills of Granford, Massachusetts? Until a month ago, she had had trouble keeping her apartment in Boston neat—and had been happy to call the building manager at the first sign of a leaky faucet or balky electrical switch.

No more. Boston was her past, and she was now a resident of Granford, albeit a temporary one. Her mother had decided that this little project was just the thing to do while Meg waited for that perfect job to fall into her lap. Then again, her mother hadn't seen the place in decades. When she had inherited the house and land from those aged aunts, she'd considered selling the place, but the real estate market had been soft back in the 1980s, so her mother had simply rented it out to a series of tenants with the help of a local Realtor, and more or less forgotten about it except as a tax write-off. And since she hadn't needed the money, and owned the house free and clear, she had been content just to collect the rent, which easily offset the tax bills. Maybe Meg's mother had inherited a Yankee thrift gene and couldn't let go of a property easily. Or, Meg reflected, maybe it was just a case of "out of sight, out of mind."

But the last tenants had moved on a couple of months earlier, and nobody else had expressed an interest in a decrepit house in the middle of nowhere, so it had sat empty until Meg's mother had had her little brainstorm. And as she had pointed out, Meg could job hunt from just about anywhere, couldn't she, in this Internet era?

But now Meg wished she had been a bit more specific about who was footing the bills for this renovation. Of course, part of that had been her own stupidity: She had had no idea what this "little" project was going to cost, or how long it was going to take. She had blithely assumed that she could dip into her severance pay, slap a coat of paint on the place, and put it on the market. She had learned quickly how wrong she had been. But now she was reluctant to go back to her mother and ask for assistance. Meg was the banker, wasn't she? And she was supposed to be smart about money, wasn't she? Maybe the events of the last few months had hit her harder than she had realized and muddied her thinking. So here she was, stuck—and spending money left and right.

But if she was honest with herself, Meg had been ready—no, eager—for a change of scene, so she hadn't looked too hard at what she was getting herself into. Being downsized out of a job was the last straw in a not-so-good year. A few months before she'd lost her job, she'd also been unceremoniously dumped by her so-called boyfriend, Chandler Hale. Being somewhere else for a while had appealed to her. And she wanted to do something that would wear her out enough to sleep at night without wondering why she had apparently repelled both a lover and an employer in the space of a few months. Mom's plan had offered the ideal opportunity, and Meg had conveniently ignored the fact that she barely knew which end of a hammer to hold. She had taken herself to Granford with high hopes—which had lasted until this afternoon's visit with Frances. Three weeks of blissful ignorance had just come crashing down around her head.

Meg had a dim memory of visiting the Aunties with her mother once, many years earlier, but she had no memory of the house. What she remembered best about the visit was being bored. The ladies were unimaginably old to her five-year-old mind. Worse, they were cranky and unaccustomed to children. They had offered tea in brittle china cups and dry store-bought cookies, and then had shooed Meg out to explore the yard while they chatted with her mother. Meg, dressed in her finest for this ceremonial visit, had had little interest in exploring the drafty barn or the muddy fields, and instead had spent most of the time kicking at clods of dirt and feeling much put upon. Meg's mother had finally given up: her duty done, she had made quick farewells to Lula and Nettie, then collected Meg and scooted her off to the nearest ice cream place.

Even fortified with a substantial sundae, Meg remembered whining, "Why did we have to come? I'm missing Andrea's birthday party."

Her mother had sighed. "I know it's been dull for you, sweetie, but they're our relatives. And they're old and alone. The house is lovely, though, isn't it?"

"I dunno." Meg had poked at her melting ice cream, and her mother had dropped the subject.

Funny thing—she didn't remember seeing the orchard.

Almost thirty years later, here she was. It was a good thing she hadn't remembered the house, or she would never have agreed to her mother's scheme. Western Massachusetts in January was cold and damp when it wasn't snowing; the house was correspondingly cold and damp. And she was beginning to wonder if the house resented her: from the day she had arrived, things had started to fall apart. First she had discovered that the heating system was on its last legs (if heating systems had legs), and she couldn't use the handsome fireplace in the front room unless she relined the flue, which would cost a few thousand dollars. And all the original multipaned windows leaked like sieves, sending eddies of cold air through every room in unexpected locations, but storm windows would cost another few thousand dollars.

What had she been thinking? *Meg, you're an idiot! You should have taken one look and gone straight back to Boston and found yourself another nice, safe—clean! warm!—job in finance.* She had solid skills, a good track record, and connections—she could have found something. Let Mom worry about renovating this dump—or maybe just razing it and letting some college professor build the minimansion he wanted, full of brushed steel and plate glass. Meg was beginning to wonder if she could possibly make enough money out of the sale to justify all the work she was putting into the place, not to mention the cash. *Right, Mom— a little cleanup, a few touches here and there, and call the Realtor. Ha!* Why would anyone want to buy a house with wonky heating, plumbing, and wiring? And even if they were crazy enough to overlook those not-so-little flaws, it was hard to see past the flaking paint, peeling (and hideous) wallpaper, cracking plaster, creaking boards . . . the list went on and on. Any sensible home buyer would take one look and run.

But still . . . Meg drifted over to the parlor window that overlooked her driveway. Beyond it, past the level patch of lawn, the far side of the rustic split-rail fence, the ground sloped down to a sea of grass, golden now in winter, and then to the dark tree line. It was soothing, peaceful, lovely.

With her luck it was a swamp, complete with a population of monster mosquitoes.

The to-do list just kept growing. She had blithely assumed that it would take only a couple of months to whip the place into shape and put it on the market. But she hadn't taken into account the fact that there was no way to paint the exterior until the weather warmed up. Or deal with the roof and gutters. Or repoint the foundation—the latest addition to the list, thanks to Frances. As the to-do list lengthened, the projected renovation expenses increased, and the bottom line scared Meg, especially since she knew the tally was still incomplete.

But then, there was the orchard . . .

Meg lifted her chin. If she couldn't tackle the outside projects now, that left all the inside chores. Unfortunately, every time she took a step forward, something fell on her head. She had been looking forward to stripping off the tacky wallpaper in the parlor, but when she had pulled at a loose corner, she found the plaster underneath—apparently original to the house, if the clumps of horsehair in it were any indication—was crumbling, and if she wanted to paint or paper it over again, it would have to be repaired, filled in, spackled—whatever the heck it was called. And she was scared to start stripping paint off the interior woodwork when she couldn't open the windows for ventilation. She had visions of herself overcome with fumes, and no one finding her body for months. Although her corpse would probably freeze before it rotted.

So the calendar kept shifting forward. Frances said May was a good time to sell, so she was going to focus on putting the house on the market then. Lots of families looked to move at the end of the school year when the weather was nice. This house would be great for a small family, if the school district was any good. Meg had no idea about that. And she liked Frances's idea about researching the place. Maybe some famous person had lived here or slept here or walked by here, and that might make a buyer overlook a few of the house's more egregious shortcomings. Maybe the blooming orchard would distract the buyers from the peeling paint.

May. Right now she was going to concentrate on being ready to sell by May.

3

 Lunch was out of the question—she wasn't going near the reeking kitchen right now. Thank heavens she had even *found* a plumber: it had taken three tries to reach a human instead of an answering machine.

"Chapin Brothers," a cheerful male voice had boomed.

"Oh, hi, thank goodness. Look, my kitchen sink is spewing, uh, nasty stuff, and I haven't dared look at any of the other plumbing, but I really need help, like, right now." Meg knew she sounded desperate, which was probably not a smart bargaining strategy, but then, she *was* desperate.

"Yep, sounds like you've got a problem. Where are you?"

"Eighty-one County Line Road—the big white house."

"Oh, yeah. I know the place—the Warren house. Can you hold out for an hour or two? I've got to wrap something up here, but I can swing by after." The male voice on the other end was reassuring.

"That would be wonderful," Meg had replied. "Thank you so much. I'll be waiting right here. Oh, let me give you my number in case you need to call me or anything." She rattled off her cell phone number. "See you soon, then." She realized after she had hung up that she hadn't asked about the cost, but what choice did she have? She knew zip about plumbing, beyond changing the odd faucet washer now and then.

She checked her watch: it had been two hours since she had called, and no sign of this Chapin plumber person, but she didn't think calling him again would help. What to do while she waited? Nothing that involved water, clearly. Maybe she could rip up the ugly green shag carpet in the parlor. No doubt if she started something, that would be the precise moment the plumber would arrive.

Unfortunately she had miscalculated how much dirt, dust, and other unknown filth could accumulate in and under cheap carpeting over a few decades, so after she had spent an hour dislodging the bilious shag from its tacking bars, she was filthy. *Bad idea, Meg, especially when you don't know when your next shower will be.* She was beginning to wonder if the dirt would embed itself permanently in all her creases, a lifetime souvenir of her epic battle with the house. And the stains in the carpet and the wood floor beneath suggested that the Tuckers and their predecessors had owned pets—poorly trained ones. Now there was a whole new aroma of antique cat pee mingling with the sewer stink wafting from the kitchen. Worse, true to her prediction, she was interrupted by a knocking at her front door. Meg sent up a quick prayer: *let it be the plumber*. She swiped sweat off her forehead and hurried to yank open the door.

"Thank goodness you're here! It's in the . . ." Her voice trailed off as she processed the fact that it was not a plumber who was standing on her granite steps, but someone else. Someone she knew well. Her ex-boyfriend Chandler Hale.

He appeared as startled to see her as she was to see him. "Margaret?" he asked, his voice incredulous.

"Chandler," Meg answered, trying to keep her voice level. "What are you doing here?"

Chandler still looked bewildered. "I was looking for the Tuckers—I understood they lived here. But I've been sending them letters and they haven't responded."

So he hadn't been looking for her, Meg thought, not sure if she was relieved or disappointed. "They rented, and they've been gone for over three months. I assume they had their mail forwarded. What did you want with them?"

"May I come in?"

Meg wavered. She had left Chandler behind in Boston, and she wanted him to stay there. She looked past him to see a woman standing by his car. Her clothes were elegant and completely inadequate against the bitter wind, and her high-heeled boots were more decorative than practical. She paced as she talked on a small cell phone plastered to her ear. Meg nodded toward her. "What about your friend?"

Chandler glanced behind him. When he caught the woman's eye, he waved her over, and she picked her way across Meg's uneven path. "Yes, Chandler?"

"Meg, this is Lucinda Patterson, my assistant." He turned to the woman. "This is Margaret Corey—I may have mentioned her."

Lucinda gave Chandler a brief and enigmatic look before extending her hand to Meg. "Please, call me Cinda. Chandler?"

"Why don't you finish up those calls while I talk to Margaret? I won't be long. Sit in the car and keep warm." Chandler was clearly dismissing her and Cinda knew it, but she didn't argue.

"Nice to meet you, Margaret." She turned and stalked back to the car.

Chandler turned back to Meg. "Aren't you going to invite me in?" While no hair was out of place, and his finely tailored Brooks Brothers wool overcoat was flawless, Chandler was shivering and the tip of his aquiline nose was red. Meg didn't have the heart to leave him standing in the icy breeze on her granite stoop, even if out in the cold was where she'd most like to see him. She stepped back reluctantly and let him in, closing the door behind him. This time it took two tries. She followed him to the center of the parlor, where he had stopped to take in the shredded wallpaper and mound of mangy carpet in the middle of the floor.

"Um, what a lovely place you have here." His voice was tinged with a hint of sarcasm.

Meg had no patience for chitchat. Right now she wanted a plumber, not an ex-lover. Even from two rooms away she could catch a whiff of sewer gas, and she was sure that it hadn't escaped Chandler's refined sensibilities. "You don't have to be polite—I know it's a pit. Chandler, what are you doing here?"

"My apologizes for dropping in unannounced, but the phone number I had wasn't working—the absent Tuckers again, I assume. I certainly didn't expect to find you here."

"My mother owns this house, or rather, we both do now. Can you get to the point? I'm expecting someone."

"Of course. May we sit?"

Meg looked around. The elderly overstuffed chairs would do. She stalked over to one and swept the sheet off. "There. Sit." She did the same with another chair and sat facing him.

Chandler settled himself gingerly into the dusty depths of the plush-covered chair. "I saw what must be your mother's name on the property records, but I never made the connection. I'd hoped the Tuckers would know how to contact the owner, which now turns out to be you." He smiled. "So, are you empowered to act on your mother's behalf with regard to this property?"

Whatever she had expected to hear, this was not it. "Yes. Actually, as I said, I'm co-owner now, and I have her power of attorney. Why do you want to know?"

"What do you know about the Granford Community Development Project? Granford Grange?"

Meg shook her head. "Not a thing. I've only been here a few weeks, and I haven't read the newspapers or talked to anyone. I'm fixing up the house to sell." Looking around her and seeing the place as Chandler must see it, she felt the full idiocy of her statement.

"Ah. Well, then, let me give you the bare outlines. Puritan Bank is providing financing to a consortium of developers who are planning a commercial project along Route 202."

"That's nice," Meg said neutrally, as her mind churned. Chandler's presence here meant that Puritan Bank must want something. The house? For a moment Meg saw all her plans crumbling. Then her banker's side kicked in: if the bank offered a good price, she could be rid of the white elephant sooner rather than later, and she could skip all the messy renovation. She realized that Chandler was still talking.

"In order for this to happen," Chandler went on, "the developers need to acquire the parcels of land that lie along the highway, and that includes a portion of this property."

"The house?"

"No, just a strip that lies along the highway. Unoccupied land, and you can't even see it from here. If you're concerned, it wouldn't affect the value of this place much at all. In fact, it might be a good thing for you in the long run. I understand that the market for rural homes is somewhat depressed, and the presence of more modern shops and other amenities nearby might be a plus."

The orchard. That must be the piece of land that Chandler was talking about. Meg felt a pang of disappointment. She'd barely had time to take in its existence, and now Chandler was aiming a bulldozer at it. Christopher would be so disappointed. And she was annoyed that Frances hadn't mentioned anything to her about this project—unless it was totally hush-hush. "This is all public knowledge?"

"Oh, all quite public—open and aboveboard. We are working closely with the town to make this project happen, and let me tell you that there's a lot of excitement about it." He looked pleased with himself.

"So what do you want from me?" Meg asked.

"At the moment, very little. There are some administrative formalities to be completed by the town, and you—or your mother—as owner of record will no doubt be contacted by the proper authorities when the time comes. Oh, and there should be an official vote of approval by the town, at a Town Meeting scheduled for next month. You might want to attend, although it's not required."

A Town Meeting was something else Meg had never heard of, but she wasn't about to ask Chandler about it. She had no desire to prolong his stay. "I'll think about it," she said curtly. "Is that all?"

Before he could answer, Meg's cell phone rang and she grabbed it, holding up a finger to Chandler. "Hello?"

"Meg, it's Seth Chapin. I'm awfully sorry, but I've gotten kind of tied up with something and I won't be able to make it today after all."

Meg felt a stab of despair, although she wasn't exactly surprised. Nothing had been going her way lately. She watched as Chandler drifted around the room, a contemptuous half smile on his face. He picked up a book that had emerged from under the dust cover and leafed through it idly.

She turned away from Chandler and spoke. "When can you get here?"

"First thing in the morning, I promise. I'm sorry to do this to you, and I'm usually much more reliable."

Yeah, right. "All right, if that's the best you can do."

"Thanks. Eight o'clock all right with you?"

"Fine. See you then. And thanks for calling."

Meg turned around again to find Chandler looking at her. "Plumbing crisis—the plumber can't make it until tomorrow."

"Then perhaps you could join me for dinner?" Chandler asked.

Meg considered. She had no desire to spend any more time with Chandler, but it would be childish to say no—particularly since the alternative was sitting here in a cold and stinking house without water. "I guess."

"Such enthusiasm." He chuckled. He looked at his elegant watch. "I have a meeting with a local contractor, but I could swing back and pick you up at, say, seven?"

"Fine. By the way, how did you come to be interested in Granford?"

"Something you said once—about how you'd been through here as a child and had always remembered it as the perfect sleepy New England town. Puritan Bank was looking for a likely place to invest, so I took a run out this way, scouting for locations, so to speak. And here we are."

Meg had no memory of such a conversation, but it could have happened. She remembered more than once spinning out tales to entertain Chandler, and perhaps she had colored her recollections a bit too brightly, to keep his attention. *Sorry, Granford.* Although she had to agree: this was a prototypical small town, with its steepled white church overlooking the small-town green surrounded by tidy eighteenth- and nineteenth-century houses. Unfortunately it also suffered from many of the ills of small towns that time had passed by, including deteriorating infrastructure and an inadequate tax base. Obviously it was ripe for exploitation by someone like Chandler Hale and his merry band of developers. Still, that wasn't any of her concern, except as it affected the value of her property—and if the deal went through, it could be a good thing for her. As long as she didn't need to see much more of Chandler Hale.

"I'll need to be going now," he said, neatly buttoning his coat. "I can give you more details on the project over dinner. Oh, and may I borrow this?" He held up the book.

Meg peered at the book's spine. "Oh, that history of Granford." She had pulled it off a bookshelf in the house, thinking to read it, but had mislaid it under the drop cloths. "No problem—it came with the house. It's probably been here since it was written. I think there's an inscription from the author to the last owners. So, I'll see you at seven."

"I'm looking forward to it," Chandler replied, and Meg wondered if he was being sarcastic again. "I'm glad I stumbled on you here." He tucked the book under his arm and headed for the door, Meg trailing in his wake. She watched as he made his way back to his car, where Cinda waited, the cell phone still at her ear, then shut the door firmly. No sense in wasting any more of the air she was paying too much to heat. Then she leaned against the door and shut her eyes. Damn: Chandler Hale. She thought she had left him behind in Boston, yet here he was. And six months was not long enough to purge him from her system.

She heard Chandler's Mercedes exit the driveway with undue speed, sending up a spray of gravel. *Thank you, Chandler, for digging another hole in my poor driveway.*

Damn him. Meg looked quickly at the kitchen clock. She had two hours to clean up, and if she wanted to wash off the grime, it would have to be out of a bucket. A shower was out of the question and her hair was a mess. She should have said no to dinner, but Chandler had caught her off guard. Still, what did it matter how she looked this evening? She didn't need to impress Chandler Hale.

But she had standards—and she didn't want to face Chandler's critical eye. People had managed in this house for at least a century without plumbing, and she'd just have to improvise. After all, she came from hardy New England stock, didn't she? She took a deep breath before venturing into the kitchen to look for a big pot in which to boil water.

Upstairs, doing what she could with a sinkful of hot water, she considered Chandler's ad hoc invitation. Six months earlier, after nearly a year of dinners and concerts, just when she had begun to wonder if it was time to take their relationship to the next level, he had suddenly announced that he thought they should stop seeing each other, leaving her hurt and bewildered.

Well, she had to admit that maybe her pride was more hurt than her heart, but the rejection still stung, all the more because she hadn't seen it coming.

And in the Boston banking community, it had been hard to avoid running into him, or someone who knew him. If she was honest with herself, that was one of the reasons why she had been so happy to take her bank's severance package, why she had jumped so quickly into a venture that took her halfway across the state, away from Boston. Away from Chandler's measuring eyes, which always made her wonder just how she had failed.

And now he had insinuated himself into her new life in Granford. Why?

She was dressed too early, and sat at the dining room table leafing through a tattered magazine, waiting for Chandler. When he knocked, Meg wrenched open the door to find him standing on the step, impeccably dressed as always. She was suddenly conscious that she hadn't had a decent haircut in months, and her short brown hair probably looked like a haystack.

"Are you ready? I thought we could go to the Lord Jeffery in Amherst."

Didn't she look ready? She bit back a sarcastic response—no point in starting off on the wrong foot. "I am. I'll just get my coat."

As she collected her coat and gloves, she reflected on why Chandler always managed to get under her skin. She was a competent woman, and she didn't need to flinch at Chandler's scrutiny. Besides, he was the one who had asked her to dinner; therefore, there must be something he wanted from her. At least she'd get a nice meal out of him before he laid out just what his real motive was.

He didn't ask for directions to Amherst, which prompted Meg to say, "You know your way around here. Have you spent much time in this area?"

"Recently, yes, getting this project started. But I must say, it's lovely, peaceful—a welcome change from Boston."

"I thought you loved Boston. And you couldn't see the point of the country—you know, all those trees and cute little towns with fake antique stores and ersatz colonial pubs?"

"Perhaps I've reconsidered. But what about you? Are you enjoying your bucolic interlude?"

Meg laughed. Even if she had hated it, she wouldn't admit it to Chandler. "Yes, I am. As you say, it's a pleasant change."

"Do you like Granford?" Chandler's smooth baritone could easily be heard over the velvet purr of his Mercedes' engine.

"I do. Although I'm just beginning to meet people." A real estate agent and a professor, so far. Not exactly a huge social circle.

"Is it a close-knit community, based on what you've seen? How do they respond to newcomers like you?"

Meg reflected for a moment before speaking. "I'm not really sure. From what little I've read or heard since I've been here, there's been a good deal of turnover in recent years, new families moving in, so outsiders aren't as rare as they once were. But I'm sure you know that—you were always good at doing your homework for a project."

"Ah, is that a compliment? But of course you're right—I and my staff did a good deal of research on this town and its demographic profile." Chandler shot a quick glance at her. But he lapsed into silence until they arrived at Amherst, a town that Meg was growing increasingly fond of. It was collegiate—not that it had much choice, with Amherst College smack in the middle, and the much larger UMass Amherst only a mile or two beyond. The Lord Jeffery Inn faced the town green, rambling over the better part of a block. Meg had heard that the restaurant there emphasized its homely colonial roots, but the extensive menu impressed her. She indulged herself in what the menu called *caneton aux pommes et poivre vert*—duck with apples and green peppercorns. Maybe she had apples on the brain, she mused, but it sounded tempting.

She decided she deserved a little pampering, and sat back and let Chandler take charge of the evening. He did it so well, with or without an ulterior motive. Their conversation flowed smoothly, as did the excellent wine. Toward the end of the meal she realized he was watching her. "What?"

"You're blooming. This country living seems to be good for you."

Chandler's words always seemed to hold more than one

meaning. Was he mocking her? She decided to take his statement at face value. "I'm enjoying myself." She twirled her wine-
glass, catching the candlelight, and said, without looking at him,
"Chandler, why are we here?"

He sat back in his chair. "I can't pass an evening with an old
friend?"

She ignored his choice of the word "friend" and cocked a
skeptical eyebrow at him. "You were happy not seeing me in
Boston. Why here, why now?"

"Ah, Meg, you underestimate yourself. But you're right—this
is more than touching base. But before we get into that, tell me:
don't you miss playing a part in bigger things? You were doing
well at the bank. I know they let you go, but you could have
found something else at your level."

"Chandler, I don't miss it. I like what I'm doing at the moment. It's not permanent—once I've sold the house, I'll move
on, find a new job. But maybe it was a good thing that I got
pushed out of my rut." She was mildly surprised at her own response. Did she really believe that? However, that wasn't the
most important issue at the moment. "Why are you asking? Were
you planning to offer me a job?"

Chandler took his time responding. "The thought had crossed
my mind. I could use someone in place here for this project, long
term, and someone of your intelligence and experience would be
ideal. But short term I need to know where the support for the
project lies, as well as who is opposing it. No matter how strong
or convincing the proposal looks on paper, there is still a human
element to be considered. I'd rather have the local people supporting this project than fighting me every step of the way. Of
course, you know this will come to a public vote."

"Really," she said noncommittally. But his question interested her. Chandler was asking for her help. Did the project need
help? Meg resolved to find out what she could—for her own
sake, since her property was involved. "You want me to be your
local informant? And what would I derive from this?"

"I could see to it that you receive an advantageous price for
your property."

She stared at him, and as she did, anger percolated to the surface. Chandler was asking her to spy on her neighbors, the peo-

ple of Granford, for a price. Worse, for all she knew he was offering her a bribe, although he had chosen his words carefully. She could see his viewpoint: she had no ties to the community, and she had already told him of her intention to leave when she sold the house. Why should she care about the people here? And yet ... she did. The local citizens weren't numbers on a page, they were people who had owned and farmed these fields for generations. To Chandler, they were percentage points in a demographic analysis, but as far as she was concerned, they deserved to have a voice in the decision-making process, and she wasn't about to tip the balance in Chandler's favor by giving him information so that he could run around sweet-talking the naysayers.

"Chandler, I'm not interested. Even if I did have stronger local connections, it doesn't feel right to me. I'm sure you'll have no trouble finding someone else to be your mole." She stood up abruptly, surprising both of them. "And I'd like to go home now. It's been a long day."

He stared at her for a long, silent moment, and Meg wondered if she saw anger lurking in his eyes. Chandler was used to getting what he wanted, particularly from her. She found she didn't care.

"I'm sorry you feel that way," he said at last, in a neutral voice. "I'll settle the bill."

As she stalked off to the ladies' room, she saw Chandler make a peremptory gesture. The bill appeared, a credit card flashed. By the time she returned, the beaming waitress had returned it to Chandler in record time. He helped Meg into her coat and held her elbow lightly to guide her out of the restaurant. Always the gentleman, was Chandler Hale, even when thwarted. Outside the air was icy, but Meg inhaled deeply. It felt good: clean, fresh.

They spoke little as Chandler drove back to Granford. The roads were mostly empty, but he concentrated on his driving. When he pulled into her driveway, Meg got out of the car before he could help her, and went before him to open the front door. He followed her, and on the doorstep she turned to him.

"Thank you for a lovely dinner, Chandler. I enjoyed it, and I appreciate your asking me. But I don't think we have anything more to talk about. Good luck with your project. Good night."

And without waiting for his response, she went inside and shut the door, then turned and headed back to the kitchen. She dumped her coat on the back of a chair, then, holding her breath, helped herself to a glass of juice and fled back to the dining room table, trying to sort out what had just happened. She felt a small bubble of glee well up inside her: she had stood up to Chandler. She had said no to him. Let him find someone else to spy on this town. And there was more: she felt proud of her decision. Maybe she was finally done with Chandler.

She was wrong.

4

It was still a few minutes shy of eight o'clock the next morning when Meg heard a vehicle pull into her driveway. Peering out through the dining room window—after a brief plunge into the stinking kitchen to make some essential coffee, she had retreated quickly—she saw a large white van with "Chapin Brothers" emblazoned on the side. Meg waited until the plumber climbed out, then went to her front door and held it open for him, studying him as he approached. Early thirties, a little taller than she was, with sandy hair and a lot of freckles. "Hi. You're the plumber?"

"That's me. Seth Chapin. You're Meg?"

"Yes." She slammed the door shut behind him, bemused. He was not what she had envisioned as a plumber. Her mental image ran more to a middle-aged guy in a baseball cap, with a gut hanging over his low-slung jeans. Seth was about her age, in good shape, and clean. And not bad-looking.

Seth was looking around her hallway with clear admiration. "Nice. Sorry about bailing on you yesterday, but something came up at the last minute. So, what's the problem?"

Meg sighed. "I just moved in a couple of weeks ago, and things have been falling apart ever since."

"Yeah, these old places'll do that. Gotta love 'em."

"Well, yesterday's happy surprise was the plumbing."

Seth was in no hurry to follow her, but was studying the architecture. "You've got a great place here."

So everyone kept telling her. Meg was torn between pride and impatience to get on with the nasty business at hand. "You've seen it before?" she said, edging toward the kitchen and hoping that he would follow.

"Sure. I think my dad did some work on the place years ago. My brother and I used to tag along. So, where's the problem?"

"What I've seen so far is in the kitchen. I'm scared to look any further."

Seth followed her to the kitchen and headed directly for the sink. He took one look at the pool of noxious sludge in the sink and shook his head. "Yep, that's what I thought. Septic system's backed up."

That did not sound good. "I have a septic system? What does that mean?" Feeling stupid, Meg tried to keep her voice from quavering.

Seth turned and leaned against the counter, regarding her with a look of pity. "Where did you think your waste went?"

"Sewers?"

He shook his head. "Nope, you're too far from town. You've got a septic system here. Your drains flow into a holding tank, and then there's a septic field beyond that where it disperses. I don't suppose you know where your lines are? Your holding tank? Or maybe how old it is?"

Meg wrestled with a feeling of desperation. "No to all of those. But why did it just stop like this? I haven't done anything to it."

"It happens. This has been a hard winter. Really cold, and the ground froze and stayed frozen. Those old cast-iron pipes get brittle, and sometimes you get tree roots working on them, too. Maybe that was just the last straw for the system. Let me poke around outside a bit and locate the parts of the system and where a break might be."

"But what am I supposed to do?" She could avoid flushing for only so long.

Seth looked amused. "You got a friend you can stay with?"

"No. I'm new here, and I haven't met many people yet. Look, what's the worst-case scenario?"

"Replacing the septic system."

Ouch. That sounded ominous. "That's the most extreme solution?"

He nodded. "How many baths you got?"

Meg counted quickly in her head. "Two, and one's just a half. There's the kitchen. And a washer, out there." She waved vaguely at the door at the back of the kitchen, which led to a rather ramshackle room that linked the main house to the sagging barn.

"Pretty standard, then. A few thousand, anyway. Depends."

Meg shut her eyes. Sure, another few thousand. *Ka-ching, ka-ching* went the cash register in her head. She wanted to cry.

"Hey, you all right?"

Meg opened her eyes to find the nice—if expensive—plumber looking at her with concern. She nodded. "Sure, I'm fine. I think my checkbook may be seriously ill, though." Surely he must see this response a lot if he threw around figures in the thousands just to clear up a drainage problem.

"Listen, can I take a look at the basement?"

"Oh. Right. Basement." It took Meg a moment to recall where the door was—she had been avoiding the basement since she had arrived. She had been down there once, reluctantly, to take a look at the ancient furnace, and had no intention of going down again. She had even let Frances check it out unaccompanied. She led Seth into the hall. "That's it. Watch your head. I think the stairs were built for someone about five feet tall."

"Not a problem," he said, plunging down the rickety wooden stairs.

Then she could hear him banging on pipes. She refused to think about what Seth might find in the way of new plumbing disasters. Blast the man, he was whistling. At least he enjoyed his work.

Meg sat down at the dining room table, resolutely ignoring the mess in the parlor and the stink emanating from the kitchen. She gazed out the window that overlooked the grassy field—the view was pretty, though it offered little comfort. Her eye fell on the bowl of apples she had set in the middle of the table a couple of days earlier. She'd found the bowl, an old salt-glazed blue one with an ominous crack, in the sideboard; the apples were Red Delicious she had picked up at the market outside of town. The colors had looked pretty together. How often had she bought apples without giving a thought to where they had come from? Now she had to think about that, with Christopher's condemnation of commercial apple varieties ringing in her ears. She wondered what varieties she had growing in her orchard. Christopher would know—she'd have to ask him, the next time she saw him.

A few minutes later Seth reappeared, looking less cheerful than before, and Meg's heart sank. "All right, hit me with the bad news."

"Doesn't look good. Like I guessed, the system's just plain old. If we're lucky, could be as simple as a broken pipe near the house. That'd be the easiest and cheapest thing to fix. If you have to replace the septic tank, it'll run you about two thou. If you need a new leach field, that's another two or three thou. If you have to reinstall the existing field, it'll get a lot more expensive. But let's not worry about that just yet, okay?"

"I don't suppose you can stick a Band-Aid on it?" Meg said faintly.

"Nah. The system's at the end of its useful life. Sorry." He looked at his watch. "Listen, today's clear. I could have this done by the end of the day, if you can handle that."

"Do I have a choice?" Meg asked faintly.

"Not really. Outhouses aren't exactly approved anymore."

"Then I guess you'd better go ahead." Meg felt sick. How many more four-figure fixes were going to sandbag her like this?

"Let me poke around outside, then, get the lay of the land. The good news is, there's plenty of room for a new septic field, if you need one. How much land is there, by the way?"

"Somewhere around thirty acres, I think. About fifteen acres is orchard, I'm told. Up that way." Meg waved vaguely.

"Oh, right—the grove." Seth had pulled a PDA out of his pocket and was scrolling through something. "Let me make a couple of calls—I'll need to bring in a Bobcat to dig a trench, so I can get a look at things. And if we need to go for the new tank, I'll line someone up to bring it over."

We? At least it looked like Seth was someone who could get things done. Meg sighed.

Seth looked up and grinned. "Don't worry—you can pay it off in installments."

Meg mustered a smile. "Thanks, Seth. I don't know what I would have done if I hadn't found you."

"Hey, that's what neighbors are for."

"You're a neighbor?"

"Yup, just over the hill there—for the last three centuries, give or take."

"Wow," she said, feeling stupid. One more thing she didn't know about her house: who the neighbors were.

When Seth started punching numbers into his cell phone, Meg turned to survey her latest mess. She couldn't use the kitchen. The rug she had pulled up still lay in a crumpled heap in the front room. One more thing to add to the discarded stuff she had been piling up in the barn. She made a mental note: find out about trash collection, or whether there was a town dump. While Seth was making calls, she might as well finish clearing out the rug and its shredded underlay, and pry out the tacking bars.

After half an hour or so, she heard the sound of machinery outside. Looking out the window, she saw what she assumed was a Bobcat, with a narrow shovel attached in the back. She heard a rapping at the front door, and hauled it open to find Seth. "We're going to dig a trench now," he said, looking for all the world like a boy with a new toy.

"You guys want some coffee or something? Is there anything I need to do?"

"Coffee'd be great, but let's see how the trench goes, with the ground frozen and all. You're lucky—we can keep it narrow. And it's a good thing you don't have a paved driveway, because then you'd have a real mess."

Meg laughed. "Thank heavens for small favors. You mind if I watch?"

"As long as you stay out of the way. I don't want you falling in."

Meg bundled up and stood on her back steps, bouncing from foot to foot to keep warm, and observed while the small machine slashed into her driveway, as well as into the flower bed under her kitchen window. She sighed inwardly: she hadn't been here long enough to know what might have been growing there, but whatever it was wasn't going to grow again.

Seth kept a critical eye on progress, but occasionally he would bend down and pick something up. After the third time, he motioned her over. "You want to get a box or something?"

"Why?" Meg had to shout over the noise of the machine.

"Anytime you dig around these old places, you turn up artifacts. I thought you might want to save them."

"Sure. I'll get something." In the kitchen she located a shoe box she had been using for receipts and brought it out to him. He emptied his pockets of several unidentifiable lumps.

Chilled and bored by the process of digging, Meg went back inside and busied herself with small chores. In less than an hour she realized the machine had fallen silent. She went out the kitchen door and contemplated the trench that ran some twenty feet from her foundation to the lawn. Peering in, she could clearly see that the system was in trouble: a heavily rusted cast-iron pipe had fractured, and even now yuck was seeping out through the dirt that had clogged it. Seth came over to stand beside her.

"Sorry, it's not good. The main pipe gave out, and the septic tank is pretty well shot."

At least he'd prepared her for the worst. "How long will it take to replace them?"

"Tank's on its way, and I've got pipe in the van. The vendor'll haul the old tank out and drop the new one in. I can have things hooked up by the end of the day. I'll give my brother Stephen a call, tell him to head over here and help out."

Meg had no idea if the speed of this process was normal for plumbers, but she had the feeling Seth was making a special effort. The least she could do was let him warm up. "Are you ready for coffee now?"

"Sure. Oh, and here's your archeological trove. No treasure chests loaded with gold, I'm afraid, but some neat stuff."

"Thanks." Meg eyed distastefully the sodden clumps in the shoe box he handed her. He followed her into the kitchen, where she laid the box on the table and filled two sturdy mugs with hot coffee. She heard the Bobcat start up again, and then the sound faded into the distance. "He's leaving already?

"Yup. Tight schedule—I had to sweet-talk him into fitting you in. Look, I'm sorry about yesterday . . ."

"You've already apologized, you know."

"Yeah, but I try to avoid screwups like that. Gives us plumbers a bad name, you know." Seth pulled the shoe box of artifacts toward him and poked around. "This is part of the job I love. You never know what's going to turn up. Let's see." He rummaged through the muddy fragments with one finger. "A coin—looks like an 1895 Indian head penny, nice. A spoon, definitely twentieth century. A couple of marbles. You know, it seems like any place where there's been a kid over the last century, I end up finding marbles. And here's a nice piece of china. Too bad it got broken." He handed Meg a shard. He was right: it was a pretty piece of blue willowware, almost half of its original bowl shape. It looked old.

"Neat. Don't you find yourself wondering how these things got lost? Did somebody miss them? Or was it trash? What did they do with trash in the old days, for that matter?"

"Threw it down the privy, up to a point. Then town dumps. You have to remember, people didn't make as much trash as we do now. And there were plenty of thrifty Yankees around here— if you could save something or reuse it, you did. So I'd guess this pretty little bowl was broken a long time ago, from the look of it."

Meg pointed to a piece he hadn't mentioned, a much-rusted, large, and ornate multitoothed gear. "What's this?"

Seth picked it up and turned it in his hands. "Part of a—" He stopped himself and grinned at her. "Maybe I'll let you figure it out." He dropped it back into the box with a thunk, then turned his head to listen. "That'll be the guy with the tank. Damn, where's Stephen?" As Seth left the kitchen, he was pulling out his cell phone again. Meg peered out at the newly arrived truck carrying a bulky concrete object she assumed was her new septic tank. For its cost, it was disappointingly prosaic, but if she was lucky she'd never see it again anyway.

The truck was soon joined by a dented, not-new sports car. The man who climbed out bore a clear resemblance to Seth, although his hair was darker and he walked with a swagger. *This must be the brother, Stephen.* Seth approached him, clearly annoyed, and they argued briefly before Seth directed him toward the Chapin van while he went to talk to the truck driver.

In short order the old tank was hauled out, and the new tank was off the truck and in the ground, even though Stephen looked a bit sulky about taking orders from Seth, and moved slowly.

It was little more than an hour later when Seth knocked again. "You're good to go. Want to try out your drains?"

"With pleasure," Meg answered. She went to the kitchen sink and turned on the tap. The water disappeared with no hesitation. "Hallelujah! It works! And it'll keep working, right?"

"Of course it will. Chapin Brothers does good work."

"I hope so. Hey, listen—can I get you something?" Meg racked her brain to recall if she had any food in the place.

Stephen had come up behind Seth on the step, crowding him. "Hey, I could use something hot. It's freezing out here."

Grudgingly Seth moved into the room, and his brother pushed past him. "Hi," he said to Meg with an engaging grin. "I'm Stephen Chapin, the other half of Chapin Brothers. I'd offer to shake hands, but . . ."

Meg waved at her sink. "Please, wash! It's such a treat to be able to use the water again. And let me make some fresh coffee." She waited while Stephen washed his hands thoroughly, then she filled the pot and set the coffeemaker brewing. She was pleased to find a forgotten bag of cookies in a cupboard, and distributed a handful on a slightly chipped plate, which she set in the center of the table. "There. Sit down, you two. Coffee'll be done in a minute."

As she waited for the coffee to finish, she studied the brothers. The kinship was evident in their bone structure, but there were clearly differences. Seth had been unfailingly cheerful, at least around her. Stephen was another matter. He was darker in coloring than his brother, and seemed more intense. He was also fidgety, tapping his fingers on the table. When Meg set a mug of coffee in front of him, he flashed her another smile. "Hey, thanks. Seth says you're new to the area. I'd be happy to take you around, show you what's fun around here."

Was he flirting with her? "Thanks for the offer, but I unfortunately don't have much time for fun, Stephen. I don't know if Seth told you, but I'm trying to get this place ready to sell, and it keeps me busy."

That smile came again. "Ah, come on. You need to get out of the house now and then, don't you? Why not?"

"Stephen, she said no." Seth's voice was mild, but there was an edge to it.

Stephen turned to look at him. "Oh, yeah, right. She's one of you worker bees, right? No time off for good behavior. Sorry, Meg—big brother here has put the kibosh on fun."

There was a clear tension between the two brothers, and hidden currents that Meg didn't understand—or want to. It was none of her business. All she wanted from them was working plumbing.

Seth made an obvious effort to change the subject. "Have you ever looked into the history of this place, Meg?"

Meg shook her head, confused by his abrupt shift. "Haven't had time, but I suppose I should. The Realtor asked the same thing. She thought it might be a good selling point."

"Who's your Realtor?"

"Frances Clark."

Seth nodded. "She knows the market around here—she'll do a good job for you. But as for the history, it's definitely worth doing. Some of the land grants around here go back to the 1600s, when this part of the country was first surveyed. The records should be in Northampton or Springfield, if you ever have a free afternoon. Ask at the library in Northampton first—they have a lot of material on local history. You know, this whole area used to be called Warren's Corner, after that intersection of this road and what's now the highway. They changed the name to Granford in the early nineteenth century."

"I'll put it on my to-do list." Which now covered several pages. "How do you know all this, anyway?"

"I've lived here all my life, and I like history. But I mentioned it because there's a meeting of the Granford Historical Society tonight, and you might be interested in going and talking to some of the local historians. Maybe they could help. I'd be there myself—I'm on the board—but I promised my sister I'd help her install a new sink. She runs a B and B over toward Amherst."

Stephen drained his coffee cup and stood up. "Well, then, we'd better head over there. Wouldn't want to keep Rachel waiting, would we? And I'm sure Meg here will have a rip-roaring good time at that society of yours." His tone was snide.

Seth gave him another exasperated look, then stood up more slowly.

Meg followed them to the back door. "Seth, where's this meeting, and when?"

"At seven, first Tuesday of every month. The society owns a building on the green in town, but they meet in the basement of the church next door, because the heating's better. They're a good group. You'll like them." He checked his watch. "Oops, gotta go! I'll send you the bill, no hurry. Let me know if you have any more problems. Oh, and watch out for the open trench, if you decide to go out tonight. And you're probably going to need some more gravel for the driveway, unless you're thinking about paving it. I know a guy . . ."

Meg laughed. Seth seemed determined to solve all her problems. "Let me know later, okay? You've got places to be."

Stephen grinned at her as he followed Seth out the door. "Have fun with the old fogies tonight. You would have had a better time with me."

And then they were gone. With a start, Meg realized that she could shower now, and went upstairs to take advantage of that immediately. While she soaped and rinsed—and made a mental note to replace the trickling shower head—she debated whether she really wanted to go out that night, much less to a meeting. But she'd spent far too much time indoors of late, and it could be a good business move. After all, the more she could find out about the house, the better. For a brief moment she wondered what it would be like to have the kinds of roots in a community that Seth had—three hundred years, hadn't he said? But she had no intention of staying in Granford long enough to put down any kind of roots. She'd go to the meeting for information only.

5

Meg bundled up well before she headed out for the meeting: down coat, scarf, hat, heavy gloves. The wind was cutting. She had lived in Boston for years and hadn't minded the cold there. Maybe the stone and concrete of the city held the heat; maybe the buildings blocked the worst of the wind. Here in Granford, icy blasts swept across open fields and seeped through her coat. She hurried to her car, which was freezing but out of the wind, then started it and sat shivering while the heater came slowly to life.

Seth had told her that the Granford Historical Society met at the church on the green, in the center of town. There were a few cars in the lot when Meg pulled in, and she hurried to the door to get out of the wind. Inside it was marginally warmer, and she wandered through the poorly lit corridors looking for the meeting room. Luckily it was the only one with lights on. Meg poked her head in tentatively, to be greeted by a woman of about forty or so who was wrestling with an elderly slide projector. She looked up quickly when Meg entered, and her gaze was frankly curious.

"Hi! I'm Gail Selden. You looking for the historical society meeting? I haven't seen you here before."

Relieved that she had found the right place, Meg entered the room. "No, I'm new in town. I just moved to the house at 81 County Line Road."

"Ah, the Warren place. Welcome! You wouldn't know anything about projectors, would you? I go through this every time we use this old monster."

Meg shook her head. "Sorry, no. Now if it was PowerPoint, maybe."

Gail laughed. "Heaven forbid we should use anything that modern! This thing is approaching antique, and I'm not sure we can still get bulbs for it, but I just keep my fingers crossed that it'll keep going, because we can't afford a new one. Take a seat. I think a few more people said they planned to come—it's not every month we have a guest speaker."

Meg looked around at the twenty or so folding chairs that had been set up in rows, less than half occupied. "What's the talk about?"

Gail had apparently succeeded in bringing the projector to life, and was fiddling with the switch that advanced the anticipated slide carousel. "There, got it. There's a professor from UMass who's going to be talking about nineteenth-century agriculture in this area. I brought along some old tools from our collection so we can get a sense of how things were done. So, what brings you here? Please, sit."

Meg took a seat in the front row, while Gail leaned against a folding table covered with rusty farm implements. "As I said, I just moved in, and I thought maybe I should find out more about the house, its history. My real estate agent said it might help when I sell it."

Gail's face fell. "You're selling? I was hoping that someone would stick around this time. I know it's been rented out for quite a while, and the tenants have been okay, but they just don't put much into keeping the place up, you know?"

Meg smiled, while feeling a pang of guilt. "Tell me about it! Every time I get something fixed, something else falls apart. Today it was the drains. Actually, it's my mother who owns it, so I guess she's the one responsible for renting it out."

"Well, maybe when you sell we'll get some long-term people in. It's a great house, and it comes with a lot of the original land. The wetlands on one side are protected, you know."

Meg nodded, but Gail had already turned to greet a couple of new arrivals whom she obviously knew. Meg studied the room: low ceilinged, wooden floor, the walls covered in paint-crusted bead board. How old was the church? This room looked as though it hadn't changed in a hundred years. She turned in her seat, keeping an eye on new arrivals. A few people headed for a table set up at the side, where a large coffeemaker burbled, and set down cakes or plates of cookies covered with plastic wrap. Meg checked her watch: ten past seven. Apparently the schedule was flexible.

She heard Gail's voice again. "Ah, here you are! I was beginning to wonder if you'd bailed out on us."

"Not at all, dear lady, but I must confess I was tardy in assembling all my slides. But I wouldn't miss this—the subject is dear to my heart."

Christopher? Meg knew of his interest in orchards, particularly hers, but she hadn't thought he was an historian as well.

Christopher handed a tray of slides to Gail and made his way to the front. "Meg! How delightful to see you again, and so soon."

Meg stood up to greet him. "Christopher, I had no idea you'd be here. Seth Chapin—my new plumber—thought I might be interested in learning a bit more about the history of my place, so here I am."

"So your plumber arrived at last. And your problems are resolved?"

Meg nodded. "They are, I hope. I have a new septic system."

Gail came up to Christopher and laid a hand on his arm. "We ought to get started—I think this is everyone."

Christopher surveyed the sparse crowd. "Ah well, I guess it's to be expected. But you know me. I'm always happy to talk about farm history. You've met Meg here?" When Gail nodded, he went on. "She's graciously promised to allow us to continue to use her orchard for our research."

"Assuming, of course, it survives the proposed changes," Gail said, shaking her head. "But let's not get started on that again. You go on and talk."

"With pleasure." Christopher went to the front of the room and took a position beside the rickety screen. Gail went to the projector and clicked on the first slide. Christopher began. "As I'm sure you all know well, Granford, like so many early New England towns, was founded by a small group of farmers in ..."

Meg listened as Christopher spoke knowledgeably without notes. The slides he had brought ranged from early deeds to bills of sale and advertising flyers for various farm products. After a while she found she was finally warm—and struggling to stay awake. She was jerked from a near doze by the sound of a cell phone.

"Oops, sorry—it's mine," Gail said, pulling the phone from her pocket. She strode toward the back of the room and spoke quietly into it, then returned. "Sorry, folks, I'm going to have to duck out on you—crisis at home. John, can you talk about the stuff I brought over, and make sure the items get back to the society building? Tomorrow's plenty of time. And can anybody here work this dang projector?" A couple of hands went up. "Next meeting's the fourteenth of next month, and we're going to have to review the budget. I'll send you a reminder, with the details. Christopher, please go on. I'm sorry I'm going to miss the rest of your talk. Bye, all."

Gail bustled out of the room, and Christopher resumed without a hitch. It was clear that he loved his subject, and the small crowd listened patiently; some people asked intelligent questions. Finally Christopher wound down, and John moved quietly to the front, demonstrating various tools that Meg didn't recognize. Christopher seized on one that had a wickedly curved blade at one end, and proceeded to demonstrate how to use it, swinging it with enthusiasm and putting John in some peril. Meg sighed with relief when Christopher put it down—as did John.

After a few questions, the group stood up and moved en masse toward the refreshments. Meg hung back. She felt awkward trying to break into the group, all of whom obviously knew each other. Nor did they make any effort to approach her. Was this a sample of Yankee reticence?

Christopher noticed her hesitation and came over. "Did you enjoy that?" he asked.

"Yes, I did, although I have no idea what most of that stuff is. Easy to forget our agricultural beginnings, isn't it?"

"It is indeed. We're so accustomed to stopping in at the market and finding whatever we need, we've lost sight of where it comes from. Which these days may be Mexico or China, all too often."

"You don't approve?"

Christopher shook his head, more in sorrow than in disagreement. "We live in a global economy, I know, but I don't think a journey of a thousand miles improves the flavor of a tomato. And I fear the next generation will not know what they're missing. But I do what I can in the orchard. You're in for some happy surprises come harvest time, I assure you."

Meg didn't see any point in reminding him that she didn't expect to be around in the fall. Together they drifted toward the table with the food and helped themselves to coffee and cookies. Extrovert Christopher had no trouble engaging several people in conversation, and Meg listened and smiled and sipped her coffee. When she looked at her watch, she was surprised to find it was nearly ten. Christopher did the same, then exclaimed, "Heavens! And I've an early class. Good people, thank you for putting up with my obsession this evening."

People laughed and thanked him, then turned to clearing away the tables and packing up the projector. Meg was left standing alone, unsure whether she should offer to help but recognizing that she didn't know where anything went anyway. She was relieved when Christopher turned to her again. "Shall I see you to your car?"

Meg smiled gratefully at him. "Thank you. I should be getting home myself."

"Well, then, let us take our leave. Good night, all!" Christopher escorted her up the stairs and out to the parking lot. The temperature had dropped yet again, and emerging from the relative warmth of the church, Meg shivered.

With a cheerful wave, Christopher headed for his car. Meg climbed into hers quickly and turned on the engine and the heater, full blast. She looked around at the town. No lights showed, and there were few cars on the road. Sleepy didn't begin to describe it. Moribund, maybe.

What had she learned tonight? Gail seemed pleasant. The others ... She'd have to reserve judgment about them, because she hadn't talked with most of them. But what did it matter? She didn't plan to stay around long enough to make friends. She'd have to get back together with Gail, find out what she knew about the house. Funny that everyone she met seemed to know it well. Better than she did, certainly.

The drive home took no more than five minutes, and when

she approached the house, she was glad she had left some lights on. This was not the city; this was open country, with houses spaced widely. From the looks of those she had passed, most people were already tucked into bed.

Meg, you're not in Boston anymore.

6

The following morning Meg came down to the kitchen feeling satisfied with herself. She had dealt with her plumbing crisis efficiently and successfully, and now she could tell prospective buyers that the septic system was in good shape. Moreover, she had gotten out of the house, gone to the meeting, and even enjoyed herself.

She filled the coffeemaker with water, then scraped off the dishes she had used for a sketchy dinner the evening before. As she rinsed, she looked out over the meadow, trying to imagine it in spring, in summer, with grasses blowing in the wind, the trees in full leaf ... She looked down to see water rising in her sink, topped with greasy scum.

"Damn!" To think she had believed Seth when he said he'd fixed it. Had he taken her for a gullible idiot and done a shoddy patch job? At least she hadn't paid him yet, and the trench was still wide-open. Well, he had said to call if there was a problem, and she was looking at one now. She grabbed her cell phone and punched in the number she had come to know far too well.

Seth answered on the second ring. "Chapin Plumbing." Damn him, how could he always be so cheerful?

"Seth, it's Meg Corey. Something's screwed up with the plumbing again. Like last time. You told me it was going to be fine!" She was mad, in large part because she had been feeling so good about things just minutes before. And Seth had said it would work, and she had believed him.

"Hey, slow down. What's the problem?"

Meg stalked over to the sink and recoiled. "The sink's backing up again. I don't want to look any further."

"Okay, I'm on my way. Sit tight."

Meg devoted the ten minutes it took him to arrive to building up a good head of steam. When Seth knocked at the back door, she opened it before he could lower his hand. He took a look at her face and nearly backed away. "Okay, show me."

Wordlessly she pointed to the sink, where the problem was obvious. He looked at it and his brow furrowed. "This should not be happening."

"Tell me about it."

"No, really. This system was clear yesterday; there's no way it should block up like this. You used it last night?"

Meg nodded. "I even took a shower before dinner."

"I'm going to have to go take a look. Sorry about this, Meg." Seth strode quickly out the back door. Meg closed the door behind him and watched as he stared at the muddy trench where the tank sat. He shook his head, then went to his van and emerged with a long pry bar, which he used to lever up the top panel on the tank. Then he knelt down next to the open porthole and poked around into the dark depth of the tank.

Even from the kitchen door Meg could see his expression change.

He stood up slowly, clambered out of the hole, and approached the kitchen door. Meg opened the door and stepped outside to join him. His face was almost green. "What?"

He took a deep breath. "Meg, you'd better call 911. I think I've found your problem. There's a dead body in there."

She stared at him in horror. "What do you mean?" He couldn't mean what she thought he did, could he? No, she didn't want to believe that.

He spoke with slow precision. "When I opened the clean-out for the tank ... There's a body in there. That's what caused the blockage. Human. A man. I didn't look any more closely, but it's pretty clear whoever it is ... was ... is dead. Make the call, will you? I'd do it myself, but my hands are kind of muddy."

Silently Meg backed into the kitchen and fumbled for the phone. She punched in 911 and waited a few moments until someone answered. "This is Meg Corey in Granford—81 County Line Road. There's a dead body in my septic tank. No, I don't mean an animal—a man. The plumber just found it. Him. Seth Chapin. He's here now. Right. No, I know it wasn't there yesterday. The tank was just installed yesterday. I don't know who you need to send, but just do it, please."

She put the phone down and stared at nothing for a moment. Then she shook herself and, pulling on her coat, made her way out the back door. When she sat down on the step next to Seth, she was surprised to find she was trembling, which seemed silly. She hadn't even seen the body.

"They coming?" Seth said without looking at her.

"I guess. Who ... how long ... ?" She fumbled for the right question.

Seth looked down at his hands, hanging between his knees. "I'm going to guess that this wasn't an accident or a suicide. Which means it's a homicide, and that means it'll involve the state police in Northampton, the county seat. But the police chief'll be here first, since he's only a mile or so away."

"Ah." Meg couldn't think of anything better to say, so they sat silently, contemplating the gash in the driveway, and the tank, and the dark hole in the top, and what lay inside. She was startled when Seth stood up abruptly.

"Well, we've got company," he said. "Here's where the fun starts."

Meg dragged her eyes away from the trench to see a police car pulling into her driveway. It stopped, and a rangy man in uniform stepped out of the car, buttoning his coat. He seemed to be in no hurry: he looked up at the house, then at Seth and Meg, then at the hole in the driveway. After completing his thorough survey of the scene, the officer walked over to the back door.

"Seth." He nodded before turning to Meg. "You Ms. Corey?"

Meg stood up and held out her hand. "Yes, Meg Corey. I moved here last month."

The officer took her hand and shook it briefly. "Art Preston, Granford chief of police. Nice place you've got. So, where's our victim?"

Seth pointed across the driveway. "In the septic tank. I'm the one who found him."

"Ah." The officer turned and once again scanned the scene before approaching the crater. "New installation?"

Seth moved to stand beside him. "Yeah. It went in yesterday.

The old one was shot to hell. Jake didn't have time to fill in the trench yesterday. He was going to come back this morning."

"Don't suppose you want to confess to stuffing the body in there when you hooked it up?"

"Sorry, Art, it wasn't me. You want to take a look now?"

The chief grimaced. "Let's wait for the ME and the rest of the team. Detective's on his way from Northampton. I don't want to mess with the scene any more than necessary, not that it's going to make a rat's ass worth of difference. Jake dig the hole?" Chief Preston pulled a notebook out of his pocket and opened it to a new page.

"Yeah."

"Ah." Chief Preston made a note.

"Chief?" Meg's voice sounded feeble to her own ears. "You have any idea who it might be? I mean, is anybody missing?"

"Can't say, ma'am. Man can't have been there more'n twenty-four hours. Right, Seth?"

Seth nodded, but then Meg interrupted. "Less than that—I was here until after dinner."

The chief made another note. "And you went out after that?"

"Yes, to the historical society meeting." *Where plenty of people saw me*, Meg reflected. "I arrived home about ten."

"You didn't notice anything out of the ordinary?"

"No. It was dark, and I came in by the front door. I didn't go anywhere near the trench."

They all stood silently for a moment, until Meg asked, "What happens now?"

"We wait for the state crime scene unit—they need to get pictures. And the medical examiner, of course. Maybe you'd rather wait inside, ma'am?"

Meg couldn't decide whether she should go inside: she was sure she didn't want to see whatever it was they were going to pull out of the septic tank, but on the other hand, the police chief, who couldn't be more than ten years her senior, was treating her like she was a fragile flower of womanhood. Seth still looked unnerved by his gruesome discovery. The police chief just looked thoughtful. She stayed put.

Five minutes later an unmarked van pulled into her driveway

and parked behind the police car. A stocky gray-haired man climbed out and approached the group.

"Hey, Art, Seth. What've you got for me? And who's this nice young lady?"

Much as she appreciated being called "young," Meg thought she ought to assert her rights on the scene. "I'm Meg Corey, and I'm the new owner." Meg was getting tired of trying to explain the ownership, so she decided to keep it simple. "You're the medical examiner?"

The man nodded briskly. "That's me. Samuel Eastman, at your service. I heard the Tuckers left, but I didn't know anyone was here. What a mess, eh?"

Meg summoned up a faint smile. "Well, the septic system was a goner, but the body's new."

"We'd better take a look." He went back to his van, rummaged around, and emerged a few moments later with a mask and latex gloves, which he pulled on. Feeling useless, Meg went back to the steps again and watched as the three men went over to the trench and stared into it. They conferred, their expressions serious and intent. Then the ME knelt and poked around the depths of the septic tank, inserting his arm deep into the opening. He emerged clutching something triumphantly, and Meg guessed it was the victim's wallet. Still gloved, the ME opened it, reached in, and extracted a driver's license.

After a word to the other men, Seth came over and sat next to her again. "You okay?"

Meg nodded. "So far. You know who it is?"

"Chandler Hale."

7

Interesting, Meg thought. The world seemed to be rotating clockwise, and there were green sparkling spots on the fringes of her vision. Did this mean she was going to faint? She had never done it, so she had no basis for comparison. Chandler Hale was lying—or did she mean floating?—dead in her new septic tank. It was a lot to take in. *Snap out of it, Meg!*

The spots cleared, the whirling slowed. Seth was watching her, clearly concerned. Meg tried to summon up a smile. "It's okay, Seth. I'm not going to pass out on you. Are you sure it's Chandler?"

"That's what the ID says, although since he's facedown we won't know for sure until we get him out of there. We're going to wait for the detective for that." He hesitated, as if wondering how to phrase his next question. "You knew him?"

Meg laughed, without humor. "You could say that. Until about six months ago, we were ... seeing each other, in Boston. Wait a minute—you knew him?"

"He is, or I guess he *was*, heading up the Granford Grange project. I'm on the Granford Board of Selectmen, and we've been involved from the beginning."

"Small world. I don't suppose you happened to notice how he died? Like is there a stake through his heart or something?"

"Sorry. It's kind of dark in there, and I admit I didn't want to look too closely. I didn't see any blood, though. The ME will take him away and figure it out."

Meg fought a hysterical giggle. "Poor Chandler. He was always so ... fastidious. He would be appalled by this."

Chandler, dead. Someone she knew, had known well. Someone she had seen only two days earlier—and someone with whom she had parted on less-than-happy terms. Someone who might possibly have been killed right here. Why would anyone kill Chandler? And why here?

Seth was still watching her. "I'm sorry."

"Why?"

"I mean, I'm sorry he's dead. And I'm sorry it had to be here that he was found."

Something about his tone made Meg look at him curiously. "You didn't like him much, did you? But I don't suppose you killed him."

"No, of course not. And by the way, if I had killed him, I wouldn't have dumped the body in your lap. Besides, it's not a great recommendation for my plumbing efforts, is it?"

If Seth was trying to be funny, he fell flat, but the effort was endearing. Meg studied him: he wasn't green anymore, but he looked as rattled as she felt. "You didn't ask if I killed him."

"Did you?" Seth gave her a ghost of a smile.

"No. And just for the record, I had no reason to want him dead."

"Then that's all right."

It was a funny way of putting it, but suddenly Meg was very glad that she had Seth sitting beside her. "What happens now?"

Seth leaned back and stared at the sky. "The state detective is on his way. Art's just here to keep an eye on things, since it's in his jurisdiction. The detective will probably want a statement from you, and I guess you can ID Chandler."

Meg sat up straighter and turned to face Seth squarely. "You know, I hadn't seen Chandler in months. And then he showed up at my door here, two days ago. We had dinner that night. Uh ..." Meg paused, wondering how much more she should say.

"What?" Seth prompted, casting a quick glance at the men huddled by the trench. No one was paying them any attention.

"We had an argument, a minor one, at the restaurant that night. All very civilized—Chandler wasn't the type for public scenes—but someone might have noticed we weren't happy. Then after dinner we came straight back, and he dropped me off here and left. That's the last I saw of him."

Seth waited a moment before responding. "I don't mean to

pry, but was there anything about your argument that might be important? I mean, were you rehashing old stuff, or was there something else?"

"We'd both agreed that the past was past. He wasn't trying to rekindle things, if that's what you're asking. His real purpose for inviting me to dinner was to find out if I'd be willing to feed him inside information about Granford and about how the development deal was going—to be his spy. I told him I wasn't interested, although I think I said it in slightly stronger language."

Seth looked relieved. "Shouldn't be a problem, then. There are a lot of people around here who weren't real happy with Chandler Hale. The detective'll keep busy interviewing them all."

"I'm sorry, I hadn't realized what a big thing this project was around here. I haven't been here long, and I haven't been paying attention. You'll have to fill me in, after we take care of ... all this." Meg waved vaguely at the scene before her: police chief, ME, corpse.

Seth stood up. "Meg, you're turning blue. Why don't you wait inside, at least until the detective arrives?" He peeled off a grimy glove and held out his hand. Meg took it and struggled stiffly to her feet.

"Thanks, Seth, maybe I will. And maybe I should make some more coffee." She seemed to spend half her life these days making coffee, but she wanted something hot, and it would give her something to do while she waited. "I can offer these guys coffee, right? Or would that compromise the investigation?"

Seth smiled. "I think it's a good idea—I'm sure they'll appreciate it. Go on inside, now."

Gratefully Meg fled into her kitchen, and went about the mundane tasks of grinding beans and pouring water into the coffeemaker. She was so lost in thought that she was startled by a loud pounding on her back door a few minutes later. At the kitchen door stood a man she didn't recognize. Art Preston and Seth stood behind him.

"Ms. Corey? I'm Detective Marcus. I'd like to ask you some questions."

"Of course." Meg opened the door, and the three men entered, taking up a lot of the free space in the kitchen. "Shall we sit in here?" The trio moved to her kitchen table, then stood there expectantly. Meg realized with a start that they were waiting for her to sit down first. "Can I get you some coffee? You must be cold."

"No, thanks." Detective Marcus spoke decisively, and the others took their cue from him. She poured herself a cup of coffee and sat, focusing on the detective.

He spoke quickly. "The ME has suggested a possible identity for the victim, based on identification found on the body, and Chapin here has confirmed it."

Meg's stomach unclenched; she hadn't realized that she had been dreading looking at Chandler, dead. She'd have to thank Seth later.

The detective was still talking. "Did you know Chandler Hale?"

Meg folded her hands in front of her on the table. "Yes. We had a personal relationship when I lived in Boston, and we were professional colleagues."

"You a banker?" the detective asked. "Did you know why he was in Granford?"

"I previously worked for a bank in Boston. But I haven't been here very long, and I've had little contact with the rest of the town, so I was unaware of the development project until the other day, when Chandler showed up here."

"He came here?" the detective asked.

"Yes, with his assistant. He said he was looking for the former tenants. He was surprised to find me here. We had dinner together Monday."

"Here?"

"No, we drove to Amherst."

"So you two went out. What time did you get back?"

"About nine, I think."

"And then he left?"

"Yes, Detective, he did. I did not invite him in. We had a disagreement at the restaurant, and I asked him to drive me home. I didn't see him after that." Meg wondered if she should be angry about what the detective might—or might not—be insinuating, and she decided to turn the tables. "I assume you're going to check if anyone saw him the next day?"

"You said something about an assistant?"

"Yes. Lucinda something, I forget the last name. We spoke only briefly. But she should know what Chandler's schedule was on Tuesday."

The detective made a note, then turned his attention to Seth. "You installed the septic tank, right?"

"Yes. It went in yesterday. I had a guy coming to fill the trench this morning, but Meg called to say she was having problems again, so I came over to check it out and found Hale."

Detective Marcus was silent for a few moments, making some more notes. Seth and Art shifted in their chairs but didn't say anything. Finally the sheriff looked back at Meg.

"Who else knew about the installation?"

Meg stared at him. "I don't know."

"Where were you yesterday?"

"Here, mostly. Once the tank was installed, I cleaned up, had something to eat, and went to a historical society meeting in town after dinner. I returned about ten."

"Did you notice if the hole had been disturbed at all?"

"No. It was dark when I came back, and I went straight inside through the front door."

"But you knew it was going to be filled in this morning."

"Yes, because Seth told me. Look, can I ask what happens now?"

"We're waiting for the forensic team. They'll want to see the body in situ, and then they'll extract it and process it. I expect they'll want to drain the tank and look for any further evidence. Seth, you can get someone to clean it out?"

Seth nodded. "Sure. Your team will have to tell us what they need. But it's only been used for a day, so it shouldn't take long."

Meg realized that the detective was eyeing her with curiosity. "Did you have more questions?" she asked.

"Ms. Corey, are you sure you've told us everything about your relationship with Mr. Hale?"

"Of course."

"You both worked in Boston in the same profession, right? Yet you weren't aware of his activities in Granford?"

"My bank in Boston merged with another one last year, and I

was let go last fall, so I was out of the loop. Look, I was a municipal analyst, and he was involved in corporate projects. I didn't have anything to do with real estate or property development. And we didn't talk much about business even when we were seeing each other. Certainly not since."

Seth interrupted. "Detective, you can't think she had anything to do with this. She wasn't around that night—she was in town, with a bunch of witnesses."

The detective fixed Seth with a stare that Meg found hard to read. "You know what time he died? Didn't think so. We have to look at all the possibilities. She knew the victim—we'll be looking into that. She certainly knew that the tank was sitting there, open. The time frame is loose, and it's unlikely that we'll be able to narrow it down much. So we have to consider her. And you as well."

"Me?" Seth said.

"You also knew about the tank. And you have a certain interest in the development project, don't you?"

"Fair enough. But we've been working on that in a public forum. Why would I want to kill the man?"

"I can't say. All I am saying is that we're going to look into it. You can start by giving us a list of people who knew that there was a convenient hole in the ground where they could hide a body—and assume that it wouldn't be discovered too fast."

Another van pulled up outside, and the detective stood up abruptly. "That'll be the lab guys. Ms. Corey, I don't have to tell you not to leave town, do I?"

Where else would she go? "I'll be around. You can reach me here or on my cell phone."

"All right. Seth, when's your guy due?"

"Anytime now."

"I'll go check in with the team, and then they'll let us know what they need. Ma'am." He gave Meg a cursory nod, then let himself out the door.

Meg, Seth, and the police chief sat silently for a moment. Art was first to break the silence. "Damn, what a mess—in more ways than one. I'd better get out there and do my duty. Seth, the guy's got a point. You've got as much reason as anyone around here to try to derail this project. Not that I think you'd go so far as to kill anyone. But still, he's got to check it out."

Seth sighed. "I know. Remind me again why I ran for office, will you?"

Art smiled. "You're a glutton for punishment. Ms. Corey, nice to meet you. I just wish the circumstances had been a bit more pleasant." He followed the detective out the door, leaving Meg and Seth alone in the kitchen.

"What did he mean, you've got issues with this project?" Meg was trying to make sense of the undercurrents among the men.

Seth met her look squarely. "As a Granford selectman, I have to consider the needs of the town. Heck, I encouraged bringing in outside investors. We need them. But it's a big chunk of my land that they're talking about. That didn't become clear until we were well into discussions. So I'm caught in the middle. And then the project kept growing, and so did the part of my property they wanted. Marcus could see it as a motive. He knows how these things work."

Meg laughed grimly. "Funny thing—part of my land is affected also, although I didn't even know that until the day before yesterday, and I'm not sure how I feel about it. And I suppose the detective could point to other motives for me. Maybe I'm supposed to be the jilted woman who killed Chandler for revenge. I just snapped when he showed up unexpectedly. Or maybe I killed him because he made unwanted advances. Or *didn't* make advances but spurned *my* unwanted advances. Do I make a more convincing murderer than you do? Maybe you and I did it together. Or did one of us hire somebody else to do the dirty work?" Meg could sense hysteria bubbling up in her chest and managed to shut herself up.

Seth gave her a small smile. "Look, let's not get ahead of ourselves. We'll see what they find when they pull out the body and clean out the tank. We've got a lot of questions to answer before we start worrying about how suspicious we look. Right now, I'd better get out there and do some damage control." He hesitated, and Meg wondered what he wanted to say.

"Yes?" she prompted.

"Look, I can't imagine that you want to stay here tonight. How about you spend the night at my sister's? I think I told you she runs a B and B, and I'm sure she'll be glad to have you."

"I don't want to be any bother," Meg protested. *And I don't want to pay the going rate for a room either.* It had already been an expensive few days, and it would get worse if she had to find herself a lawyer.

He seemed to read her thoughts. "It's off-season, and if Rachel hasn't got a booking by now, the bed's going begging anyway. She won't mind."

"All right, I guess," Meg said. Much as she hated to admit it, she felt profoundly relieved that she didn't have to stay in the house, at least for this one night.

"I'll give Rachel a call." Seth went into the dining room to use his cell phone, and Meg cleared away the untouched coffee mugs while keeping an eye on the activities outside.

He was back in under a minute. "You're all set. Why don't you let me drive you over when we're done here? I can swing by tomorrow morning and bring you back. Okay?"

"Isn't that out of your way?"

"It's no trouble."

Meg sighed and said, "Thank you. That'd be very kind of you."

"Well, then, I'd better go out and see how the clean-out is going."

Meg watched him as he joined the rest of the men clustered around the hole in the driveway, and then she turned away. She didn't want to see what came out of it. She couldn't allow herself to think of that sodden corpse as Chandler, someone she had known intimately, someone she had once cared about. Whatever had happened between them, he didn't deserve to die that way. And she didn't deserve to have to clean up the mess.

8

The afternoon dragged on interminably. The light was fading from the sky before the various teams of people finished collecting whatever they thought might be evidence, and the body was bundled up and carted away. After the last official vehicle had pulled away, Seth reappeared at the back door. "Listen, you have any plans for eating?"

Meg realized she had completely forgotten lunch. "No, I haven't even thought about it."

"You look like you could use some food. I thought maybe we could stop in Northampton on the way to Rachel's."

Seth looked like an embarrassed schoolboy, and Meg was touched. And she realized she *was* hungry. "Okay, sure. Let me grab some clothes for tonight, and I'll be good to go. Give me five?"

"Deal." He smiled more openly this time.

She made her way to the bedroom at the back of the house that she had been using since she arrived. Based on the out-of-date flowered wallpaper, she guessed that the sisters Lula and Nettie had staked out the two front rooms, and subsequent tenants hadn't bothered to change anything. From the look of the back bedroom, there had been few guests. The room reeked of mothballs and abandonment. Still, it was reasonably clean and quiet, and it suited Meg for now.

She sat heavily on the creaking bed, glad for the moment of silence. She felt numb. Chandler was dead, and all she could summon up was a combination of sadness and annoyance. Not exactly overwhelming grief. She had never met any of his family, and she wondered who the police would notify of his death—and who would actually miss him.

Being suspected of killing him was unsettling. If it weren't so personal, she would have found it amusing: Chandler's last joke. She was the most law-abiding person she knew, and the idea of committing a murder, much less wrestling with an inert body, was beyond her comprehension. But how was she supposed to convince the detective of that? He didn't know her. Nobody in Granford knew her, and they couldn't vouch for her. And her Boston friends ... would remember when she was with Chandler. What would they say?

Enough, Meg! Right now she was tired and hungry, and those were things she could do something about. She scrabbled through the drawers of the walnut dresser, hunting for clean jeans and a shirt without paint streaks, then rummaged through the pitifully small closet and tossed the change of clothes, a nightgown, and some toiletries into a bag.

Suddenly she sat down hard again, slammed by another unwanted thought, one that she had managed to avoid thinking about all afternoon. Was Chandler's death going to put a damper on selling the house? Who would want a house where a murder had happened? Maybe if she was lucky it hadn't happened here. Maybe the detective would find that he had been killed somewhere else. Unfortunately this would always be the place the body had been found. And then there was the community development project, which might or might not have died along with Chandler. How would local people feel about that? And if the project wasn't dead, she might lose the orchard she hadn't even known about a few days earlier.

"Everything okay?" Seth called up the stairs.

Meg shook herself. If nothing else, she had found herself one friend in town, and luckily he was one who was willing to help her. Of course, he might turn out to be the killer. How was she supposed to know? Still, she had a hard time visualizing Seth as a murderer—and how could her luck be that bad? No, she was going to consider him one of the good guys and hope for the best. For the moment, at least she knew where her next meal was coming from and where she would sleep that night.

"Be right down," she answered, and finished packing.

When she headed down the stairs, Seth was waiting at the

bottom, apparently engrossed in a study of the construction of the stair spindles. When he saw her coming, he nodded toward them. "Nice. Not the originals, but probably mid–nineteenth century. Looks like they upgraded the place then, added some fancy touches."

"I wouldn't know. I haven't really looked into it." Feeling somehow apologetic, Meg collected her coat and her purse, and led the way to the front door and yanked it open. Seth politely held it open for her, which surprised her. *Why are you surprised?* she wondered. *Plumbers don't have to be boors.* In fact, Seth kept surprising her. He was clean, courteous, intelligent, a whole list of Boy Scout traits. She was going to have to rethink a lot of her preconceptions about plumbers.

"Hope you don't mind riding in the van," he said, unlocking the passenger door for her.

"Not at all." She peered over her shoulder at the materials and tools in the back, neatly arrayed. "My, this looks almost like a workshop. You have everything right here."

"Pretty close. You never know what you're going to run into, and it saves time if I don't have to run back to the shop for parts." He started the engine and turned on the heater. "What do you like to eat?"

"Almost anything. I haven't had a chance to try most of the restaurants around here, so feel free to pick something you like."

"Let's head for Northampton, then. They've got something for everyone." Before pulling out, he took another look at her. "Hey, I know you didn't kill him. And from what little I knew of him, there are probably plenty of other candidates."

"I'm not sure that makes me feel any better. I mean, I was involved with him, for a while. Even if I didn't kill him, what does that say about my judgment, if he was so widely disliked?" She caught herself. "Don't answer that. It's a stupid question, and nothing you have to worry about. And Chandler and I were over a long time ago, no matter what happened in Granford. I guess it's just the shock of seeing him unexpectedly and then finding him dead. It seems so unreal." Meg hesitated for a moment. "Did anyone say how Chandler was killed?"

Seth kept his eyes on the road. "Apparently the old standby 'blunt force trauma'—a blow to the head. That's all they could tell for the moment."

"Oh. So he was dead when he went in?"

Seth nodded. "Looks like it. I can't imagine anyone could get him in there if he wasn't. But don't worry about it, Meg. Let the police do their job, and get on with your life. How are you enjoying your house?"

Meg was relieved by his change of subject. "I don't think 'enjoying' is quite the right word. Sometimes I feel sorry for it—people have done such tacky things to it."

Seth smiled, his gaze still on the road. "If you can tell that, you can see what lies beneath. And the place has good bones."

Meg turned in her seat to face him. "That's an interesting way to put it. You said you had been inside before?"

"Sure. More than once, in fact, now that I think about it. When the Warren sisters, uh, passed on . . ." He paused, uncertain.

Meg interrupted, "Hey, it's okay. I only met them once, and my mother barely knew them."

He looked relieved. "Well, when the place was rented out, you can guess that the tenants had some problems now and then. The sisters had never done anything to upgrade the plumbing—I think their father had it put in, and I won't even guess when. We were the nearest plumbers, so we were the ones who got called when something went wrong."

"That's right—you said you live close by."

"Yup, just over the hill from you."

The trip to Northampton was brief. Seth concentrated on the road, tossing a question at Meg now and then. "You said you hadn't been around here long?"

"Just since the first of the year. You heard what I told the detective: I used to work at a bank in Boston, but they got bought out and then they downsized. I guess I came out better than most, and at least I didn't have to worry about supporting a family. Then my mother had this bright idea that fixing up the house would keep me busy while I sorted out what to do next." *I'm still trying to figure out just how to thank my mother for that*, Meg thought sarcastically.

Seth chuckled. "An old house'll do that, all right."

He skillfully navigated his large vehicle into a parking lot behind the main street in Northampton. "Here we are," he said. "Hop out."

Meg opened the door and climbed down from the high seat, looking around her. "Where are we going?"

"I was thinking of this great Argentinian place just up there. Unless you want Tibetan, or Thai, or vegan—well, you get the idea. Ever eaten Argentinian?"

"Can't say that I have."

"Well, there you are, a new experience. Come on." Seth led the way down the street, then up a series of steps to a small restaurant that smelled wonderful. He greeted the owner by name, and they were quickly escorted to a table.

After they were settled with menus, Meg asked, "You come here often?"

Seth was reading the specials for the day. "What? Oh, sure. I like to eat in Northampton. You never know what you're going to find."

"Maybe you can give me a list—in case I ever have a chance to eat out again. I haven't seen much in the way of restaurants in Granford."

Seth laughed. "No, there's not a lot to choose from. Certainly not like Boston. But this isn't far, and there are more good places in Amherst. Want me to order?"

"Please. You know what's good here."

Meg watched Seth as he conferred with the waitress, who looked like a college student. He didn't wear a ring, so she assumed he wasn't married. But maybe a ring would get in the way of plumbing activities. Still, he hadn't had to call anyone to say he wasn't going to be home for dinner . . . *Meg, stop it!* She wasn't looking for a new relationship, especially since she didn't plan to be around for long. She sighed.

"Problem?" He cocked an eyebrow at her.

"No, nothing. I'm just worried about everything that's happened, I guess."

"Well, you can't do anything about it right now, so why not just relax and enjoy dinner?"

With a smile, she said, "You're right. So, you've lived here all your life?"

"Born and raised—and as I told you, my family goes back a whole lot of generations. Didn't even go far for college."

Politely, Meg asked, "Oh, where did you go?"

"Amherst College." He didn't elaborate.

Sure, it was just down the road, but wasn't it also one of the top liberal arts colleges in the country?

Seth was watching her face with clear amusement. "That's okay, you can go ahead and ask. Why does an Amherst grad work as a small-town plumber?"

She felt herself blushing. "I'm sorry—I feel very petty. But you're right. Why?"

"Simple. The money's good, and I can work as much or as little as I want. I'm my own boss. Besides, it's a family business. My dad started it, and my brother Stephen works with me. How about you?"

"Brown undergrad, then an MBA at the Sloan School at MIT. I always liked numbers. Although you wouldn't know it at the moment. I had no idea how much this house overhaul was going to cost . . ."

Their meals arrived after only a short wait, and the good food was a happy surprise to Meg. They chatted amiably as they ate, but the eating took up as much time as the talking. By dessert, Meg was feeling much more right with the world. Amazing what a difference a well-filled stomach could make.

"Ready to go?"

Meg looked at her watch. She was surprised to find how late it was, and they still had a drive ahead of them. "Sure. How far is it to Rachel's?"

"Maybe twenty minutes."

"I feel bad, taking you out of your way like this. I could still go to a motel, you know."

"Forget it. Folks around here help each other out. You'll like Rachel, and she'll never forgive me it I don't bring you over and let her pump you about the murder."

Meg sobered for a moment. "It is a murder, isn't it? Nobody commits suicide in a septic tank, and it certainly would have been Chandler's last choice." She shook herself. "Well, let's hope the detective knows what he's doing and gets this cleared up fast."

"Amen to that," Seth said, rising from his seat. He quickly paid the check, and after they'd bundled back into their coats, he escorted her back to his van.

Rachel turned out to be a brisk, no-nonsense woman who looked very much like her brothers, only shorter and rounder. She gave Meg a quick once-over and grinned, looking even more like Seth in the process. "Welcome! How're you holding up? Seth gave me the bare outlines. Are you exhausted? Your room's ready, if you just want to go to sleep. But if you want some coffee or dessert or something . . ."

Meg didn't have the heart to squash her eagerness. "I can't thank you enough for this, Rachel. I'm sorry to just land on you on such short notice. And I think I can stay awake a little longer, if there's coffee."

"How about this? I don't want the kids to hear all the gritty stuff, so why don't you go up and get settled, and I'll get my family sorted out, and then you can fill me in. Okay?"

"Sounds good to me."

"Great. It's up the front stairs, second door on your left. Give me ten minutes, maybe, and then come on down to the kitchen. Seth, you want to say hi to the little monsters?"

"Sure." He followed Rachel toward the back of the house, and Meg trudged up the stairs. The room was lovely, and she wondered if she could ever create something as nice in a home of her own. The contrast with the faded wallpaper and scuffed woodwork in her current bedroom depressed her. She went into the small attached bathroom and splashed water on her face, then prowled around the room. Rachel had left an eclectic assortment of books, and Meg picked up one with the appealing title *Till the Cows Come Home* to read before bed. Not that she expected to have any trouble sleeping tonight. In fact, she would have been happy to collapse on the high ruffled bed right now, but it seemed rude not to give Rachel the inside scoop, since she was doing her a huge favor. Meg waited another few minutes and then made her way down the stairs and followed the sound of voices to the kitchen at the rear.

Seth and Rachel looked up when she entered the room.

"Seth's been filling me in on what happened! How awful. Not just a body but someone you knew. If you don't want to talk about it, I'll understand, believe me."

Meg sat down at the table with them. "No, it's fine. I mean, it's not, but I don't have any trouble talking about it. Chandler and I parted ways a while ago—we just weren't a good fit. And I still have trouble visualizing him around here. Country was definitely not his thing. He must have thought there was money to be made."

Rachel poured Meg a mug of coffee and set a plate of home-baked cookies on the table. "Seth's been keeping me up-to-date about the development project, but you might know more from the banking side. What'll happen now?"

"I don't know the details so I'm just guessing, but I assume the bank will have people ready to step into Chandler's shoes. If it's a financially viable project—and Chandler didn't get involved with shaky deals—then they'll want to go ahead."

Through a mouthful of cookie, Seth mumbled, "So if anyone killed him to stop the project, they're out of luck?"

"Most likely, although whoever it was might not have known that. But yes, you're probably right. Is that good or bad?"

"For Detective Marcus, it doesn't help. For Granford, it's not clear. The project hasn't come to a vote yet, and won't until the Town Meeting. You know about that?"

"Chandler mentioned something about it, but I'm a little unclear about the details," Meg said.

Seth looked at her with mock horror. "You don't know what a Town Meeting is? Good heavens, woman."

"No. And before you ask, I've never been particularly interested in local politics. Local finance, maybe. I lived in Boston for most of my adult life, and I don't remember running into anything about town meetings. So go ahead: educate me."

"With pleasure." Seth took another cookie and settled back in his chair. "I'll give you the short form, but I expect you to do your homework. The history of the Massachusetts Town Meeting goes back over 350 years. Regrettably most people—like you—don't pay much attention to them. Which means, in effect, that a very small percentage of residents gets to make the decisions for everyone in a town. Town officers are elected at

Town Meetings, and the budget is approved. I told you I'm a selectman for Granford."

He looked at her to make sure she was paying attention before going on. "Every town has to have an annual Town Meeting, and there are also Special Town Meetings, which the selectmen may call, or if enough voters want one, they can request one themselves. That's where the vote on the project comes in. It's a Special Town Meeting, with only one article on the warrant: approval of the Granford Grange project."

Meg took another cookie and tried to look alert. "Can we cut to the chase? What's going to happen at this Special Town Meeting?"

Seth sighed. "The article is basically a request for approval of the seizure of certain properties by the town through eminent domain to permit the construction of the project. And believe me, a lot of people are interested in that. It should be quite a meeting."

"Hold on—the town is planning to seize the land? I've seen eminent domain applied only when the state wanted to take land for a new highway or some other municipal project."

"You haven't run into this before?"

"You mean when I was working at the bank? Actually, no, or at least, not directly. I dealt mainly with bond structuring, debt issues, that kind of thing. We were usually brought in to handle the financing once the deal was in place. Although I do recall reading something about a Supreme Court ruling about implementing eminent domain for commercial purposes. That was a couple of years ago, wasn't it? I haven't seen much about it since, but I guess I'm not surprised that Chandler would take a run at it."

Seth nodded. "That's what's going on here. And you're right. Hale suggested it when he first approached the town. He thought he could make it work, if he could convince the voters. That's why there's a Special Town Meeting scheduled."

"And that means my orchard and part of your land?" Meg didn't like the way this sounded.

Seth nodded. "It does. Problem is, the idea has galvanized the town and splintered its good citizens into a lot of factions. The younger ones, who've moved here recently, are all for having more amenities—they'd love to have a Starbucks around the corner and more stores. But then there are the ecologists, who are worried about environmental impact, and the preservationists, who are worried about the historic properties in the way and the threat to the character of the town. And the landowners, who feel strongly about their property."

Rachel spoke for the first time. "Seth seems pretty cool about it, but our family has been on that land since it was first settled back in sixteen-whatever. The developers want a chunk along the highway. Which could mean a strip mall in the front yard, and all the lights and trash and noise that come with it."

Seth turned to her. "Rachel, you're exaggerating. The selectmen wouldn't let that happen—we have the right to control what kind of development takes place. But I may have to recuse myself from the debate, since I have a direct interest." He looked at Meg. "Listen, are you registered to vote?"

It took Meg a moment to grasp the question. "I was in Boston. Not here."

"You'd better, then. You can't attend the meeting unless you're registered, or at least, you can't cast a vote," Seth said promptly.

"So I need to attend the meeting?" But registering to vote meant declaring that she actually lived in Granford, and Meg hadn't been willing to admit that. On the other hand, she did have a personal stake in the outcome, and it made sense to keep an eye on the process.

Seth looked outraged. "Of course you do. It's democracy in action, in the best sense. And you're a local property owner."

"Okay, tell me what I need to do. Will tomorrow be soon enough?"

Rachel started collecting cups. "Seth, time for you to go home. Can't you see this poor woman is falling asleep?"

Seth stood up quickly. "Sorry, I get kind of carried away about all this. Meg, I'll swing by around eight, if that's okay?"

"No problem." Meg managed to make it to her feet, far more slowly. It had been a very long day.

Rachel was quick to notice. "You have everything you need? Then go to bed. We can chat more in the morning. Seven thirty good for you?"

"Fine." Meg was happy to have everyone else make her decisions for her. Right now all she could think about was that big bed with the cool white sheets. "See you then."

Seth led her out into the hallway. "Will you be all right?"

"Yes, I'm fine. Just tired. And I'm sure there's more to come."

"Count on it. Well, see you in the morning. Get some sleep."

Upstairs, Meg changed into her nightgown and then tried to read the book she had set aside. But she gave up the effort after a couple of minutes, turned out the light, and tried to ignore the distant voice in her head: *Chandler's dead, Chandler's dead . . .*

Think about something else. Seth. The plumber with an Amherst degree. Who took finding a corpse in stride. And who had been kind enough to worry about how she felt. That was nice. Rachel was nice, too. Plenty of nice people around here.

She drifted off to a troubled sleep.

9

Meg awoke with a start at six thirty, even though she had forgotten to set the alarm. It was still winter-dark outside, but she could hear distant clatter somewhere below her in the house. Rachel fixing breakfast, no doubt. She swung her legs out of the bed, walked to the bathroom for a quick shower, then toweled off and pulled on her clothes. She threw the few things she had unpacked back into her bag, and in minutes she was ready to follow the enticing scent of baking down to the kitchen. There she found a scene of controlled chaos: Rachel shifting pans on the stove and in and out of the oven, while serving breakfast to what Meg deduced to be her husband and two children.

"Matthew, eat your muffin. The bus'll be here in ten minutes. Chloe, do you have your lunch money? Hi, Meg, have a seat—this crew will be out the door in a minute. Oh, right, you haven't met my husband. This is Noah."

Rachel's husband, a gangly man with disorderly dark hair, sprawled in his chair, clearly amused by the hubbub in his kitchen. He extended his hand across the table. "Noah Dickinson. And before you ask, no relation." He grinned.

"What? Oh, you mean Emily. Nice to meet you, and thanks for taking me in for the night. I'm Meg Corey."

"I know. You're the celebrity of the day. The murder was on the local news."

Meg quailed inwardly. She hadn't even thought about that. She sat wordlessly and waited while Rachel herded her family out the door. In less than five minutes, a blessed silence fell, and Rachel dropped into a chair with a sigh of relief.

"End of round one! Thank goodness I don't have any guests

at the moment, but the spring season will be starting soon enough. With all these colleges in the area, there are always people looking for a place to stay." Rachel bounced up again and went to the stove, where she waved a coffeepot in Meg's direction. Meg nodded in response to the unvoiced question, and Rachel poured two mugs of coffee. "What do you want to eat?"

"Those muffins smell wonderful. That'll be plenty for me."

Rachel took a basket, lined it with what looked like an antique linen napkin, then added six large muffins, and brought the basket and the mugs to the table. She went to the refrigerator for butter, retrieved a silver-plated jelly tray and some mismatched antique butter knives, and placed them on the table. Finally she sat down again. "There," she said triumphantly. "So, talk, before Seth shows up and eats all the muffins. If you don't mind, that is. I have a tendency to ask a lot of questions, and Seth says I pry."

Meg took a warm muffin and sliced into it, then slathered it with butter. If she had wanted to speak, she couldn't have: she was too busy inhaling the homemade apple muffin. Between bites she managed, "These are wonderful!" She took a second muffin and quickly finished half of it before responding to Rachel's curiosity. "No, I don't mind, and anyway, I owe you. I don't know what Seth has told you, but here's the outline. My mother inherited the house from the last of the Warren family maybe thirty years ago, and held on to it. I came out here to fix it up, and a couple of days ago the septic tank went kerflooey—that's how I met Seth."

Rachel smiled at her. "The old Warren house. It's a great place."

"That's what everyone keeps telling me. You know it?"

"Sure—remember, we grew up just over the hill. I've been going by the house most of my life. You're lucky. You've got the wetlands protecting you on one side, which means your views are safe."

Gail had said something like that, but Meg suspected that the term "wetlands" more likely meant "bog." "And, it seems, an orchard on the other side." Meg eyed a third muffin. After all, she needed to keep up her strength.

"Of course! Warren's Grove. It's so pretty in the spring! And you know what? There's a good chance you're eating one of your own apples right now, in that muffin. I think the people who were living in the house sold the whole crop to the co-op group not far from here. The co-op holds a street market in Northampton on Saturdays, come summer. You should check it out, when they reopen." Rachel paused to study Meg, then grinned at her. "Go on, have another. You know you want to."

Meg smiled back. "I do, and I will." No need to mention that she didn't expect to be around in summer.

As Meg buttered the muffin, Rachel went on. "So, tell me, you just picked up from wherever and plopped yourself down in this house?"

Meg smiled through the crumbs. "More or less. I was in Boston, out of a job, and there wasn't much to hold me there. I'm here to figure out what I want to do next, and Mom thought the house would keep me busy. She was right about that. But so far all I've learned is how much I don't know about houses— particularly what can go wrong."

They heard the slam of a door, and Seth barreled into the kitchen. "Hi, Rach—smells good in here! Hello, Meg." Without ceremony he helped himself to coffee, sat down, and snagged a muffin from the basket.

"Hey, Seth. We were just talking about Meg's house, and the orchard."

Meg swallowed the last of her muffin with regret. "I didn't know the orchard had a name. Warren's Grove?"

"Sure," he replied, taking a second muffin. "That's right—we got a little distracted yesterday, and you never had a chance to tell me how the historical society meeting went. And before you ask, no, there's no news about the murder."

Meg sighed. "The historical society people seem nice enough, but I didn't get to talk to many people."

"You met Gail?"

Meg nodded. "I did, but she was kind of busy, and then she had to leave early."

"She's the best person to talk to about the house. Have you done a title search?"

"No, of course not. I figured the Realtor would take care of that, when the time came."

Seth snorted. "That's just the legal stuff, not the history.

Aren't you curious to know who lived there before you? Or before the sisters?"

"Not particularly, unless it helps me sell the place. Look, Seth, I appreciate that you're interested in the house, and you probably know it better than I do, but I'm just not into old places." She added, "I'm sorry," when she saw Seth's face fall. Obviously he thought she should care more. Maybe he was right; maybe she was missing something. Maybe she'd been so wrapped up in scraping twentieth-century dreck off every surface that she had missed seeing what lay beneath. It was something to think about, if Chandler's murder didn't throw a monkey wrench into everything. Should she touch base with Frances and see what her reaction was? She almost laughed: would it be possible to translate the value of Chandler's life—or death—to the reduction of her asking price? She had a feeling he would not be pleased by the result. She tuned back in to realize that Seth was apologizing.

"Don't worry about it. I know I can be kind of pushy, but I really love the old places, and I hate to see them torn down and replaced with modern trash. Or even—what is it they call it? Remuddled?"

Rachel laughed. "That's the word. And kind of pushy? You're a bulldog, brother of mine. I'm just glad it's up to you to keep the family place intact, not to mention this one."

"You have a beautiful place here, Rachel," Meg added. "But aren't Victorians even more work than colonials?"

"You bet. That's why it helps to have a brother like Seth. Me, I stick to decorating."

Meg noticed that Rachel didn't mention Stephen. He wasn't into old places? Or helping out?

Seth stood up. "Meg, we've got to get going—I'm supposed to be in Hadley at nine. Rachel, thanks for helping out. I'll let you know what I hear about the project."

"You bet you will. Meg, it was nice to meet you. Listen, if you need to talk or something, I'm here. I mean, you knew the dead guy, and that can't be easy for you."

Meg felt an unexpected prick of tears. She wasn't sure whether it was for Chandler or for Rachel's simple kindness. "Thanks, Rachel. I appreciate the offer."

Rachel smiled. "No problem. How about I give you a call in a couple of days, and maybe we can get together later this week, or next?"

"That would be great. And maybe later you can give me some tips on how to make the place presentable to buyers. I'm ready, Seth—just let me grab my coat."

The scent of Rachel's apple muffins followed them out into the crisp morning air.

After Seth dropped her off at the house, Meg looked up at the building, trying to see it objectively. If she could ignore the peeling paint, it was handsome, if not particularly noteworthy. To her unskilled eye, it looked like every other colonial house she had ever seen, old or new. Rectangular, with a simple roofline. Doors and windows, symmetrically distributed. The proportions were harmonious—and at least the roof didn't appear to be sagging—but there was little to distinguish it.

She glanced around, trying to spy any newshounds, but the two-lane road in front was all but empty. A white van with a green logo went by, headed toward the orchard. A UMass truck—Christopher? She dropped her overnight bag on the front steps, avoided looking at the trench, still marked with crime scene tape, and set off up the hill toward the orchard. She needed to work off that last muffin, and she wasn't ready to face the chaos inside the house.

She was puffing by the time she reached the crest of the rise, but not as badly as the last time. She stopped and surveyed the land before her, trying to visualize a strip mall. It wasn't a pretty mental picture. No matter how tastefully executed it might be, it would still be ... unnatural. Buildings and asphalt and bright lights—and paper trash, and smells wafting from fast-food places. She shook her head to clear that picture and focused on what was there now. She'd guessed right: the van was parked along the verge of the road, and she could spot Christopher's silvery hair. He was surrounded by a clutch of seven or eight students, looking for all the world like a flock of ducklings in their bulky winter jackets. Her breath regained, she decided to join them and see what was going on.

As she came closer, Christopher saw her and beamed. "Welcome, Meg. Come to see us at work?"

"Just wondered what you all were up to."

"This is my class on pruning fruit crops. Of course, it's still early to prune, but I wanted them to familiarize themselves with the trees and the lay of the land. Would you care to join us?"

Why not? She could learn something. It occurred to her that she should try to snatch a private word with Christopher: she wanted to know what he knew about the development scheme, and what he thought about it. "Sure, if you don't mind."

"Not at all—I'm delighted to have you. Now, my young friends, if you will turn your attention to the nearest row of trees ..." Meg hung back, watching as Christopher warmed to his subject, catching a phrase now and then. "Control growth ... control size ... encourage earlier blooming ... increase the size and quality of the fruit ..." The students didn't take any notes, no doubt trying to keep their hands warm in their pockets. But at least they were there: somebody was still interested in learning about fruit cultivation. Although maybe they'd all go seek jobs at the huge orchards on the West Coast, rather than nurse along small plots like this one.

As they ambled between the rows of trees, one male student sidled up to Meg. "Hey, isn't this where they found that body yesterday?"

"Yes, down near the house." Meg braced herself for a slew of questions, and was both relieved and disappointed when the boy just said, "Cool," and turned his attention back to his professor. Meg moved closer to the group, both to shield herself from the wind and because she was becoming interested in Christopher's spiel. He pulled down a midsize branch and began explaining its various parts to the cluster of students.

"The tree is dormant now, but you can see rows of buds on the branches, particularly on the smaller twigs. You'll want to direct growth by choosing a bud that's pointing in the direction that you want your branch to grow, and then cutting just below it. This is the terminal bud, here—cut that off and you encourage the buds behind it. And you want to select buds that point outward from the trunk, so that the growing branch will have space and light."

He looked around to make sure he had everyone's attention, and then he looked at Meg and winked. Meg smiled back at him as he went on. "When you make a cut, keep it as small as possible, to minimize access for pests or disease. And we'll be doing the majority of the pruning in a month or two, when the buds begin to swell. That way, the new growth will heal any cuts more quickly."

The longer Christopher talked, the more Meg realized how little she knew and how much expertise was required to maintain an orchard. So many decisions to be made, and Christopher hadn't even touched on insect and animal pests and their treatment, much less the apples themselves. And the orchard seemed so vulnerable—there were so many things that could go wrong: weather, diseases, things she didn't even know about.

Or a developer could raze the whole orchard and put in a parking lot.

Christopher was finally winding down, and the students were shivering in the cutting wind. At last he noticed and announced, "All right, students, that's enough for today. Back to the van, the lot of you." They moved quickly away, and as Christopher lagged behind, Meg joined him.

"Did you enjoy my lecture?" he asked.

"I did, although I'm a bit overwhelmed by everything I don't know. But there was something else I wanted to talk about—the Granford development project."

Christopher stopped and turned to her, his face desolate. "I wondered if you knew, last we met, since you said nothing. It would be an awful thing if it were to go forward."

"If?" Meg asked in surprise. "It seems to be moving along fairly well, from what I've heard."

Christopher shook his head. "It's early days yet. There are many hurdles still to be crossed. And with the death of that young man . . ."

"Word travels fast around here," Meg said. "You heard about it on the news?"

"No, the Springfield daily paper. I have little time for television."

"What did the article say?"

"It was rather sketchy. Merely that the body of a Boston banker had been found on a local farm, and police suspected murder. A bit about Hale's involvement with the proposed development project in Granford. Please don't be concerned, Meg—your name did not come up."

Thank goodness no one had come looking for her, or had found her. Meg wondered briefly if Seth had considered that when he had spirited her away to Rachel's for the night.

"But you and the students know his body was found here?"

"We do. I'm sorry that you had to deal with that, although less sorry that he's gone."

"You knew him?"

"We'd met. I attended a meeting or two in Granford, when the project was first proposed. I can't say I warmed to the man—he was an arrogant one."

Whether or not Christopher knew that she had known Chandler, Meg agreed with his quick assessment. "But his death wouldn't stop the project. He had the backing of his bank, and I'm sure they'll send someone to replace him."

"We'll see. Still, for the near term I shall proceed as if all's right in the world, and train these eager lads—and a lass or two—in apple management. It's been a pleasure to see you again, my dear. Perhaps I may stop by at some point and we can chat at greater length?"

Meg laughed. "Only if we can do it inside where it's warm."

"Delightful. Then I'll let you go, for now. Oh, I nearly forgot. I brought something for you, hoping I'd find you in." He dove into the passenger side of the van and emerged holding a bulging paper bag, which he presented with a flourish.

Meg peered inside. Apples. Rather yellowish, and mottled with rough brown. She looked back at Christopher. "Isn't it kind of late in the season for apples? I thought you didn't approve."

"Ah, but there are those few that actually improve after a few months. Those are Roxbury Russets, one of the oldest American varieties. They ripen late, and keep well. You'll enjoy them."

"Thank you, Christopher."

"My pleasure. Ta!"

Meg watched him rejoin his class, and then the van pulled

away, leaving her alone with her trees. *Her* trees. It felt odd to think in those terms. She'd never owned a tree before, much less a whole field of them, dependent on her for their well-being. She had trouble keeping an African violet alive on a windowsill; an orchard was a whole different universe. One she wasn't sure she was ready or willing to deal with.

But nothing was settled yet. She still had a lot of work to do to get the house into shape, and maybe by then the whole development project issue would be resolved. Only Meg wasn't quite sure what outcome she wanted.

10

Reluctantly Meg gathered up her bag from the step and let herself in the front door. Nothing had improved since the day before: the house smelled damp and musty. In fact, yesterday she hadn't even noticed the trail of muddy footprints that the various representatives of the law had added to her less-than-pristine kitchen floor. And she wasn't sure if she could run any water, or if her entire plumbing system was considered a crime scene. She amused herself by picturing the Granford police impounding all of her pipes as evidence, but sobered quickly. Should she call someone and ask? Or would they call her? She fished her cell phone out of her bag and discovered that her battery had died. She set Christopher's bag of apples on the countertop, plugged the phone into the kitchen charger, then put on some coffee. She'd had only one cup at Rachel's, and then she'd been tramping around the orchard in the cold, and she really deserved some hot caffeine.

She had just filled a cup when there was a rapping at her front door. *I thought Granford was rural and quiet. I've had more visitors over the past few days—dead and alive—than I had in years in Boston,* she reflected as she hurried to answer. She wrestled the door open to find her real estate agent, Frances, looking slightly less sleek than she had on Monday.

"Sorry to barge in like this, but I was in the neighborhood . . ." She looked strangely forlorn.

"Come on in. I've just made some coffee—want a cup?"

"If it's no trouble."

"Not at all." Meg led the way to the kitchen, and Frances sat heavily in a chair at the table, without invitation. Meg poured a second mug of coffee and joined her at the table. "Did we forget to check something out?"

Frances sighed. "No. I'm sorry, I shouldn't be bothering you. But I guess I figured you'd have questions about selling, now that they found Chandler Hale ..." She looked as though she wanted to cry.

Meg was mystified. "Did you know him?"

Frances sipped at her coffee, struggling to regain control. "Of course. He was buying land in Granford, or at least he was connected to the ones who were. How could I not?"

"Ah," Meg said. Frances's comment in no way explained the tears. "So you were working together?"

Frances shook her head vigorously. "No, nothing like that. In fact, he cut me right out of the loop—cost me a nice chunk of change, too. After ..."

A horrible suspicion popped into Meg's mind, and she hurried to squash it. Chandler and Frances? Unlikely. Frances might be a nice woman, and reasonably attractive for what Meg estimated was her forty-something years, but she came nowhere near meeting Chandler's exacting standards for partners, long or short term.

Unless, of course, Chandler had wanted something from her.

If she was going to be honest with herself, Meg had always wondered why he had dated her. Meg was nice enough to look at, but not in his league. She was intelligent and capable, but she was no Wall Street darling. Maybe she had been filler—someone to amuse him while he scouted out his next trophy blonde. She had been flattered, sometimes amused, sometimes exasperated, but she had never felt any real, intimate connection with Chandler. They had dated for the better part of a year, and she still didn't feel that she had known him. He had always kept secrets.

Meg stared at her coffee, troubled by her thoughts. Chandler had asked her to spy for him; what had he asked Frances to do? And what had he promised her? Whatever it was, it must have fallen through. But was it any of her business? She took a swallow of coffee and changed the subject quickly.

"All right, Frances, you might as well tell me what impact finding a body on the property is going to have on my chances of selling the place."

Frances dragged herself back from wherever her thoughts had taken her. "What? Oh ... We said May, right? Months away. Once they arrest someone, the whole thing will blow over. Shouldn't be a problem. Unless, of course, you did it?" Frances scrounged up a token smile at her own weak joke.

"No. And if I had, I would have put him somewhere a little farther from home, obviously. Frances, why didn't you mention the development project the last time we talked? And what do you think about it? Obviously it's going to make a difference when I sell."

Frances didn't meet her eyes. "Sorry about that. I just thought you had enough to worry about, without dealing with something that might not ever happen. Honestly, I think the project might be just what this town needs. You've seen the main road—not much to look at, is it? Mostly car repair places and pizza joints. People drive through, but they've got no reason to stop. Now, don't get me wrong—I love this place. Born here, grew up here, and I'm still here. But I know we need change. Heck, I go to Town Meetings, and every year we keep whittling at the programs that need the money most, like the library and the schools. Library's only open three days a week now. It's not right, and the money's got to come from somewhere."

Frances's lecture on the community had apparently pulled her from her funk about Chandler's death, Meg was glad to see. "I agree, in principle. But this is in my backyard, quite literally."

"Meg, you can't eat scenery, or pay your bills with it. The world changes. So will Granford. But that's not your problem, is it? You'll sell this place to some nice couple with two kids and a dog, and they won't remember what the old Granford was like, and everyone will be happy. Right?"

"I suppose." In fact, that had been Meg's intention, and she was sure the family with two kids and a dog would be very happy here. But she could also see the old-timers' viewpoint. It was always hard to deal with change. She'd weathered plenty in the past year, and she had expected her interlude in Granford to be something of a retreat, a time to regroup and recharge her own batteries. Instead she had found herself embroiled in a major public controversy, with a dead body on her hands. So much for planning.

But Frances had a point. The sooner the murder was cleared up, the sooner the public would begin to forget about it. After all, Chandler had been an outsider, and he wouldn't be missed. As she had told Seth and Rachel, the bank would see to it that the project went forward uninterrupted. For them it was a business deal, plain and simple.

So why was Frances sitting in her kitchen? The clear morning light was not kind to the grooves bracketing her mouth, or the bags under her eyes. Or were those new? Was she really taking Chandler's death that hard?

As if in answer to her question, Frances asked, "You knew Chandler before, right?"

How did word travel so fast? Sure, Granford was a small town, and murder had to be big news, but how did her personal connection get dragged into it so quickly? "Yes, in Boston," Meg replied neutrally.

Frances pressed on. "I mean, you *knew* him, if you know what I mean."

This was getting worse and worse. Meg barely knew Frances and had no way of guessing whether she was discreet, or whether she was the town crier for gossip. But apparently the word of her relationship with Chandler was already public property. Might as well make sure the right story got out. "Yes, we were seeing each other, but we broke it off last year."

"He dumped you," Frances said flatly.

Meg stared at her. "Yes, he ended the relationship. We both moved on. Frances, what are you asking?"

Frances shook her head. "Sorry, it's none of my business. I guess I'm just upset. Look, Meg, one of the pluses—and minuses—of living in a small town is that everyone knows everyone else's business. And people remember things. Like the time you went joyriding in your brother's car in high school, or the wonderful cupcakes your mother baked for PTA meetings in

1983. You're new here, so people are curious. And you haven't spent much time getting to know your neighbors, which makes them even more curious. Please don't think they mean it unkindly—they're good people. But they'd be a whole lot happier to pin this murder on you than on one of their own. See what I mean?"

This was an angle Meg hadn't considered. "Unfortunately, I guess I do. I'm sorry I can't oblige. Yes, I knew Chandler, but until Monday I hadn't seen him in months. I was totally surprised when he showed up here—I didn't know about the project or his involvement in it. We had dinner, and then I sent him packing. The next thing I knew, he was dead. And that is the sum total of what I know." Meg wasn't sure how believable she sounded, even though it was the truth. She had to admit that the coincidence of her connection with Chandler was hard to dismiss. "What am I supposed to do?"

"Hey, don't get defensive. You didn't do anything wrong. It's just that it would help if you let people get to know you a little better. Get out more. And the fact that Seth vouches for you helps."

What? When had Seth talked about her, and to whom? He'd known her a total of three days. But there was no point in asking Frances about that—better that she take it up with Seth. "Look, Frances, I don't mean to cut this short, but I've got to make some calls."

Frances stood up. "Sorry, I didn't mean to keep you. Don't worry, whoever buys this place will probably be from somewhere else, and the murder will be ancient history by then. You just work on cleaning the place up, and get in touch when you want me to check it out again. Deal?"

"Sounds good to me. And thanks for what you said about the town. I'm used to living in a city, and the rules are different there, I guess."

"Welcome to small-town Massachusetts. Oh, and you might want to see about getting that front door of yours planed down— first impressions matter, you know . . ."

Meg escorted Frances to the balky front door and watched as she pulled away. What was her visit all about? But before she could puzzle her way through Frances's behavior, her phone rang. It was the detective's office, requesting her presence in Northampton ASAP.

"Oh, before you hang up, can you tell me if I can use my drains?" Meg pleaded. Too late: the line had gone dead.

11

Half an hour later Meg arrived in the center of Northampton; the detective's office was housed in the County Courthouse. Another new experience—and one which she would happily have avoided. With trepidation she entered the lobby and stated her business, then sat in one of the molded plastic chairs bolted to the floor in the bleak waiting area until Detective Marcus appeared. He nodded to the person at the desk, then silently escorted Meg through multiple sets of heavy automatic doors to his office. Inside, he gestured toward a chair in front of the desk, and Meg sat.

He took his time before addressing her, lining up the papers on his spartan desk, pulling out a couple of pencils and inspecting their points. Finally he began. "Ms. Corey, I asked you here to confirm the details of what you told us the other day. Often people omit critical details under the stress of the moment, and perhaps you can fill in anything that has occurred to you since."

"Of course. I'm happy to help in any way I can."

"Let me review the basics, to save time. You have resided in Granford for approximately a month now? And you lived in Boston before that?"

Meg nodded, and recited the basic details of her move to Granford once again. She clamped down hard on an urge to elaborate. Better stick to the facts, even though the laconic man across the desk made her want to babble.

"Why were you fired?"

Was he deliberately trying to provoke her? "I wasn't fired. I was laid off because my position was declared redundant. My former employer merged with another bank, and after the merger they eliminated a number of positions. They offered a reasonable compensation package."

"Your mother is the owner of record for the Granford property?"

"Yes, for about the last thirty years or so. She added my name to the title recently, when I agreed to renovate and sell it."

"Tell me about your relationship with Chandler Hale."

"When we were both in Boston, we ... dated for approximately a year, maybe less." Meg struggled with finding the appropriate term to describe their relationship. Everything sounded so stilted. "We ended the relationship about six months ago."

"Before you lost your job?"

"Yes. There was no correlation between those two events. Chandler worked for another bank."

"You didn't work together?"

Meg shook her head. "No. We worked for different, competing banks."

"And he never discussed the Granford development project with you?"

"Not that I recall. As far as I know, his involvement in the development project postdated our relationship."

"You didn't expect to see him in Granford?"

"No. It was a complete surprise to me."

Detective Marcus said nothing for several beats, his eyes never leaving her face. Meg forced herself to meet his cold gaze. Finally he said carefully, "Is it possible that you followed Hale to Granford, in hope of rekindling your relationship? And that you took it hard when he indicated that he wasn't interested?"

Meg was stunned, then angry, but she kept a tight grip on her emotions. "I assure you, that was not the case. And you can check the property records—my mother's owned this place for decades. That's the only reason I'm here."

He ignored her. "So you deny that sequence of events?"

"Of course I do! Listen, Detective, Chandler and I were no longer involved with each other, and I had no idea what he was doing, in Boston or in Granford."

But even as she voiced what she knew to be the truth, she could see all too clearly how someone else might see it differently. At least, someone who didn't know her, or someone who wanted to do her harm or use her as a convenient scapegoat. But she wasn't a hysterical, jilted lover, and even if she were, she would never have killed Chandler, either in the heat of the moment or with—what was it they called it?—malice aforethought. Anyone who knew her would attest to that. The problem was, no one around here knew her.

"You had dinner with Hale at the Lord Jeffery on Monday?"

"Yes. When he and his assistant came by the house and found out that I was living there, he invited me out. We caught up on what we'd been doing, discussed impersonal things, and then the Granford project." Meg hesitated a moment before going on, wondering if she was handing him more ammunition for his suspicions. "At dinner he asked me if I would keep an eye on things locally and report to him, before the town voted on the project. I gather there are people in Granford who aren't thrilled by the project, and he wanted to know what the opposition was saying. I told him I wouldn't be comfortable doing that."

"The waitress at the restaurant reported that there was some hostility between you."

Naturally she would have to have noticed that. "Yes. I was angry that Chandler had asked me to spy for him, and I told him so. He put me in an awkward position, and I didn't like it. I asked him to take me home, and he did. He left after dropping me off, and I didn't see him again after that. All this should be in your notes, right? And haven't you found anyone who saw him later? Where was he staying? Didn't he have any business meetings the next day? You must have talked to his assistant by now. What did she tell you?"

"Ms. Corey, I'll ask the questions. But no, so far you're the last person to have admitted to seeing him."

Meg wondered if she looked uncomfortable. "Not what's-her-name?"

He was definitely unhappy with that question. "Lucinda Patterson. Ms. Patterson has been in Boston since yesterday. I'll be speaking to her later this afternoon."

So he hadn't managed to track her down, which made him look bad. Meg wondered exactly when Lucinda had gone to Boston, but she didn't think the detective was going to volunteer that information. "Detective, how long had Chandler been dead when he was found?"

The detective looked startled by her question. "Hard to say, given the conditions. He'd eaten dinner. ME puts it at maybe twelve hours."

Meg suppressed a "gotcha." "So you're saying he was alive for at least a full day after I had dinner with him?"

The detective nodded, looking pained.

"Then surely you'll be able to find someone who saw him in those twenty-four hours? You are looking, aren't you?"

"We know our business here, Ms. Corey, even if this isn't the big city."

"I didn't mean to imply otherwise." They sat silently for a moment until Meg asked, "What happens now?"

"We continue to investigate. We are interviewing people both here and in Boston. People who knew both of you." He stood up. "Thank you for coming in. We can reach you at the Granford address?"

Meg stood as well. "Yes, of course. Please let me know if there's anything else I can do. Oh—one last thing. Is my place still a crime scene, or can I use my water?"

"We've got all we need."

One small blessing, at least. After the detective had escorted her out of the building, Meg sat in her car for a few moments. If she was going to be fair to him, she could see how it would look: poor Meg, her guy dumps her, she loses her job, and now she's stuck out here in the boonies with no friends. Then Chandler shows up to rub her nose in it, and she gets mad and whacks him with the proverbial blunt object. No shortage of those around her place: tools, assorted pieces of old lumber, tree branches. Of course the detective would consider her a likely candidate for murderer.

But if she had killed Chandler, why would she do such a lousy job of hiding the body? How stupid did the detective think she was? No, bad argument: until a few days ago she hadn't even known she had a septic tank, much less how it operated and what effect a body might have on it. Clearly there were gaps in her intelligence. And she had to admit that tank was certainly convenient—if she had been the person who killed Chandler.

She wasn't, but Chandler was undeniably dead. So who had killed him? She gnawed at the question like a dog with a bone for the duration of her trip back from Northampton, but came up with no answer. She didn't know enough about the town of Granford and its people to make even a wild guess.

Rather than go back to her cold, messy, empty house, Meg decided to make a detour to the nearest market and stock up on groceries. She wanted comfort food. Cooking in general didn't excite her, but maybe the smell of a burbling pot of soup or a hearty stew or even an apple pie—would those apples Christopher had given her be any good for pie?—would make the place more welcoming and provide a tantalizing reward for her labors. She had earned it. And it would mask the less appealing smells of dry rot and mildew that had become the backdrop to her days.

Decision made, she pulled into the parking lot of the supermarket along the highway outside of Granford and parked. As she approached the door, she noticed a colorful sheet of paper taped at eye level. On closer inspection, she found that it was an announcement from Puritan Bank about a meeting at Granford Town Hall that evening, to update the citizens of Granford on the future of the Granford Grange development project. Odd name for the project; as far as she knew, a grange was a building, not a strip mall. Still, it sounded pretty and vaguely historic. In any case, it was clear that the bank wasn't wasting any time, or maybe they were worried about losing momentum. Should she attend? Well, why not? She had a stake in the project, and she was curious to see what spin the bank would put on Chandler's death. And on a more personal level, maybe she could test the waters and see if those worthy citizens treated her as though she were the prime suspect in his murder. Not a comforting thought, but she needed to know.

Which reminded her: she had promised Seth that she would register to vote. She searched her memory about how she had gone about that in Boston and came up blank. But she was sure that the town clerk would know, and that meant a trip to town hall. She could do that on the way home.

She filled her cart with groceries, shocked to realize how depleted her cupboards were. Had she eaten at all over the past few weeks? Or was she turning into one of those weird old maids who existed on cereal and the occasional can of cat food? She was beginning to understand how that could happen. Or maybe she was channeling Lula and Nettie, but at least they'd had each other to talk to. Frances was right: she needed to get out more, talk to other people, just to keep some sort of perspective. The historical society meeting had been pleasant enough, but sparsely attended, and they didn't meet again until the next month. At least she could get a library card. Maybe there was some sort of adult-education program around, and she could learn something useful, like how to use a table saw. She snorted at that thought, drawing a startled glance from a teenage clerk shelving cans.

Groceries safely stowed in her car, Meg drove back to the center of Granford. The municipal offices occupied a stately Victorian house perched on the low hill overlooking the town green. The town clerk's office turned out to be on the ground floor. Inside, Meg waited while the two men in front of her took care of various licenses and permits, then she stepped up to the desk. "I'd like to register to vote."

The clerk, a woman about Meg's age, looked up at her in curiosity. "New in town?"

"Yes, I'm Meg Corey, and I just moved to a house on County Line Road. That's within the town limits, isn't it?" Was it her imagination, or did the clerk's expression change?

"Sure is. You registered anywhere else?"

"In Boston, but I don't live there anymore."

"Granford is your official residence?" When Meg nodded, the woman fished out a form from under the counter and pushed it toward her. "Fill this out. And I'll need some ID with your current address on it."

"Oh," Meg said, feeling absurdly disappointed. "I haven't been here long—my driver's license still has my old address. What else would work?"

"Photo ID, bank statement, paycheck, government check, utility bill," the clerk recited in a monotone.

"I changed the address on my bank account, but I haven't gotten a statement yet. Wait! I know." Meg fished in her purse, where she remembered stuffing a batch of bills she had grabbed from her mailbox. She leafed through them. Half of them had been forwarded from Boston, but then she struck gold. "Aha!

My first utility bill—I wanted to make sure the lights stayed on."
Meg smiled at the clerk, who responded with tepid enthusiasm.
She handed her the driver's license and the bill, and concentrated
on filling out the form, then handed it back to the clerk, who re-
turned her ID. "Does this make me eligible to vote in the Special
Town Meeting?"

The clerk laughed briefly. "Oh, yeah, no problem. You and
half the town—never seen so many registrations in a short
period. Have a nice day now."

Since there were people waiting, Meg gathered up her documents and turned to leave. At least she'd accomplished one
tangible thing today. Seth would be pleased. She certainly
was pleased. And the message waiting on her phone also
cheered her.

"Hi, it's Seth. Don't know if you saw the flyers about the
meeting at town hall tonight, but if you want to go, I can swing
by and pick you up. Six thirty? Let me know."

She punched in his number but got his voice mail. Before she
could change her mind, she said, "Hi, Seth, it's Meg. I'd like to
go to the meeting. Six thirty is fine, unless you'd like to stop by
for supper before. I think I'm making soup."

12

Now she had a plan for the evening, and she had committed herself to making a pot of soup. Meg set about gathering her ingredients and went scrounging for a large pot. Surely the daughters or granddaughters of farmers would have a pot large enough to feed a crowd? Her search was rewarded with a battered but serviceable stockpot lurking in the back of a deep cupboard. She made another mental addition to her to-do list: inventory cupboards. And clean them, she added dubiously. The grease on some of them was probably older than she was.

After starting a hearty vegetable soup, she went back to the front parlor and surveyed her domain. So far she had been approaching the renovation project in a rather haphazard fashion—mostly assessing what needed to be done, rather than doing it. The net result was a lot of bald patches, as though the house had a case of mange. Of course, most of the work had involved removing modern crap, and there was still plenty of that left to do. She was undecided about some of the wallpaper, and Frances had viewed it with scorn. Downstairs, it would definitely have to go: it represented the worst of the early 1980s, when the sisters had died and her mother had inherited the place. That was probably the last time anyone had done anything to the first-floor rooms. She couldn't believe her mother had been responsible for it, but she might have hired someone local to pretty up the place for tenants. It was clear that either she hadn't spent much on it, or her delegate had pocketed half the money.

Meg wandered slowly from room to room, looking at the sun-filled spaces with a critical eye. Seth had said the place had good bones, and she was beginning to understand what he meant. The proportions of the rooms were pleasing. The ceilings weren't low enough to be confining, as she understood was often the case in old colonials, and there were plenty of good-sized windows. Much of the original woodwork had survived, although she wasn't sure what its condition was, and the wide-board floors were in surprisingly good shape. She had already checked out the fireplaces, and they were salvageable—for a price. In the hallway she ran her hand over the stair-rail. Seth had said the stairs were a nineteenth-century addition, but that still made them at least a hundred years old. Meg tried to imagine the number of hands that had passed over the satiny old wood. So much history. So much she didn't know.

The smell of cooking onions and carrots and celery drifted from the kitchen. It made the house seem more lived in, somehow. *Okay, Meg—what now?* She checked her watch: almost two thirty. What could she do in the three or so hours before Seth arrived? She couldn't face one more half-finished project left in a muddle, so she wanted to find something that she could actually finish; she wanted progress, not more mess. So maybe the kitchen was the best place to start. She wondered just what else she would find lurking in the dark corners of the cabinets. *Note to self: mousetraps?*

After two hours of steady work—interspersed with tossing more chopped vegetables into her soup pot—Meg had reached bedrock in all the lower-tier kitchen cabinets. She had divided her finds into two piles in the middle of the kitchen floor: things she wanted to keep, by far the smaller pile; and things that she couldn't imagine anyone in the world using, past, present, or future. These included various pieces of bakeware, now welded together with rust; pans with holes; pans without handles; cookie sheets encrusted with black ick. A lot of sad, cheap stuff that nobody had wanted and had left behind. She would be glad to get rid of it.

She gave her soup a final stir, threw together a batch of cheese biscuits and popped them in the unpredictable oven, then took herself upstairs for a quick shower and to change into something respectable—something that didn't make her look like a murderer. Not that she knew what a murderer would look like. She had never met one, to her knowledge. Though she might well have met one without knowing it, she realized. *Somebody* in Granford was a murderer.

Back downstairs in the kitchen, she was surveying the piles she had created when she looked up to see Seth at the back door. She opened it quickly. "Hi! I wasn't sure you'd gotten my message, but I've made enough for an army. Come in out of the cold."

He followed her into the kitchen, after stamping his boots on the step. "Smells good. Looks like you've been sorting stuff."

"I have. The things that people save! It never ceases to amaze me. What's the routine for trash pickup around here? Mostly I've been leaving stuff out in the barn or the connecting el, but the piles keep growing, so that won't work for long."

Seth laughed. "Actually, that's a two-part question. Regular trash pickup you have to contract for, with an independent provider. But you might want to think about getting a Dumpster in, for the bigger stuff. Cheaper in the long run, and you can get rid of it all at once. I can call a guy I know."

"I hadn't even thought that far, but you're right. No municipal service for trash, though?"

Seth shook his head. "Costs too much. There's the town dump. You can get yourself a dump permit and haul it over there yourself."

"I guess I'll need to figure something out. Oh, before I forget—the detective said they're done with my place as a crime scene, so I guess we can fill in the trench now."

"No problem. I'll call Jake first thing tomorrow."

One more item she could check off her to-do list, Meg thought with relief. "Great! Why don't we go ahead and eat? Sit down, and I'll dish up."

Seth sat at the kitchen table, after removing a pile of precariously stacked pans. Meg set a bowl in front of him. "Hey, this is good!" he said, spooning soup.

She added a basket filled with hot biscuits to the table. "You're surprised? Thanks a lot." She smiled. "Oh, wait a sec—I found something."

Seth continued to eat as Meg rummaged through the pile of stuff she had moved to a counter.

"Ta-da!" She said, holding up her find. "Remember that metal gear thingy you found the other day? It goes to something like this, doesn't it?"

"Got it in one. You know what that is?"

"I deduce ... that it's an apple peeler. Makes sense, doesn't it, with an orchard just outside?"

"It does. And I'll bet it still works—got any apples around?"

"In fact, I do. Christopher brought me a whole bag, and I was thinking about making a pie, but I ran out of time. But I'm sure I can figure out how to use it. Anyway, let's worry about that later. Don't we have a meeting to go to?"

The meeting took place in the largest room that town hall had to offer, but it was more than large enough to handle the twenty or so people gathered there. Meg recognized a couple of faces from the historical society meeting, but the rest were strangers to her. They were old and young, male and female, and their expressions ranged from curious to wary to angry.

"Are you involved in this?" She whispered to Seth as he led her into the room.

"No," he replied in the same low tone. "This isn't the town's meeting, it's the bank's. The bank requested a meeting with the selectmen, to discuss what happens now. We suggested they make it an open meeting, although we really didn't have enough lead time to get the word out. But we told as many people as we could, posted an announcement on the town website, stuck up flyers around town. I'm just here to listen."

Three people huddled in conference at the front of the room. Meg nudged Seth again, after they had sat down in rickety folding chairs. "Who are they?"

Seth leaned toward her. "The one on the left is the chair of the Granford selectmen, Tom Moody. Don't know the guy in the middle, but the blonde on the right came to a couple of meetings with Hale, so I'm guessing she's with the bank. I've forgotten her name."

Meg recognized her from Chandler's visit. Lucinda Patterson, his "assistant." Meg wondered if Detective Marcus had talked to her yet. If so, she didn't look particularly ruffled. While waiting for stragglers to find seats, Meg studied the body language of the people in front. Cinda was conferring with—and deferring to—the man next to her. Another banker? Cinda smiled, laid her hand on the man's arm, nodded, then stepped back with the proper deference. But Meg saw her scan the room, her expression calculating. Meg nodded as Cinda's eyes passed over her and on to Seth sitting next to her.

By ten minutes past the hour, only a few more stragglers had arrived, and the board chair must have decided no one else was coming. He cleared his throat. "Thank you all for coming on such short notice—I'm glad to see you here, Andy—give you something to plug into the paper next week, right?" A subdued laugh swept the room, and Andy laughed with them. Seth leaned toward Meg and whispered, "Editor of the local weekly."

Tom Moody went on. "I won't waste any of your time. John Cabot here is the one who requested this meeting, and he wants to fill you in on what's going to happen with the Granford Grange project, after the unfortunate death of Chandler Hale. I'll let him do the talking."

With almost palpable relief, Moody stepped back and crossed his arms. John Cabot replaced him at the podium, and Cinda assumed a position a discreet pace behind him.

"I apologize for the short notice of this event," Cabot began, his voice properly grave, "but I thought it was important to quell any rumors that might be circulating. Chandler Hale was a valued member of my team at Puritan Bank, and he had been doing a wonderful job for us—and for you—in the planning of Granford Grange. I'm here to assure you that he was a thorough and careful man, and left his records in admirable condition. There will be no interruption in the planning and execution of this community's project—you can count on that. One of the reasons I called this meeting was to introduce you to Chandler's former assistant, Lucinda Patterson. Some of you in town will have met her at various meetings, but I wanted to announce that she will be taking over Chandler's role in moving this project forward. She has the full support of the bank behind her, and she is more than qualified to represent us. But I'll let her speak for herself." Cabot smiled perfunctorily, then waved Cinda forward. She quickly moved front and center.

"Thank you, John," she began. Her voice was low but easily heard, and she spoke with assurance. "I appreciate your kind words and the confidence that the bank has placed in me." Then she turned to face the small crowd, addressing them directly. "The death of Chandler Hale was a tragic blow to our department, and he will be missed. But he was part of the team, as I have been, and I know that he would want to see his work go on. He kept me fully informed on all aspects of this project, and I've had the pleasure of speaking with a number of you in the past few months—Fred, Martin." She flashed a smile of her own, showing off her perfect white teeth. "I look forward to seeing this through to completion. And I will be available, now and in the future, for any questions you might have. Yes?" She pointed to someone seated toward the rear of the room, where Meg couldn't see.

Seth leaned toward Meg. "Do you know her?"

Meg moved closer and whispered, "I met her the other day with Chandler, the first time he came by. I don't know how long she's worked for the bank, but I can't recall Chandler ever mentioning her. Not that he would have, I'll bet. She's, uh, easy to look at."

Meg wasn't sure Seth had heard the last part of that, because he was flagging Cinda's attention. "Ms. Patterson?"

Cinda dimpled to a carefully calculated degree. "Cinda, please. It's Seth Chapin, right?"

"Yes. Tell me . . ."

Meg tuned out Seth's informed but technical question while watching Cinda at work. Blonde, yes, but not dumb. She was saying all the right things, and in a properly subdued tone. Chandler had done all the hard work—or had he? Perhaps Chandler had fronted the project, but had Cinda actually put the deal together? The next few weeks should prove interesting. Meg wondered how well connected Cinda was to the local population, and how she would handle dissenters. From what she had seen so far, Cinda looked up to the challenge.

The meeting didn't last more than half an hour, clearly intended more to reassure the townspeople than to provide any new information. Outside the town hall building Meg inhaled deeply: the air was chill, with a hint of wood smoke. Seth had hung back, exchanging a few words with his colleagues, but he joined her quickly and guided her back to his truck.

Once they were settled and he'd turned on the engine, he asked, "What did you think?"

"The message I got was that the bank wants this project to go forward," she said slowly. "If they didn't, they could have taken this opportunity to bow out gracefully. I take it to mean that the financing is in place. Which is a good thing, if that's what the people here want. Do they, do you think?"

Seth pulled out of the parking lot. "That's still an open question. I have to say ..." He hesitated a moment.

"What?"

"We've still got some time until the Town Meeting, time that I'm sure the project's supporters will use to try to persuade the people who are on the fence about it. And I think that Ms. Patterson is going to win over more of them than Chandler did." He grinned. "At the risk of sounding sexist."

"You mean, she's going to flash her pretty smile and toss her blonde hair, and the old codgers of Granford are going to fall all over themselves to go along with anything she wants?"

"Something like that."

"You may have a point. I'd guess that Chandler's attitude probably turned off a lot of people—he could be pompous, and he usually thought he was right. Cinda will be a pleasant change."

"And she's smart enough."

"You think that, too? I agree—whatever the outside package, I don't think Cinda's lacking in brains. And Puritan Bank doesn't hire people just for their pretty faces. So I'd say the bank is still behind the project, and no matter who's in charge, they'll see that it keeps moving."

Seth pulled into her driveway and stopped. "Assuming the town votes for it."

Meg put her hand on the door handle. "Thanks for asking me along. I wish I knew more about what was going on, and how it might affect ... well, to put it bluntly, the value of this property. I know you have other concerns, but I'm not here for the long haul."

"Understood. Look, Meg, you know more about how this works from the financial side than I do, and you've got an outsider's eye. I'd appreciate any insights you can give me. If Granford is selling its soul, I want to be sure that the town gets the best deal possible. One we can live with in the future."

"Fair enough. And I'm happy to help, if I can. Well, I'll let you go. Thanks again, Seth."

Meg watched his truck pull out of her driveway. *Note to self: get more gravel for the driveway, before the mud season—as soon as the trench is filled.* She let herself in the back door, locking it behind her. Then, shrugging off her coat, she stacked the dishes from dinner in the sink and filled a bowl with hot, soapy water.

Scrubbing the dishes gave her time to think. Seth had asked her to look critically at the deal, as an outsider. A smart move on his part, but what surprised Meg was that she didn't resent his request for help the way she had Chandler's. She wasn't sure what that meant. The fact that it was Seth who had asked her wasn't important, was it? But she trusted Seth's motives, where she hadn't trusted Chandler's.

Seth had called her an outsider. Yet the town clerk had demanded proof of address—proof that, in effect, she was an insider. Filling out a form stating that Granford was in fact her one and only residence felt like a significant step, but she wasn't sure in which direction. It had driven home to her yet again that she had nowhere else to go. But that meant she was free to go anywhere, right?

If only she knew where that was.

13

By the next day Meg was beginning to understand the term "cabin fever." She didn't want to spend a day cooped up with her thoughts, much less staring at the open trench in her driveway, which looked far too much like a grave; she needed a distraction. Then she remembered the historical society. Research on the house—that would be a good excuse to get out and talk to someone, anyone. It would also advance at least one of her goals: getting the house ready to sell.

After breakfast, Meg set out for the Granford Historical Society. She knew from the handout she had picked up at the meeting that the place was open at odd times, depending on the availability of its director or other volunteers, but she hoped she would get lucky. When she pulled into the drive that passed in front of the building, she was gratified to see that a paper sign hung crookedly on the door, proudly proclaiming "Open." After parking in the empty lot, Meg mounted the single slab of granite that served as the front step and knocked firmly. For a moment there was silence, then a distant voice called out, "Hang on, I'm coming." This was followed by a crash and some creative if muffled curses. Meg waited patiently until the door finally opened, and then she was confronted by Gail, dressed in jeans and a grubby sweatshirt, her hair disheveled.

"What?" Gail barked.

"I'm sorry. Have I come at a bad time? You are open, aren't you?"

Gail gave her a grudging smile. "Oh, sorry. You're Meg, uh, Corey, isn't it? You came to the meeting last week. Yes, we are—open, that is. We! That's a joke. The place is, and I'm it. The staff, I mean. Sorry. So, welcome. Gail Selden, director, curator, archivist, and apparently, housekeeper, at your service. Sorry I snapped at you. What can I do for you today?"

"I was hoping to find out some more about my house, the Warren place?"

Gail's smile broadened. "Oh, right! You're the one with the body." Meg nodded. "Oh goody! Now I can get the straight scoop. Come on in. Oh, watch where you put your feet. And your hands. Heck, just keep your eyes open. I don't know how much our liability insurance covers."

Meg stepped into the building, then stopped dead. There were two rooms in front of her: a vestibule perhaps ten feet deep stretched across the front of the building, and beyond that, through a pair of tall doors, Meg could see a single large room. Both were crammed to the rafters with stuff. Gail was right to warn her, and Meg took a moment to reconnoiter. The place looked like no historical institution she had ever seen. The lowest layer of stuff appeared to be mid-Victorian furniture, based on the dusty plush and peeling veneer. But then there were books and papers and framed prints, and a couple of headless mannequins wearing tattered Civil War uniforms, and some large flags hanging haphazardly on the walls. But that was not the oddest part: distributed throughout was a collection of stuffed animals—not toys, but birds, foxes, what looked to be a bobcat. There was nowhere Meg could turn without meeting the beady glass eyes of ... something. She took a tentative step forward and nearly tripped over a shellacked armadillo on a pedestal.

"Wow," Meg said. Not much heat, either. Despite the chill, the room smelled like the inside of an old sock. One that had been kept in a trunk for a century or so.

"Yeah, I get that a lot." Gail grinned cheerfully. "So, what are you looking for?"

Meg tore her eyes away from a compulsive inventory of the contents to answer the question. "Well, I thought if I'm going to be putting the house on the market, buyers might like to know about its local history. I guess I'm interested in the people who built the place and who lived in it over the years."

"Beats discussing murder with them, doesn't it? Is it true that the guy was stuffed in your septic tank?"

Meg flinched. "Unfortunately, yes. And, no, I didn't do it, and I don't know who did do it. I really can't tell you much."

"But you knew him?" Gail eyed her shrewdly.

Word certainly gets around, Meg thought again. "Yes, I did, back in Boston. But I didn't know he had business here."

"My condolences, if any are due. You don't look too broken up about it. Anyway, why don't you come in and sit down, and I can tell you what information I've got and where else you can look."

"Great." Meg followed her guide into the big room, and they wove a path toward the far end, where an ancient rolltop desk spewed papers. There were two chairs in front of it, miraculously clear. Meg fell into one, grateful that she had avoided destroying any vital pieces of Granford history along the way. A stuffed skunk at eye level glared at her.

Gail took the other chair. "All right. Before we get started—you're family, right?"

"What do you mean?"

"You're related to the Warrens."

"So my mother tells me. Not exactly directly."

"You know, the house has been in the same family since it was built, and it's a shame to let it go to strangers now, after some two hundred and fifty years. Anyway, I know the house—built by Stephen Warren in the 1760s, before he marched off to war with his two sons, Stephen Junior and Eleazer. Stephen got to keep the house, and Eleazer built one next door, to the east."

"That's interesting. I knew it looked similar, but I didn't know it was the same family that built it."

"Sure. And have you seen the Chapin house? The original one, I mean?"

Meg shook her head. "Same family again?"

"Yup. A Warren girl—Stephen's daughter, if I recall—married into the Chapin family way back. That house is only about thirty years newer than yours, and I'll bet her dad put up the money. And they kept the name in the family—hence, Stephen Chapin."

Meg laughed. "And you keep all this straight in your head? Are you related to any of these families?"

Gail shrugged. "One way or another. It's a small town."

"Then you can probably tell me if there are any Warrens still around?"

"The house next door to you passed out of the family long ago. Sad to say, the last of the Warrens were those old biddies, Lula and Nettie, and they hung on about forever. Into their nineties, I think. And then a series of renters." Gail made a sour face.

"I keep feeling I have to apologize for that," Meg said quickly, "even though I didn't have anything to do with it. My mother inherited the house, and she couldn't be bothered to sell it, so it was easiest just to rent it out."

"No doubt. You wouldn't know if anyone cleared out the attics, would you?"

"I can't say, because I haven't been up there, but given what I've seen so far it wouldn't surprise me to find that they're full of old stuff." Suddenly Meg made the connection and grinned at Gail. "I promise you and the society first crack at whatever I uncover up there."

"You're an angel! You have no idea how much local history ends up in the trash. So, what else are you interested in?"

"You tell me. There must be deeds and wills and such in Northampton—that's the county seat, right?" Gail nodded. "So I should check out the documents there. But I guess I wanted something more human. You know—what living was like around here in the eighteenth century, what people did. Were the Warrens farmers?"

"Early on. Crops, orchards, some grazing land. But the problem was the swamp on the east side. Oh, sorry—we're supposed to call it the 'Great Meadow.' You may have mosquito problems, come summer. You might think about putting in some bat boxes on your barn. Bats do a good job of keeping the mosquitos down. So, anyway, the farming wasn't great because a lot of the property was wet at least part of the time, and there sure as heck wasn't a lot of industry around here, even in the nineteenth century. That all happened over in Ware, Springfield, Chicopee, but it never made it this far. There were a couple of generations of carpenters at your place—they even had a small sawmill at the back. Oh, hey, wait a minute!" Gail bounded up, crossed the room, and started rummaging through a pile of things stacked against the far wall. "Got it. Come over here a minute."

Meg joined her and looked down on a large slab of wood. "What is it?"

"Guess."

Meg studied it for a moment. She was looking at a single plank, not a joined piece. Not something one would see very often these days—the trees that could supply that kind of width were long gone. Then she noticed that there were lines and figures inscribed on it, but they made no sense to her. "I give up."

Gail grinned. "It's a measuring board for sizing coffins. It came out of your barn. The renters were going to throw it out when they wanted to get a car into the barn, but somebody noticed it and brought it here. I hope you don't want it back."

"Heavens, no. But I've never heard of such a thing."

"Well, carpenters made a steady living building coffins, so one of the Warrens—I'm guessing Eli the younger—decided to set himself up a template. Cool, huh?"

"It is," Meg agreed.

"Have you found anything else interesting around the place?" Gail's eyes gleamed with the lust of a true collector.

"I really haven't had time to look. Odds and ends keep popping up. You know, a piece of broken china here, an old coin there. I really should check out the barn, see if there's anything lurking there, but I've had other things to do. None of the Warrens left a convenient Bible or a batch of diaries?"

"Nope. Least, not that I've seen. But never say never! There's a lot of stuff here that's never been inventoried."

"So I suppose some of the alterations to the building were the work of Eli," Meg said slowly. "Seth said something about that—a couple of things didn't seem right for the 1760s. And of course, the barn is newer than the house."

"Yeah—probably mid–nineteenth century. Eli kept busy. Still, it's a great place. Listen, a lot of the paper files for the society are living in my attic these days. I'd be happy to take a look, see if anything pops up about the Warrens. Problem is, it's not exactly catalogued or anything."

"That would be great. Thank you. Oh, and is there anything you can tell me about the orchard?"

"That's right—Warren's Grove. That used to be a major intersection, way back, so the orchard was the first thing a lot of folks saw when they came to town. It's amazing that it's still going—although of course it's not the same trees."

"As I understand it, it may not survive much longer, if this development project goes through." Meg decided to take the bull by the horns. "Look, I know you must be dying to know about . . . the body and all. You might as well ask. But I'll trade: I want to know more about what's going on around here. And you must have an opinion about Granford Grange. What's that going to do to the town?"

Gail hesitated, chewing on her lower lip. "That's more than a two-sentence answer."

"Have you got the time to talk about it now?"

"I'll have to turn away the crowds waiting outside." Gail stood up. "I'll be happy to tell you what I know. But first, let's find a warmer place to sit."

14

Gail headed to a different corner of the room, where Meg noticed a large heating grate embedded in the floor. She shoved a pile of books and rolled documents off a pair of chairs and sat. Meg followed suit.

"Better. Much better." For a moment she studied Meg. "Okay, let's start with the body. You've got to know the murder is the biggest news to hit town in years. I had to check—the last murder here was in 1869. So take the murder and combine it with the development ballyhoo, and everybody in town has had something to say."

"I'll bet," Meg said. "But why do you know that? I mean, why do you know so much? It's not like your little museum is the throbbing heart of town. No offense intended."

"None taken. No, this is only part-time for me, and a labor of love at that—no pay. The rest of the time I work in the local insurance office, up that way." Gail pointed toward the north end of the green. "I also belong to a couple of church groups. And, hey, it's a small town. People talk. I hear things. So, come on—give me the whole story. Maybe I can make sure that everyone gets it right."

"You know who Chandler Hale was, of course?" Gail nodded, and Meg went on. "I knew him in Boston. Well, I knew him pretty well, I guess—we dated for a while. But that was over long before I moved here. I was so busy trying to figure out what I needed to do with the house that I didn't even know about the Granford Grange project, and I certainly didn't know he was part of it."

"What, you just plunked yourself down here in Granford with no clue about what the town was like or what was going on?"

Gail apparently found this hard to understand. Meg wasn't sure she did herself.

"More or less. But I figured I'd be in and out fast."

"Dreamer!" Gail grinned.

Meg grinned back. "Tell me about it. Anyway, Chandler Hale showed up at my place looking for the tenants, because nobody was answering his letters. My mother and I worked out the ownership between us, but I guess the paperwork hasn't gotten filed yet. Chandler was surprised to find me there. We had dinner in Amherst that night, and that was the last time I saw him until we found him in the septic tank Wednesday morning."

"Huh. Why the septic tank?"

"My plumbing had been acting up—pure senility, I gather—so I was getting a new one installed."

"Oh, yes, the Chapins have been taking care of that, right?"

"Of course—you know them. So they got the tank into the ground and hooked up, and they were going to fill in the hole the next morning. But before they could, someone stuffed Chandler in."

Gail sat back in her chair. "So somebody offed Chandler and hid him in a convenient hole, hoping no one would notice. Might even have worked, since with just you using the plumbing, there wouldn't be a lot passing through the system. But you didn't see anything or anybody?"

"Nobody's quite sure when Chandler went in, but it was probably while I was at the historical society meeting. It's still not clear exactly when he died. The detective is looking for people who saw him on Tuesday. Anyway, no, I didn't hear a thing. But there weren't that many people who knew about the hole."

"That does narrow things down a bit," Gail said thoughtfully.

Meg went on. "My question is, did someone kill Chandler for personal reasons or to derail the development project? Maybe you can help me there. Who around here didn't want to see this thing go forward?"

Gail sat back and tapped her chin before answering. "Let's take a step back. What do you see when you look at Granford?"

"A nice, small New England town. Pretty. Quiet. Peaceful. A sense of history."

Gail nodded. "Yes, all of those things. But what business do you see? The pharmacy there, a couple of home offices for a law-yer or two. Even farther out on 202, there's not much more—some car repair places, a gas station, a couple of fast-food joints. The hard reality is, we have no tax base. Charm don't pay the bills, and the bills keep going up. Police, fire. Snowplowing in winter. The historical society has a line item in the town budget, and every year it gets smaller. Luckily the town owns the build-ing outright. I don't get a salary, and we can barely keep the heat on in winter. Forget about a computer for cataloguing, or even funds for patching the roof. So, to answer your question, I think that the commercial strip would be a blessing. It may not be quaint and pretty, but we need it."

"But what about the land? I mean, the people whose land will be taken over for the project?"

"You mean like the Chapins? I'd say there's a mixed reaction. You know, if you dig into the records, you'll find that a lot of the property around here has been in the same family for centuries. Like your place. The Warrens lived there from the time the land was first surveyed until—what, thirty years ago? But we don't farm much around here anymore, so it's mostly sentiment and inertia that keep the plots together. That and nobody much wants to buy them. So along comes Chandler and his bank offering a nice deal: give us the land, for a fair market price, and we'll build you an income-producing complex. All you have to give up is a little of your pretty but useless green space, a few scenic views. It's a win-win situation, right?"

"Sounds like it. So is there anyone who would want to sabo-tage the project, and why?"

"Ah, that's the question. Maybe it was personal. Maybe somebody really didn't like Chandler. Shoot—I don't know. Maybe the state police will figure it out."

"Are they any good?"

"Hard to say—we've never had a murder around here to in-vestigate on their watch. But by and large I think they're decent people, and competent."

They both fell silent for a few moments. Meg felt frustrated; Gail hadn't given her much information that she hadn't already worked out for herself.

"So, what're your plans for the house?" Gail finally asked.

Meg grimaced. "I think I've got to get this murder cleared up before I can do anything about selling the place. Might be hard to do from jail."

Gail laughed. "That seems unlikely. There must be other suspects."

Meg hesitated before asking, "What about Seth Chapin?"

"As a suspect? Forget it."

"You answered that pretty fast. He does have a personal stake in this deal, doesn't he? What's his opinion?"

"You know, I can't really say. As a selectman, he's been conscientious about presenting it to the town, but I know he really cares about the family place. I'd have to guess he's torn up about it, but I don't think he'd stand in the way of the project. And, believe me, I can't see Seth Chapin murdering anybody, certainly not for a couple of acres of land." She paused. "Or maybe that wasn't the question you were asking?"

Meg sputtered. "What do you mean? Was I asking about Seth because ..."

Gail laughed. "Come on, don't tell me you haven't thought about it. You're single, right? And new in town? He's single. He lives next door to you. He has a steady job and all his teeth. You want me to believe that the thought has never crossed your mind?"

"No! Really. I mean, he has been helpful, and he's been showing me around, and he introduced me to his sister, and ..." Meg stopped. Maybe she had been misreading Seth's behavior. Maybe she had willfully shut her eyes to the possibilities. Maybe she'd been more hurt by Chandler's rejection than she realized. She had been planning a quick departure from Granford, and she hadn't been looking for any personal entanglements. But that was something to think about later—after this murder was cleared up. "Is this what small-town living is all about? The whole town is playing matchmaker?"

Gail laughed at her dismay. "Don't worry about it. But, in a way, yes. It is a small town, and people tend to look out for each other. Seth's a popular guy—people like him. So of course they wonder, especially when he's seen with you around town. Don't take it personally."

Meg pondered the wisdom of her next question before deciding to take the plunge. "So why hasn't some nice woman snatched him up already?"

"One did, years ago. Not a local girl, somebody he met in college—she went to Holyoke, I think. Nancy something-or-other. Didn't last." Gail looked at her and grinned. "Bet you're dying to know why."

"Just curious," Meg said primly. "I mean, he seems like a nice guy and all." And why hadn't Seth told her anything about this Nancy person?

Gail snorted. "He is, no question. But Nancy didn't want to be married to a small-town plumber. She thought she was getting an Amherst grad who'd go on to graduate school and get a cozy academic job. She was really ticked when he decided to come back here and run the family business. She lasted about a year in Granford and then walked out in a huff. Didn't get far, though—I think she does something administrative over at UMass. She still drops by, now and then—I think she's still hoping that Seth will come to his senses and 'live up to his full potential.'" Gail made air quotes around the last statement.

"And she's waiting to latch on to him again, when and if he does?"

"Maybe. Well, that's probably more than you need to know. But the bottom line is, Seth's unattached. If you're interested."

Meg felt simultaneously confused and pleased. If she had been thinking about it—which she hadn't—she should have wondered why a decent guy like Seth wasn't married, with a passel of kids. He was the type. So it didn't surprise her to hear that he had been married, and of course there was no reason why he should have filled her in on his life history. Not that she had any plans for him. After all, she was staying around only long enough to sell the house.

"Thanks for the background, Gail. Listen, do you think this whole murder mess will have any impact on selling the house? I mean, having a body pop up in the plumbing is not exactly good advertising."

"Depends. But I'd say no, in the long run. Maybe you're lucky Chandler wasn't found inside the house, but in any case you should be fine. In fact, when the project goes forward, there may be a lot of outsiders moving in, and they won't know a thing about it."

"You're right. Still, I'd like to see somebody arrested for Chandler's death. We don't want to lose sight of the fact that he was murdered. So, the final vote on the project is in a couple of weeks?"

"Yep. You coming to the meeting? You are registered to vote, right?"

"I am—Seth made sure of that. I wouldn't miss it. Look, I hope I'm not keeping you from anything. I really appreciate your time."

Gail laughed. "Most of the stuff has been here for longer than I've been on this earth. It's not going anywhere. And I'm glad to help out a newcomer. Feel free to ask about anything."

"Thanks." As Meg stood up, a thought struck her. "Listen, I have some free time on my hands, but it's usually unpredictable. Could I help you out with some of the cataloguing? I've got a computer at the house. I could take a couple of boxes at a time and work through them when I have the odd moment. If that would be useful."

Gail stood up, too. "Lady, I never turn down an offer of help. I made a stab at it, and I've got a good software program, but there aren't enough hours in the day, since I have to keep my day job if I want to eat. Give me a day or two to go through the boxes and find you a good place to start, and then I can show you my system. And maybe you'll learn something about the town along the way."

"Deal. Just let me know when."

15

Meg arrived home to one solid piece of good news: the trench across her driveway had been filled in. One less thing she would have to worry about, and bless Seth for remembering to take care of it.

Meg had barely taken off her coat when she heard knocking at her front door. *Who now?* She made her way to the door and started the familiar tussle. *Note to self: do something about a doorbell or knocker.* When it opened, she was startled to find Cinda Patterson.

"Hi," Meg said, staring blankly for a moment. "Cinda. Oh, sorry—come on in. And why don't you just come through to the ... dining room?" Somehow it felt wrong to Meg to entertain Cinda in the kitchen. "Can I get you something? Coffee? Tea?"

Cinda had stopped in the hallway and was looking around. "I'm so sorry to barge in on you like this, Meg. May I call you Meg? Chandler spoke of you, and I almost feel as though I know you. His death is a tragedy, for those of us who knew him." Her face assumed an appropriately somber expression. "It was a privilege to work with him. He taught me so much."

"Yes, he was a fine man." Meg almost gagged on the platitude, but she didn't think Cinda was any more sincere than she was. She looked as though she had stepped out of *Town and Country*, wearing the perfect outfit for a casual weekend.

Duty done, Cinda deftly changed the subject. "What a lovely house this is!"

"Thank you. It's been in the family for generations."

"These old places are so—I don't know—real? You feel the

weight of history—all those people who have lived here before you, and left a little part of themselves behind." Cinda sounded almost sincere, or at least well rehearsed.

Meg led the way to the dining room, where for once the table was free of clutter. "Coffee?" she asked again.

"That would be fine, if it's no trouble."

"None at all. Please, make yourself at home. I won't be a minute."

Fleeing to the kitchen, Meg thought briefly of her mother. She would have had a selection of assorted treats ready for just such an occasion, not to mention some pretty serving plates and linen doilies at hand. Meg could just about manage clean plates, period. Still, coffee she could handle, even though it had gone cold. She located a pair of matching cups and filled them, then surreptitiously heated them in the microwave. Cinda looked like the type who would take it black, no sugar, and there wasn't any artificial sweetener in the house to offer her. So much for gracious hospitality. In any case, she didn't want to leave Cinda alone any longer than necessary. She didn't trust her.

Back in the dining room, Cinda was still drifting around, apparently meditating on the woodwork. She turned when Meg entered.

"Oh, thank you! I've had only one cup today—back-to-back meetings, you know—and I'm almost useless without it!"

Meg smiled thinly, then sat down, and Cinda followed suit. "So, what can I do for you, Cinda?"

"May I talk frankly with you, Meg?" When Meg nodded warily, she went on. "You were at the meeting in town last night, weren't you? So you know that the bank wants very much to see this project go forward, and they've given me the chance to continue Chandler's work."

"Congratulations." Meg thought it was the polite thing to say, whether or not she meant it.

"Thank you. It's a real challenge for me—I've never worked on a project this big, at least not solo, but I think I'm ready. And the bank believes in me. But as a woman you must know how important it is that I do a good job. Don't you?"

Smart, Meg thought. *She's playing the feminist card.* Meg nodded. "I know it's not easy. You've got a big job here—you've got to win over the local movers and shakers, and work with the developers, too."

Cinda nodded eagerly. "You see? You do understand. And I came to you because I'd really like your help in making this work."

Meg sat back and contemplated Chandler's former assistant. Zealous, sincere Cinda. Who, if she read the signals right, seemed to want from Meg the same thing that Chandler had—insider information. Why did they think she knew anything? Maybe she was supposed to be flattered. "Cinda, what is it you think I can do for you? You have to know I'm new here. I don't have a lot of connections, and I certainly don't have any influence in Granford."

"I realize that, Meg. But you have an advantage that I don't: you own property here, property that's directly involved in the project. You can ask questions. And the townspeople will be willing to talk to you, because you share their concerns. And . . ." Cinda hesitated slightly. "I gather you have Seth Chapin's ear?"

Is that what this is really about? Meg wondered. *How would Cinda have heard anything like that?* "Seth is my plumber and my neighbor," she said neutrally. "I've known him less than a week."

"But he brought you to the meeting last night, which sends a message to the people in town. Look, Meg, all I'm asking is that you keep me up-to-date about what the buzz in town is. And maybe give me a little counsel on the financial advantages to the town. I know you have far more experience on that side than I do. Just help me strengthen my presentation, you know? I need to make my case as strong as I can. After all, I have to stand up in front of the Town Meeting and sell it."

It was a good act, Meg had to admit. An appeal to sisterhood, a little professional flattery, a touching humility. Cinda knew exactly what she was doing. Chandler had taught his protégée well. Meg's first impulse was to tell her to pack it in and go away. She had been offended when Chandler had suggested it, and she was no less offended now by Cinda's approach.

But . . . maybe it was not a good idea to dismiss Cinda as she had Chandler. Maybe she should do a little strategizing of her own. If she kept the lines of communication open with Cinda, at least she could learn something about the project and what was going on behind the scenes—a fair exchange of information. And she would have yet another reason to look carefully at the financial impact on the town—something she should do anyway, for her own purposes—and something she could report to Seth. The idea of this secret exchange pleased her.

She forced a smile. "Cinda, I'm flattered that you came to me, and I'd be happy to help in any way I can."

Cinda beamed at her. "Oh, Meg, thank you! I can't tell you how important your help will be to me. I really, really appreciate it." Her mission apparently accomplished, she stood up. "I won't take up any more of your time now—I have to get back to Boston and pick up a few things, since it looks like I'll be here for a while. But I'm so glad I can count on you."

"Of course." Meg stood up also. "Just let me know what you need, and I'll see what I can do."

Cinda was already moving toward the door. "I'll be in touch just as soon as I get back! And I love your house. It's a real treasure." As she uttered this last statement, she turned the knob to open the front door. It stuck. She pulled harder, and it gave suddenly with a jerk that sent her stumbling backward. "Damn," she said, under her breath. It appeared she had broken a carefully manicured nail. On the doorstep she turned once again and gave Meg a bright smile. "I'll talk to you next week, Meg. And I can't thank you enough. Bye!"

Meg watched as Cinda tiptoed her way along Meg's flagstone path. City heels were not intended for rough stone, and her exit was less than graceful. When she reached the car, she looked back and waved, and then pulled out too fast. Meg shut the door and sighed.

What did Cinda really want? Meg didn't doubt Cinda's professional abilities—Chandler would not have tolerated merely average performance, no matter how decorative the package. Maybe Cinda was just covering all the bases, collecting whatever scraps of information she could. Meg didn't kid herself that she had anything more than scraps to offer. Unless it was access to Seth that Cinda wanted. Was Seth the linchpin of this deal? Did his decision, to sell or to fight, carry that much weight in the community? As she had told Cinda, she had known him only a few days. There was no way she could gauge the impact of his opinions. Maybe Cinda wanted to keep an eye on him, and Meg was her best hope.

But where had Cinda gotten that idea?

16

The next morning, as she tidied up the few dishes in the kitchen, Meg was not pleased to see the state detective's car pull into her drive. With a sigh, she dried her hands and went to open the front door.

"Detective Marcus," she said as she stepped aside to let him in. "I didn't know county law enforcement worked on weekends—or made house calls. Is there something new about Chandler's death?"

He surveyed the room before he answered. "Ms. Corey, this case is high priority. I was in the neighborhood checking on a few things. I wanted to give you a copy of your statement, see if you wanted to make any changes. Let's sit down."

"Certainly." Meg led the way to the dining room and gestured toward a chair. "Can I get you something to drink?" *Stop it, Meg—this isn't a social occasion, it's a murder investigation.*

"Let's just get down to business." He stood, shifting from one foot to the other, waiting for her to sit, so she sat, and he followed suit. He pushed a large manila envelope across the table toward her. Her statement?

The detective pulled a small pad from his shirt pocket and opened it with deliberation, leafing through the pages until he found the one he wanted, then located a pen. Meg wondered if he was always this slow or if this was just a tactic to rattle her. Unfortunately it was working, which annoyed her because she had done nothing wrong, had nothing to hide. Finally he launched into his questions.

"When your relationship with Chandler Hale ended, were there any hard feelings?"

Meg stared at him. He really wanted to go over this same trampled ground? "No, it was relatively amicable."

"Had you seen him since you moved here?"

"No. I told you that the last time we spoke. He just showed up at my door last Monday."

"Maybe you two picked up where you left off?" The detective watched her.

"No." Meg fought rising anger.

"You had dinner," the detective said flatly.

"Yes, we did."

"What did you discuss at dinner?"

"Detective, I've already told you all this," Meg said tartly.

"Just answer the question."

What was he driving at? "We talked about what we'd been doing, and the development project, mainly. He asked me for my help with the project, since I was now a resident and a landowner in Granford. I told him I wasn't interested."

"How did he take that?"

"He wasn't pleased. I think he assumed I'd be happy to help him, but I disliked the way he approached the whole thing. And he implied that he could see to it that I got a good deal when I sold my land, if I went along with him. I was uncomfortable with the ethics of that. Look, Detective, I've told you all this before."

Detective Marcus ignored her comment. "How did you meet Seth Chapin?"

That was not a question she had been expecting. "I had some plumbing problems, and he was the first plumber I reached."

"You know about his involvement in the land deal?"

"Not at the time. I do now."

"What did he tell you?"

"That part of his property is targeted for commercial development, as is part of mine. And that he has mixed feelings about it, since he's both a selectman and a landowner."

"You sure there isn't anything more going on?"

Meg swallowed. What was this man suggesting? "Excuse me?"

"I have to look at all the angles, Ms. Corey. Here's one scenario: say you and Chapin had something going on, and this Hale guy shows up unexpectedly and takes it the wrong way. After all, we have only your word about how things ended between you. Or maybe Seth didn't like him putting the moves on you. Some men might not be happy about that. Might do something about it."

Incredulous, Meg realized that he was serious. "Detective," she said carefully, "are you suggesting that Seth might have killed Chandler because Seth and I are involved somehow? You're barking up the wrong tree. I barely know the man."

"Well, it would have been convenient for Chapin, don't you think? Get his competition out of the way *and* put the kibosh on a project he doesn't want anyway, all at once."

"That's ridiculous. I can't believe Seth would do something like that." Even as she said the words, she realized how little she knew about Seth.

"Maybe. Or maybe Hale decided he wanted you back and wouldn't take no for an answer, and you panicked and fought with him."

It would be funny that the detective had cast her as the femme fatale, luring—or fending off—not one but two men here in Granford, except that none of it was true. And where was he getting these ideas? Meg considered how best to answer. If she told the simple truth, would he believe her? And how could she prove a negative?

She took a deep breath. "Detective, once again, nothing happened that night between Chandler and me. I hadn't seen him in months. What's more, the idea of Chandler Hale resorting to physical violence is laughable. And I'm sure, knowing Chandler, that he had some sort of current relationship in Boston, and it shouldn't be hard for you to find out. He seldom lacked for female companionship." To her dismay, she sounded like a Victorian spinster. "We had dinner, he brought me home, and then he left. Period." Maybe it was time to turn the tables. "I didn't see him again until he came out of my septic tank, dead. Have you looked at any of the other people around here who might have a reason to want Chandler dead?"

"We're looking into a lot of things, Ms. Corey." Detective Marcus wasn't about to give anything away.

The man was infuriating. But Meg could be stubborn, too. "Have you found anyone who saw him after we had dinner that night?"

"Looks like he was in the Boston office for most of Tuesday—left there about three. Could've been back here by six if he drove straight back."

"What about his assistant, Cinda Patterson?"

The detective sighed. "Ms. Corey, I am under no obligation to report to you on the progress of this investigation, particularly since you are under suspicion. I will tell you that I spoke to Ms. Patterson on Friday morning."

Meg waited, but the detective didn't volunteer anything else, including when Cinda had last seen Chandler. "You know I went to the historical society meeting that night. It started a little after seven. I was there early."

"I know. The meeting ended close to ten. People saw you there."

So he had checked. "And then I came home and went to bed. Listen, Detective, I understand that Chandler died from blunt force trauma, right?"

"A blow or blows to the head. Where'd you hear that?"

Meg ignored the question; no need to get Seth into any more trouble. "How much strength would that have taken?"

"You mean, would it take a man to do it? A good whack with a rock or a pipe would have done the trick, man or woman."

"What about putting him into the tank?"

"He weighed, what, maybe 190? A man could do it. A strong woman could do it. Or two people working together. Or somebody in a panic. Lots of possibilities."

Since the detective seemed willing to share, if grudgingly, Meg pressed on. "Where was he staying?"

He gave her a long look, weighing his response. "Kept a room at the Hotel Northampton. Nothing disturbed there, or if there was, someone cleaned up real well."

Meg nodded. "Chandler was always very tidy. And he didn't travel with a lot of fuss. Was his car there?"

"That Mercedes? In the parking garage. Neat as a pin."

"So where do you think he was killed?" *Please, not in my backyard*, Meg prayed silently.

"Don't know yet," he said reluctantly.

They both fell silent.

"Do you have any suspects?" Meg asked finally. *Apart from Seth and me, of course,* she added to herself.

"Can't say, Ms. Corey." The detective had shifted back to stonewall mode, but at least Meg had gleaned a few kernels of information.

"Then is there anything else you need?"

He stood up. "No, I think we're done. For now. Look over the statement—if it's okay, sign it and send it back to me. And let me know if you remember anything else that might help." He handed her a business card, then looked around again. "Nice place you've got."

Everyone seemed to like her house—more than they liked her. "Thank you, Detective." She followed him to the front door.

He headed for his car, and Meg watched him through the storm door as he pulled out of the driveway. He had done everything by the book, asked all the right questions, but Meg was still uneasy. From what he had said, or hinted, it seemed that she and Seth were still the primary suspects, singly or working together. Would he look any further?

This was ridiculous. She had come to bucolic Granford for some peace and quiet, and some therapeutic construction work, and somehow had landed herself in the middle of a murder investigation—the murder of someone she knew, no less, and in which she seemed to be a suspect. It made no sense to her. Who around here had known about her defunct relationship with Chandler? Only Seth, and that was after Chandler was dead. Well, Cinda might have known. Maybe she could corroborate the fact of the breakup? The detective said he had talked to Cinda. He had to, if he was doing his job. Unless he was determined to pin Chandler's death on Meg or on Seth. But why would he be?

Meg was so lost in her own thoughts that she hadn't heard the approach of another car, and she was startled to see Seth walking toward her back door. As she opened the door she felt a stab of doubt, then shook it off. She had no reason not to trust Seth.

"Hi. Do I have a plumbing problem that I don't know about?"

"No, but I wanted to talk to you about something. Can I come in?"

"Sure." Meg stepped back to let him pass. "You want coffee?"

"If you've got it made."

"Always." At the rate people were visiting, she was going to have to get a bigger coffeemaker. Meg poured two cups, then sat down at the kitchen table, gesturing toward the other chair. "So, what's up?"

"Was that the detective I passed?"

"Yes. He wanted to go over my statement again." She waved at the sheaf of paper on the table, where the detective had left it. Meg debated with herself for a moment about bringing up his attitude toward Seth, but decided to leave well enough alone. "But that's not what brought you here, is it?"

"No. I was wondering if I could borrow your barn, or at least part of it?"

That was not what Meg had expected to hear. "Sure. I'm not exactly using it, except as a place to keep my trash. What do you want with it? Don't you have space of your own?" Oh, God, was he planning to hide stolen merchandise or something?

Seth grinned, as if reading her thoughts. "I do, but I've filled it. Or at least, the plumbing business has, but I've got this other problem . . ."

"What?"

"I collect architectural salvage. It started through the business. You know—somebody would want to remodel, and they'd say, 'Get rid of this old stuff.' So I ended up with a bunch of Victorian sinks and bathtubs, fixtures, even wainscoting—that kind of thing. And the contemporary stock takes up all the business's storage space, so I was wondering if I could use your space for the overflow. Since you're not really using it . . ."

"No problem," Meg said magnanimously. "Of course, I can't guarantee that the place won't fall down around your ears. But do you ever plan to use the stuff you collect?"

"Oh, sure. There are plenty of people who go the other way, want to restore their own places with authentic period pieces. Most of the time I can bring the old ones up to code. So you see, it balances out in the long run, but I need a holding area in between. Listen, I could swap you—check out your fixtures, maybe set you up with something more period appropriate? Like as a rental fee?"

Meg thought about the low-end fixtures that someone had shoehorned into her pathetic bathrooms. "It's a deal. What I've got now is lousy modern stuff."

"Done." Seth sipped his coffee and looked at her critically. "You okay? You look kind of down."

Meg laughed bitterly. "Why would I look down? The detective thinks I killed Chandler." *Or that you did,* she added silently. "This place eats money, and it's cold. I don't know anyone around here except you and Rachel and my real estate agent, and now I'm going to be introduced to anyone new as 'that woman who owns the place where they found the body.' Everything's just peachy keen."

"I'm sorry, Meg." Seth looked as though he meant it. "It can't be easy for you. I'm surprised you don't just bail out and leave."

And where would I go? Meg asked herself. "This was supposed to be a time to rethink my options. Funny, I hadn't included 'going to jail' on the list."

Seth looked troubled for a moment, and then his expression brightened. "Hey, I've got an idea. I've got to pick up some fixtures from this guy I know—he keeps his eyes open for salvage items I might like. Want to come along? Might do you good to get out of the house, get some fresh air and sunshine."

Was he kidding? The thermometer outside her window registered a balmy 27 degrees, and gray clouds hung low. The to-do list loomed. But suddenly Meg knew she couldn't stomach scraping another wall or ceiling or floor … "Sure. Let me suit up. Give me a minute."

As Seth finished the last of his coffee, Meg pulled on boots, found her insulated jacket, hat, scarf, and gloves. She grabbed some tissues, for her nose that always ran in the cold. Should she leave a note for the authorities, in the event Seth turned out to be a serial killer and dumped her body somewhere? She snorted. *Don't be ridiculous, Meg.*

Once in Seth's van, Meg asked, "Where're we going?"

"Eric's got a place near Hadley. Have you been there?"

"No. Should I have been?"

"Probably not. If you've driven to Amherst, you might have gone through it. There's a farm museum, and they grow great asparagus. Although this isn't exactly the right time of year for that."

"Museums haven't been high on my list lately. More like hardware stores. Is this Eric's full-time job?"

Seth laughed. "No, actually he teaches French literature at UMass. But he's like me—he loves to collect things. Junk, some people call it. Personally, I think our culture is much too obsessed by new and shiny things. Do you realize how hard it is to find anyone to repair anything these days? Most people just throw broken things out and buy a replacement."

Seth warmed to his subject, and Meg settled back to listen, watching the landscape roll by. She kept forgetting there was so much country around Granford. Gradually the land flattened out, and she could see level fields, broken by patches of trees. They passed through an intersection that seemed to be all there was of downtown Hadley, and shortly after that Seth turned left and followed a meandering country lane for a few miles, before pulling into a drive that ran alongside a gray clapboard house with a large, unpainted barn behind. At the sound of their approach, a man emerged from the barn and waved.

Seth clambered out of his seat. "Hey, Eric. Thanks for the heads-up about the stuff. Oh, I brought along some company. Be gentle with her—she's new to scavenging, but she can use some odds and ends for her place."

That was news to Meg. She climbed out of the van and joined the men. "Hello. Eric, is it? I don't know what Seth is talking about, but I'm pretty sure all the salvageable stuff has been peeled off my house."

"She lives in a colonial in Granford—lots of potential."

"Pleased to meet you, Meg. Let me guess: your plumbing gave out, and that's how you connected with Seth?"

"Right you are."

"I hear a lot of that. Well, let's get in out of the wind. Seth, I put the fixtures you might like in back ..."

Meg followed them as they wended their way through the

piles of stuff in the dim and drafty interior of the barn. She could make out a rudimentary order: stacks of multipanel doors and window sashes, a couple of mantelpieces, boxes that appeared to hold odds and ends of hardware. It was intriguing in its way, and Meg recognized a few things that looked as if they might have come from a house like hers, or maybe even from her own. She sighed. It never ceased to amaze her what people did in the name of taste, pulling out perfectly respectable materials just to replace them with something cheap and ugly.

She dawdled as Seth and Eric haggled over some sinks and tubs. She peered into a dark corner, then stopped abruptly. "What's that?" She pointed to a handsome Victorian wall clock hanging on the back display.

"Good eye, Meg." Seth gave her an amused look. "Looks to be about 1850. Let's get a closer look. Could be fake or repaired, or it might not work at all."

"Seth, you cut me to the quick," Eric said, in mock dismay. "Would I have a fake? Of course, I'm not saying it works, exactly …"

"Let's find out." Meg picked her way through the maze of materials to take a closer look. Up close, the clock was even more appealing. She had no way of guessing its date, but she could tell it was mechanical, a pendulum peeping out from behind dirty glass. She found the latch that held the door shut, opened it, and gave the pendulum a gentle push: it swung gently back and forth. The ticking noise was soothing.

"Nice, isn't it?" Eric had come up behind her. "Not high-end, but a pretty piece nonetheless. And all the finials are intact, and the glass is original."

"Does it keep time?" Meg asked dubiously.

"It might. It's an eight-day—that means you wind it once a week. It rings the hours, but you can disable that if you want. Sometimes these days people get annoyed at the noise. But there's usually some adjustment mechanism, if the timing's off. Heck, why do you need to know exactly what minute it is, anyway?" Eric grinned.

Meg was almost afraid to ask the next question. "Are you selling it?"

Eric glanced at Seth before answering. "One fifty?"

I can't buy this, Meg thought. *I'm already hemorrhaging money for the house.* Still, it was a lovely thing, and it would go so well ...

She was surprised when Seth said, "It's a fair price."

She stopped fighting herself. "I want it. Can I give you a check, Eric?"

"Fine. I'll trust you. And if it bounces, Seth can answer for it."

Five minutes later, Meg and Seth emerged into the daylight. The clock was swathed in bubble wrap, its pendulum nestled in more. Meg climbed into the passenger seat, cradling it like a baby in her arms, while the men loaded some porcelain sinks and a box filled with something that clinked into the back of the van. She wondered just what had gotten into her, but she couldn't bring herself to regret her momentary madness. It just felt right.

Seth joined her in the van and started his engine. "If it doesn't work, I can take a look at it. I like to fix things, and clocks were still pretty simple at that period."

"I'll see. I can't believe I just did that. I know my bank account won't like it."

As they passed through Hadley again, Meg searched for something to talk about. Finally she said, "Anything new on Granford Grange?" Might as well see if she could come up with a nugget to keep Cinda happy. Besides, she was curious.

"Not publicly. You said you registered to vote. You'll be at the meeting? It's a week from Monday, you know."

"I think so. You said it's just this one item on the warrant, isn't it? I've been doing a little research on the whole eminent domain issue, and I can see why it's controversial. It sure does have people stirred up around here."

"I think it should. Dollars and cents aside, decisions like this have a real impact on the character of the town, how you want to live. It's good that people feel strongly about it, and that they have a forum to air their opinions. I just wish I knew what was going to happen."

"What do you *think* is going to happen?"

"To be honest, I really don't know. Right now it's too close to call. And I'm stuck right in the middle, because I can see both sides."

"That can't be much fun. Has Puritan Bank done a good job of, uh, persuading people?"

Seth shrugged, his eyes on the road. "Probably. Hale could be a bit hard to take, but he was thorough, and he had all the numbers. And he was around to answer questions—he didn't just phone it in."

So it must have mattered to him, Meg thought. "And now?"

Seth shook his head. "There's some momentum. Once the idea is out of the bottle, it's hard to stuff it back in."

Meg turned to watch his profile. "What's your position?"

"As a selectman or as one of the landowners?"

"Either. Both."

He sighed. "As a selectman, I have to say I think it would be good for the town, as long as the size and nature of the development are reasonably controlled. As an owner, it makes me sad, but I'll survive. Oh, back to the selectman view, I have no idea how we're going to reconcile all these opinions and hammer out something that will make the maximum number of people happy. You'll notice that I don't say 'everyone,' because that's never going to happen."

Meg considered this, then asked, "So, after everyone in town has had his or her say at the meeting, what happens?"

"Well, in fact, anyone can ask that the article be put to a vote, at any time—that means discussion would be cut off. Then the people there have to vote about whether they want to keep talking, or go ahead and vote on the issue, and that takes a two-thirds majority. But if somebody cuts off the dialogue too soon, they aren't going to be very popular in town. So it's really hard to call."

"Democracy in action."

"Don't knock it—it's worked for over three hundred years. Anyway, once everybody has spoken, then it comes to a vote. Voice vote first, and if that isn't clear enough, then individuals have to stand up and be counted. That'll take a simple majority."

Back at the house, Seth carried the clock while Meg unlocked the back door and held it open for him. Inside, she turned to him. "Can we hang it?"

Looking mystified, Seth followed her into the parlor. Meg stopped in front of the fireplace. "See? There's a hook there already. Want to bet it's the right place?" She lovingly unwrapped her prize. There was a slot cut out of the wooden back for hanging. Meg held her breath and lifted the clock up over the mantel and settled it on the hook.

She had guessed right. "Look at that! Like it had always been there. Now, we have to see if it works. Wasn't there a key to wind it?"

Seth reached into a pocket, pulled out an old-fashioned key, and handed it to her. Meg opened the front of the clock's case, inserted the key, and wound carefully, stopping when she met resistance. She moved the hands to the correct position, then with one finger gave a gentle nudge to the pendulum. It swung and kept on swinging. Meg closed the front and latched it, then stood back to admire. "Voilà!" She watched the pendulum, making sure it kept going. "What's the second keyhole for?"

"Probably the chimes. If you don't wind that, it won't make noise."

"Ah. I'll have to check that out. But for now I think I'll let it settle in to its new home. It looks perfect there."

"It does. Well, I should go."

At the door, Meg said, "Seth, I can't thank you enough for that excursion today. You were right—I needed to clear my head. And look what it got me!"

"Happy to be of service, ma'am. And it does look good there. You have a good eye."

Meg closed the door behind him and turned to admire her acquisition. It was so unlike her to make a spontaneous decision like that. But the clock had called to her; she had seen it in her mind's eye, exactly where it was now. No doubt there had been one like it before, in the same place.

Then it struck her: this was the first time she had *added* something to the house. She had spent weeks throwing out unwanted stuff and peeling off later additions, and she still wasn't anywhere near done. But the clock was the first thing she had brought in—something that she had chosen. It had felt right, and it fit, as she had somehow known it would. Its steady beat echoed reassuringly in the nearly empty space. *Like a heartbeat,* Meg thought suddenly. After so long, the house was coming alive again. Meg smiled to herself, absurdly pleased.

And she had Seth to thank for it. Seth seemed to spend a lot of time looking out for other people. His sister. The town. Meg. Unlike Chandler, who had taken care of Chandler first and foremost. And paid the price?

17

Sunday Meg woke early and remained huddled under her multiple blankets, taking inventory. She could hear the balky furnace rumble to life, and after a few moments a feeble puff of warm air drifted from the heating grate. If she strained her ears, she could just hear the ticking of the clock. The sound of it warmed her.

There was so much she had to do, and yet she didn't want to move, so she lay still, running through the events of the day before. The detective had as much as said that she was a murder suspect; that meant he thought she was capable of killing a man. She didn't know whether to feel flattered or horrified.

Seth was also near the top of the detective's short list, but she couldn't reconcile the cheerful, friendly, helpful man she knew with the idea of a cold-blooded killer who stuffed his victim into a septic tank. Although, she had to admit, there would be a certain poetic justice to it, if plumber Seth were the killer. Which he was not.

Why not, Meg? You barely know him. Why have you decided he isn't a killer? Because you want him to be one of the good guys?

Because you like him? Or something more? Uh-oh.

Meg lay still and shut her eyes again. This was not what she wanted to think. Okay, so she had finally purged Chandler and his rejection from her system, which was fine until he ended up dead on her property. But she wasn't looking for another relationship, and certainly not here and now, when she would be leaving in a few months. And Seth was too nice a guy to use for a brief fling. It wouldn't be fair to him. If he was interested at all, and she had no reason to believe that. He'd been kind to her, but from what she'd seen, he was kind to everyone. Maybe he just pitied her: poor, clueless Meg, stuck in the drafty old house with no friends. Let's try to cheer her up.

Meg, you've really made a mess of things, haven't you? She had jumped into this whole improvement project with little thought and less research. If she had been thinking, she would have known that she didn't have the manual skills or expertise to do what needed to be done. She wasn't even sure she could have told someone else to do it and then oversee the project, and she probably would have been exploited in every way possible. Maybe she was depressed—beaten down by the recent blows in her life. So she had simply seized on the opportunity to flee? That didn't sit well with her vision of herself as a competent, intelligent woman. Of course, the converse would be that she had assumed that she could handle anything she set her mind to, including carpentry, wiring, and wallpapering. That thought made her laugh—surely she wasn't that deluded? Probably the truth lay somewhere in between.

The numbers still scared her. It seemed that every repair came with a big price tag, and each one somehow led to another repair that had to be done. Since she had never owned a place of her own, she had been unprepared for this peculiar phenomenon of old houses, and her naïveté was proving expensive. But it was too late to turn back now, and she had to cling to the belief that she would recoup all these expenses when she sold the house.

But she still wasn't sure what impact the Granford Grange project would have on the sale. She hadn't done any research about Granford before landing here; she had known nothing about the development controversy. Would she have been so willing to come here if she had she known that Chandler was involved? Probably not. It would have been awkward to see him, and she might have stayed away just to avoid that minor unpleasantness. She could have told her mother to hire a team of cleaners to pretty the place up and then sell it, sight unseen. They might have lost a little money on the transaction, but it would have saved Meg a lot of aggravation—particularly the part about being considered a murder suspect.

Self-pity was getting her nowhere. Time to get up and tackle the endless to-do list. Time to get serious. She'd been dabbling so far—starting a lot of things, finishing nothing. At her current pace, she'd have the house ready to sell sometime in the next decade rather than May. She swung her legs out of bed, shivering at the chill. Clothes, coffee, food, then … something she would decide after coffee.

The phone rang from downstairs. Meg debated briefly about ignoring it, but maybe it was the detective with good news. Or Frances, who'd miraculously found a buyer who loved challenges and would take the place as is. She couldn't afford not to answer. With a muffled curse she grabbed up her clothes and dashed down the stairs.

She picked up on the fifth ring. " 'Lo?" she puffed.

"Meg, darling, is that you? You sound out of breath. I'm not calling too early, am I?"

Her mother. The last person she wanted to talk to. "No, Mom, I was awake." She struggled to pull on her jeans while keeping the phone wedged against her ear. "How've you been?"

"I've been just fine, dear, but I wondered if you had fallen into a black hole?"

"Sorry, sorry. It's just that there's been so much to do here, I haven't had a minute." Frantically Meg went through a list of things she didn't want to tell her mother at the moment: house in crappy condition, land threatened by development deal, and, oh yes, dead Chandler. No, her mother did not need to know all this, not until Meg had managed to clear up a few things.

"Well, dear, I'm sure you're doing a wonderful job. You've always been so capable. When do you think you'll be ready to put the house on the market?"

Meg sighed as quietly as she could. "I'm not really sure, Mom. There's a lot that needs to be done. I talked to a local Realtor, and she said spring would be a good time. Houses always look better in the spring."

"That sounds like an excellent idea. How are you enjoying Granford? I seem to remember it was a charming little place. So New England."

"I don't think much has changed, Mom. Listen, did you ever have a genealogy for the family? The Realtor said it might be good to know more about the history of the house, and we're related to the Warrens, right?"

"Distantly. I think my grandmother applied to the Daughters of the American Revolution, and that might explain it. I'll have to look for the forms she filled out. But isn't it a lovely house?"

Mom was clearly viewing her memories through rose-colored glasses. "It's nice, but it does need a lot of work. And you never mentioned the orchard."

"My word, is that still there? I remember that from when I was a child. It's lovely in the spring. And I think Aunt Lula gave me some apple butter that she'd made herself. It's all so long ago."

As her mother fell silent, presumably lost in her memories, Meg pulled on her sweatshirt and socks. "Was there anything you wanted, Mom?"

"Why, no, dear. Can't I just call you up to chat? After all, I haven't heard from you since you took yourself up there. I just wanted to make sure you were all right."

Meg braced herself for the question she knew was coming.

"You haven't heard anything from that lovely Chandler Hale, have you? I was so disappointed when you said you'd broken up."

Mom had never met Chandler. Chandler didn't do the "meet the relatives" thing, and now it was a bit too late. Suppressing a panicky giggle, Meg answered, "No, Mom. I told you it was over. And there's no chance that we'll get back together." *Because he's dead.*

"Well, I hope you're getting out now and then. It's not good for you to stay cooped up there without any human contact, you know. You were always such a solitary girl."

"Don't worry, Mom. I'm meeting lots of new people." Like the chief of police and the detective. And a nice plumber. Somehow she didn't think her mother would appreciate hearing about any of them.

"I'm so glad. Well, I'll let you get back to your chores. And maybe your dad and I could plan a trip up there to see what you've done, before you sell."

"That would be great, Mom. Think about April. Good talking to you, and give my love to Dad. I'll try not to wait so long to call."

"Good-bye, darling. Take care."

"I will."

With a sigh of relief Meg hung up the phone. No, her mother did not need to know all the details of the past week. Maybe when Chandler's murder was resolved. Or maybe never.

She was finishing the last of her coffee when she heard a knock at the front door. If she had come here for solitude, Meg reflected as she went to open it, she had sadly misjudged the neighborhood.

When she finally wrenched the door open, she was surprised to find Rachel. "Aren't you busy with guests?" she said. "Oh, sorry, that came out wrong. Come on in! It's freezing out there."

"Nobody at the moment, thank goodness. Winter's usually slow, unless there's something happening at one of the colleges. I was headed this way anyway—the three of us try to get together and have lunch or dinner with Mom every couple of weeks. And I said to myself, I need to check out the Warren house—it's been years since I saw it."

"Any idea if it will ever stop being the Warren house?" Meg asked as she led the way to the kitchen.

"Nope. Probably never. The Warrens spent over two hundred years here, and it's going to take a while for anyone to replace them in local memory. Around here, everyone knows the Warren house. But, hey, didn't you say you were related to the Warrens yourself?"

"Yes, but only distantly."

Rachel nodded approvingly at the kitchen. "Nice. And I hope you'll keep it simple. I hate all that cutesy country stuff with gingham and ruffles and demented-looking geese."

"You're kidding me, right?" Meg laughed. "I haven't even considered decorating, and most of what's here is the worst of cheap kitsch. If I ever get around to prettying it up, I'd like to keep it as close to the real thing as I can—with a few modern necessities like electricity and plumbing."

"Ah, yes, the infamous plumbing. Come on, show me the rest." Rachel strode toward the stairs as though she owned the place, and Meg had no choice but to follow. Meg tried to see her house through Rachel's eyes. Left to her own devices, she always saw the flaws, the things that needed to be done. It took an effort for her to step back and look objectively—and to quell the deprecating comments. Her first thought was of honey: golden light, warm polished maple boards. It was very quiet; a few dust motes drifted through the light from the multipaned windows.

In the cold front bedroom, Rachel waved her hand at the side window. "The orchard, right?"

Meg joined her in front of the window. "Yes. Do you know, I didn't even notice it for weeks? I don't come into this room very often. But even if I had, I'm not sure I would have recognized it as an orchard. Doesn't look like much this time of year, does it?"

"Wait until spring," Rachel replied.

Despite the cold, Rachel insisted on seeing everything, including the somewhat ramshackle connecting el and the barn at the back. "Seth was right, you know. Good structure, nice space, lots of charm and history. And colonial lends itself to modern tastes, I think—clean lines, well-aged wood. Let the building speak for itself, without cluttering it up."

She was right, Meg realized. "Thanks, Rachel. I've had trouble seeing past the dreck."

Rachel shook her head. "That's just surface stuff. But this house was built to last. The early Warrens had money—you can tell, because they put in more windows than they had to, and big ones at that. Glass was expensive in those days, so they were making a statement."

"I hadn't even thought of that. I never paid much attention to eighteenth-century history, except for the Revolutionary War, the Constitution, all that stuff. I keep forgetting that they lived it here." That was something she had to process.

"Sorry—I grew up with it, and I forget other people didn't. But I'd be willing to bet that the Warren who built this place fought in the Revolution. I know our ancestors over the hill did, and so did most of the able-bodied men around here at the time. So now you're living in a piece of history. Cool, huh?"

Meg found herself warming to Rachel's enthusiasm. "I guess it is, at that. Thank you for reminding me."

Rachel checked her watch. "Listen, I have to leave in half an hour. If I'm not there, Mom tries to do all the cooking, and she's just not up to it anymore."

Meg felt a pang of jealousy. It would be nice to be part of a warm and welcoming family right now. Her mother just didn't fit the bill.

She led Rachel back to the kitchen and after pouring them each a cup of coffee, said, "So it's you and Seth and Stephen? No other siblings?"

"Nope. Dad died a few years ago, but Mom's doing pretty well. She keeps herself busy. And the guys don't help as much as they might—it's a man thing, I guess. They just don't see what needs to be done." Rachel sipped at her coffee. "What about you? No family around?"

Meg shook her head. "I'm an only child, and so was Mom. We used to live in New Jersey, but Mom and Dad moved to northern Maryland a while ago, and they've got plenty to keep them busy there. We talk on the phone, and I try to visit for major holidays, depending on work." Which was no longer an issue. Where would she be by the time Thanksgiving rolled around? She moved quickly to change the subject. "Mom didn't even want to come up here to look at the house. She told me to go ahead and do whatever needed to be done. I didn't realize just how much that was. She'll show up in time to move a few trinkets around and think she's done her share."

"Don't worry, you'll get it done. It just takes a lot of elbow grease."

"Tell me about it! So, do Seth and Stephen live with your mother?" Funny, she had never thought to ask.

Rachel laughed. "Not hardly. Stephen moved out as soon as he could—he wanted a place of his own so he could entertain his, uh, lady friends. Although 'lady' might be stretching the truth a little. He's got a condo a couple of miles down 202. Seth lives in one of the other family houses on the property. The Chapins ran to big families in the old days, but they stayed close to home. Convenient for the business, anyway. That operates out of what used to be farm buildings near the highway—you've probably seen it."

They chatted for the allotted half hour, and then Rachel stood up and stretched. "Well, I'd better head on over to the house. Look, Meg, if you ever feel overwhelmed, just give me a call. I can't say I've ever been a new kid around here, but I know it must be hard when you don't know anyone. And things have been kind of complicated ..."

"You mean, things like finding a dead body?"

Rachel grinned. "Exactly. But these are good people here, and once you get to know them, you'll like them. Just give them a chance. Okay, gotta run. Thanks for the tour!"

Rachel left, but some of her energy lingered. Meg went back to the parlor. Rachel was right: the room had good lines, and it was time to haul out the tacky carpet, which she had left in a heap days before, and the lumpy upholstered chairs. Once she got the room cleared out, she could tackle the faded, blotched wallpaper. The sight of the garish flowers offended her every time she looked at them.

The clock ticked steadily over the fireplace. Meg smiled at it: it kept good time.

The sound kept her company as she hauled and scraped. At least the exercise kept her warm. It also gave her time to think. She had been treating Chandler's death as both a tragedy, which it was, and a personal inconvenience, which it also was. But she hadn't considered it as a problem, one that could be analyzed and solved. And while her hands were busy, she could certainly think about it.

What did she know? One, Chandler had been murdered, by a blow or blows to the head. Two, while it might not have taken a lot of physical power to overcome Chandler, especially if he had been surprised, it definitely would have taken strength to transport him to her property and stuff him through the relatively narrow opening of the septic tank. Three, either the detective didn't know, or he was unwilling to share with her, exactly where Chandler had been killed. If it was at his hotel, someone had concealed it well. She had heard nothing but nice things about the hotel, so she assumed that any nasty evidence like blood would be glaringly obvious in a well-cleaned room. His car had been found in the parking garage, where it should have been, and the detective had checked that for evidence, so that was ruled out.

She had cleared one wall of its atrocious paper. For a break, she ambled into the kitchen and retrieved one of Christopher's latest gift of apples from the refrigerator. Back in the dining room she munched on it while contemplating how much more remained to be done to clear the rest of the wallpaper. Christopher was right: the apple was crisp and sweet. No supermarket apple would have survived in such good condition after a couple of months in cold storage.

Back to the question of Chandler's murder. She didn't have a lot of tangible evidence to work with, so maybe she needed to look at motive. Why would anyone want to kill Chandler? Was it business or personal? On the business side, she had the impression that there were people in Granford who held strong opinions about the Granford Grange project, both for and against. She didn't know those people well enough to gauge the likelihood of any of them turning to violence, but it was possible. She'd have to ask Seth or Rachel. Who else was involved—or rather, who wasn't, in a small town? Who was going to do the actual construction? What about the shop owners of Granford, who might be squeezed out by major chain coffee shops or hardware stores? The list just kept growing. Still, killing Chandler seemed rather extreme—and it wouldn't necessarily stop the project. So who benefitted with Chandler out of the way? Would the financing consortium Chandler had assembled hold together without him? Based on Friday's impromptu meeting, Cinda Patterson had stepped up to fill Chandler's shoes (Meg allowed herself a brief giggle at the mental image of Chandler in stilettos or Cinda in wingtips), and the bank was standing behind her.

And she couldn't dismiss personal motive. In another time, Chandler would have been called a "ladies' man." He liked women. *No,* Meg amended, *he liked being with women.* He liked the way a beautiful woman on his arm raised his status in the eyes of his peers. He liked the thrill of the hunt, the ultimate victory. But did he really like women as people? Meg wasn't so sure of that. He'd never been married, and he hadn't sustained any long-term relationships that she knew of. Yet he had seldom lacked for female companionship, and she could attest that he wasn't gay.

When Chandler had broken off their relationship, she had been surprised and, looking back on the episode, mildly hurt, but nothing like devastated. She smiled to herself: if the detective considered her a wronged woman bent on revenge, he was barking up the wrong tree. She had never felt strongly enough about

Chandler to consider killing him, and she certainly hadn't wished him dead. She wondered idly who Chandler had been seeing recently. She was quite sure there was someone—there always was.

She had no answers for anything. Standing up, she disposed of her apple core in the kitchen. Break over: back to the ratty wallpaper.

18

Meg slept soundly after her energetic work, but she woke up with Chandler's murder on her mind. Seth thought the detective would find Chandler's killer, but would he? She wanted closure; she wanted to be sure she wasn't a suspect, improbable though that seemed to her. She wanted to do something to move the investigation forward.

That thought surprised her. What could she do? She didn't know anyone in the area; she didn't know the lay of the land. But, she realized, she did have one advantage: she knew the banking industry and, more specifically, the Boston banks, including the one Chandler had worked for. She knew them far better than the local police ever would, and she knew what questions to ask. Maybe someone from Boston had followed Chandler out to the western part of the state and thought it would be convenient to eliminate him here, to avoid dirtying their own nest. It was worth looking into.

She checked her watch: almost eight o'clock. Her friend Lauren would no doubt be in her office. Lauren had somehow survived the merger purges at the bank and had emerged with a more exalted title and a slightly larger desk, which she deserved, and Meg didn't begrudge them to her. Would she have time to talk? At least Meg could get the ball rolling. Her mission: find out as much as she could about the business side of the proposed Granford deal. She also wanted to pump Lauren for as much personal information as she could about the late Chandler. She dressed quickly, then went to the kitchen, picked up her phone, and hit Lauren's speed-dial number.

Lauren answered the phone, clearly breathless. "Hey, Meg, you're up with the cows now? Sorry I haven't called, but things have been really crazy here. So, have you decided you've had enough of country and you want back in the game in Boston?"

Meg laughed: same old Lauren, running a mile a minute. "Hey, slow down and breathe, will you? I know you're busy, so I'll keep it simple." But having said that, Meg wasn't sure how to start. "You remember Chandler Hale?"

"Chandler? Of course—he's hard to miss. So, what about him?"

"Well, for a start, he's dead."

"What? When?" Clearly Lauren hadn't heard the news.

Meg sighed. "It's complicated, but as far as the police can tell, it was last Tuesday night. I'm surprised you didn't hear. I'm sure he'd be devastated to know he didn't make the front page."

Lauren apparently covered the phone with her hand and said something muffled to someone. "Sorry. They can't seem to function around here without my holding their hands. Back to Chandler...I've been so swamped, I must have missed it. So, tell me more. But, no, wait—why do you care? You two were over ages ago."

"Oh, yes, definitely ancient history." It was the truth. The next part was harder. "But the thing is, his body was found on my property."

Silence from Lauren's end, for several seconds. "Oh, wow! Do you need a good lawyer?"

Meg almost laughed. "No, nothing like that. But look, Lauren, I can really use your help. I know how busy you are, so I'll give you the bare outline. The detective wants to believe I had something to do with Chandler's death, because that would make his life easier, but he hasn't got any evidence, because of course there isn't any. I want to know who might have had a reason to want Chandler out of the way. Chandler was working on a commercial development deal in Granford—that's why he was here. There are a lot of people in town who feel strongly about the whole deal, and that means there are a lot of potential local suspects. The police and the detective are working on this end of things, but I thought since I knew Chandler and I know the Boston scene, I might be able to find out what was going on at that end."

"You sure you aren't a suspect, Meg?" Lauren sounded disappointed. "Because if you did it, I can think of at least six, no, seven women who would probably throw you a killer party. Ooh, bad pun."

"I suppose I am, ridiculous though that sounds. I didn't even know he was here until he came looking for the tenants at my house. And, no, I didn't have any desire to kill him. We were never that serious," Meg said. "But the sooner this gets cleared up, the sooner I can get the house on the market. I don't want this hanging over the place."

"Hey, it might bring you a lot of lookers."

"I don't want lookers, I want buyers. Or at least one. You interested in a country place?"

"Ha!" was Lauren's response. "I'll leave that to you."

I don't want it, Meg thought. "Look, can you sniff out who's involved in this deal? I know the bank but not the players, if you know what I mean. To me the whole deal seems pretty run of the mill—a strip mall in a rural area. Not a big deal by Boston terms. But is there anyone who would want to see Chandler eliminated? Was this a pet project of his, and will the bank support it without him at the helm? They're making the right noises, but that might just be PR. That's the kind of thing I'd like to find out."

"I see what you're getting at. Let me ask around. There could be more going on than meets the eye. Business has been tight lately, and there aren't that many start-up projects. If the bank is trying to establish a presence in a new market, with an eye toward bigger things, maybe the Granford deal was just the opening wedge, and somebody else wanted a piece of the action. Chandler didn't always play well with others, did he? I'll see what I can dig up."

Meg felt a surge of relief. "That's great! And thanks. I'll owe you."

"Right, you will," Lauren responded cheerfully. "Give me a day or two. They won't arrest you before then, will they?"

"I hope not." Meg wasn't even sure if she was joking.

After a pause, Lauren asked slyly, "So, how's your love life?"

"What love life? All I do is scrape, paint, and clean. I've barely had time to meet anybody, except the manager at Home Depot. Heck, I've probably seen more of my plumber than any other man."

"Is he hot?"

"Hot? I hadn't thought about it. He's nice, he's under ninety, and at least he shows up when he says he will. Actually, he's a neighbor—the next property over. And an elected official of the town. And his land is involved somehow in the development project."

"Huh. It really is a small town, isn't it? He sounds like a keeper—there can't be that many fish in your little pond there. Although if this were a novel, he'd be a likely suspect. You know, an evil heart under that squeaky-clean exterior."

"No, he's a good guy, and he bailed me out when the plumbing went wonky. Old systems tend to do that, I've learned. The hard way."

"There are things in this universe that I'd rather not know, and that is one of them." Lauren held another garbled conversation with someone at the other end. When she spoke again, she said, "Sorry, I have to rush—this place is a zoo. But I'll see what I can find out."

"Thanks. I'd really like to get this cleared up before I become known in town as 'the lady with the body.'"

"Don't worry. You'll be fine. You always land on your feet, right? Gotta go—sorry I don't have more time to chat. I'll e-mail you with whatever I find, I promise! And maybe call you over the weekend so you can tell me all about the hot plumber." She hung up without a good-bye.

Still, Meg felt encouraged. Lauren was plugged in to the banking network and had an ear for juicy gossip, which she used discreetly and judiciously. If there was dirt on Chandler—or his enemies—Lauren would ferret it out. Maybe it was a long shot, but Meg didn't want to leave any stone unturned. Plus it felt a lot better to be doing something positive, rather than sitting in her drafty house waiting to be arrested.

19

Meg found that her brief conversation with Lauren had left her both energized and confused. Had she sounded like Lauren, before she had lost her job? Always harried? She wandered into her parlor. Minus the offensive wallpaper, the walls looked kind of ragged. They were true plaster, surprisingly strong, given their age. And they had never been painted, which amazed her. What was she going to do with them? Home decor was definitely not her strong suit. Maybe she should send some photos to her mother and ask for suggestions. But something simple, definitely—she liked the room clean and bare. It reminded her of an Andrew Wyeth interior.

Looking out through the front window she noticed the UMass van pass by, heading toward the orchard. It might be a good idea to talk to Christopher, find out what he had heard—and what he would do if the orchard fell to the bulldozers. Suddenly invigorated, Meg pulled on her boots and coat and left the house, walking briskly up the hill. Outside, she realized that the sky was leaden and there was a damp feeling in the air. Snow? She hadn't been through a snowstorm here, major or minor, and she did a quick mental check of her supplies. Then she laughed—the Boston TV channels had always reported the stampede to grocery stores to stock up on bread, milk, and candles whenever a storm loomed. Half the time the storm dumped two inches of slush and everyone looked foolish. But still, she didn't know enough about her current home to know how dependable the power was. Or if she had enough flashlights or candles, or even oil lamps. Or if her furnace required electricity, and what she would do if her heat went out.

She had reached the top of the hill without even noticing—and without panting, which was a pleasant change. She spied Christopher alone in the middle of the orchard, staring intently at a tree. She headed toward him.

"Hey, Christopher. I thought I saw you drive by. What are you looking at?"

"Ah, Meg, how nice to see you—and you're positively rosy cheeked! We missed you Friday. I had the class here practicing their pruning, and I wanted to make sure they had done it right, and see what more needs to be done."

Meg smiled. "Do you grade them on pruning?"

"Not exactly, but I want to be sure they understand what they're doing. This year's group is excellent. Smart, and quick to learn."

Meg shifted from foot to foot, trying to keep warm. "Tell me, why do students go into agricultural pursuits these days? Particularly orchards? I thought the big commercial interests had taken over everything."

"An excellent question, my dear. And I think I'd have to give you two answers. The first would be that, as you've noticed, farming has become very much a corporate pursuit. But there is still need for people to run the farms, whatever their scale. Today's students focus much more on the science of it—crop genetics, for example. The chemistry of pesticides. Marketing and advertising, for heaven's sake!"

"You don't approve?" Meg asked.

Christopher's smile was wry. "Yes and no. The world will always need to eat, and the more efficiently we produce food, the better off we'll all be. I acknowledge the need for utilizing all available tools, particularly science, to make that happen. And these students will need jobs, and it's up to me to prepare them for the reality of modern agriculture."

"But?" Meg prompted.

Christopher shook his head. "Maybe I'm a throwback. But it seems to me that by treating this merely as a business, they're missing something. They have no sense of the honorable tradition of working with the soil, bringing forth a harvest. Of course it's hard, dirty work. And unpredictable—I know all too well how easy it is for a single storm, or an unexpected infestation or infection, to wipe out an entire crop, and with it, a year's work. And most smaller farmers these days operate on a very thin margin, so one such event can doom the farm, if they can't make that year's loan payments."

"And what was your second answer?" Meg said gently.

"That there are still a few romantics who want to do something basic, simple, hands-on. A generation ago they might have been called hippies, living on communes and trying to believe that they were somehow in harmony with the earth. And many of them failed miserably because they had no idea what they were doing in practical terms. So I try to give my students a balanced view—somehow blend the romance and the science. And the math and the economics. But it's not easy." He sighed.

Meg felt guilty as she framed her next question, but she had to know. "Christopher," she began carefully, "what will you do if the developers take this land, this orchard?"

Christopher dragged his eyes away from the apple trees. "Do you mean the university or me personally?"

Meg shrugged. "Both. Either. Does the university have other orchard sites?"

"Sad to say, no. Once they had an orchard on campus—which is now long buried under student housing, alas. Would they acquire a new study site? Unlikely. We were lucky to come upon this one, and to negotiate an ongoing agreement to use it. As you can guess, it takes time to develop an orchard. It doesn't happen overnight. Would the university be willing to invest in both the land and the staffing to re-create this? I can't say for certain, but I would doubt it. Perhaps they would just cede the field to the researchers at Cornell—although I don't think it's wise to put all the research eggs in one basket, if I may muddle my metaphors."

"And you?" Meg pressed.

"Ah, my dear, that is the question. I've nurtured this orchard for decades now—brought it back from years of neglect. I know it well, each and every tree. I don't know if I have it in me to start over, even if the university would offer that. I'm not far from retirement. Oh, I'm in good health—and in sound mind, I hope—but I am perhaps not the best choice to oversee a new beginning.

And I fear the university nabobs might agree with that assessment."

"Could they force you to retire? Or put you out to pasture, so to speak—teaching introductory courses or something?"

"I see you know a bit about the politics of educational institutions. To be honest, I don't know what they'd do, were this orchard to be lost. They haven't paid much attention to the situation here—being, I am persuaded, far more interested in fostering a more active football program. Which, I will admit, would be more lucrative than this little project. But I can guess that matters are coming to a head rather rapidly."

"I'm afraid so," Meg answered. "You told me you had met Chandler Hale?"

Christopher nodded. "Not to speak ill of the dead, but I seem to remember some conversation about retaining a few apple trees around the parking lot as decoration. He appeared surprised when I told him that they would not flourish under such conditions."

Meg could picture Chandler's cavalier response, the careless arrogance of his tone. Oh, certainly, he would keep some of the trees—as window dressing. Until they were killed by the exhaust fumes from the parking lot.

And Meg could also see that Christopher had every right to be angry at such an attitude. He had put years of his life into this orchard, and Meg could tell from the way he looked at it that he loved it. Take it away and he would quite possibly lose his job, as well as the object of his affections.

Was that enough motive to kill?

Meg shivered, not just from the cold, and wrapped her arms around herself. Time to change the subject. "Is the pruning done?"

"Nearly. We were out all day Friday. We keep the trees well cut back, so there is only some fine-tuning to be done."

"So, if the pruning is done, what's next?"

"These will be dormant until sometime in March. The next stage is silver-tip, followed by green-tip, which would bring you up to the first of May. Come April, we'll need to begin our spraying program, for diseases like apple scab, crown rot, and fire blight, and insects, starting with mites and aphids."

"You certainly have a full schedule," Meg said, once more appalled at how little she knew. How did any poor apple survive to maturity, with so many threats?

"That we do, my dear." Christopher cast a practiced eye at the sky. "It looks as though we'll have some snow. I don't suppose I'll get much else done today."

"Can I offer you a cup of tea or something?"

"Ah, how kind, but I think I had better get back to the university. Perhaps another time. Oh, and could you let me know the outcome when the town votes on the project? I don't want to be caught by surprise."

"You aren't going to be there?"

"I think not. You haven't attended one of these events, have you?"

Meg shook her head. "No. Boston does things differently."

"I am not a Granford resident, and while in theory I might be permitted to attend, I could not speak, nor could I vote on the matter, regardless of my interest. So I would prefer not to watch the spectacle."

"I understand. And of course I'll let you know. It was nice to see you again, Christopher."

Meg turned away and hurried back down the hill, glad to be moving again. Unfortunately she couldn't outrun her own thoughts. Christopher as killer? Laughable. He was a sweet man, dedicated to his profession—not a murderer. Or so she thought. But she kept coming back to the inescapable fact: Chandler was dead, and somebody had killed him. Just because everyone she met around here was kind and friendly didn't exempt them all from suspicion.

As she struggled to open her door, she could hear the phone ringing inside. She grabbed it up on the sixth ring. "Hello?" she gasped, out of breath.

"Hey, babe!" Lauren's cheerful voice came. "Did I interrupt you in the middle of something interesting?"

Meg struggled for a moment to figure out what she meant and then suppressed a laugh. Trust Lauren to put a lascivious spin on it. "No, I was up in the orchard and came back in a hurry. What's up?" As she held the phone to her ear, Meg peeled off her coat and walked to the kitchen to put the kettle on.

"Walking the back forty, eh? Don't you sound like a country girl. Anyway, I did some nosing around for you, about the Granford deal? Seems to be on the up-and-up. Puritan Bank's been making periodic announcements, and there are plenty of backers in place. And Chandler's erstwhile assistant has been tapped to take over management of the project, at least for now."

"Cinda Patterson," Meg said flatly.

"You know her?" Lauren responded, her surprise evident.

"We've met. And the bank made its own announcement here last Thursday, although the attending VP from the bank didn't look too happy. So Cinda's official?"

"That she is. Not that she hasn't earned it—she's been their unofficial go-to gal ever since she showed up in town. And . . ." Lauren enjoyed spinning out a story.

Meg reluctantly took the bait. "You've got something else?"

"Oh, yeah," Lauren replied gleefully. "You might just like to know about Chandler's current whatever. Squeeze? Paramour? Inamorata?"

Crap. "You don't mean . . ."

"The self-same Cinda." Lauren completed the line with triumph.

"That's interesting. I thought Chandler didn't like to muddy his own nest." The Boston banking community wasn't huge, and intraoffice romances could get sticky very quickly—and very publicly. At least she and Chandler had been at different banks, but she had been surprised how many people had known about them—and had known when there no longer was a "them."

"You said you've met Cinda? Wait till you get to know her. I haven't met her myself, but from what I've heard they must have been soul mates. She's a shark in the making. And she was his back-up on that project, and a handful of others like it. I think they were trying to put together a portfolio of small deals like that, market it as a package—you know, diversify the risk. And you know what they say about proximity." Lauren was silent for a moment. "You and Chandler split . . . what, last fall sometime?"

"More like summer, actually. Why?"

"I think they were seeing each other before that."

Meg was surprised to find she wasn't surprised. "Could be,

not that he ever said anything. Hey, Lauren, it's okay. It's not like we were an affair for the ages or anything."

"Glad to hear that. Anyway, from what I hear, Cinda comes across as . . . what was that Madonna tour, years ago? Blond Ambition? Cinda looks out for Number One. Luckily she's got looks *and* smarts, or so I'm told."

"I believe it." Meg's kettle started to whistle. "Look, I won't keep you. Thanks for digging this up so fast. And if you hear anything else, let me know, will you?"

"Sure. You playing detective now?"

Meg laughed shortly. "Just trying to cover my derrière. Thanks—you're a pal. Talk to you soon."

Meg hung up the phone and went to the stove to make tea, just as the first snowflakes hit the kitchen window, followed by a burst of wind. Cold air seeped around the rattling window frame.

Chandler and Cinda, Cinda and Chandler. Last summer. That was food for thought. And it didn't taste very good.

20

Christopher's prediction had been right. It had snowed all night, and Meg awoke to bright sunlight reflecting off a foot or more of fresh snow. At which point she realized that she had no idea what to do with snow: she wasn't even sure she owned a snow shovel, and she had no clue where it might be if she did. Nor did she relish the thought of trying to clear the driveway, even as far as her car. Still, the scene outside her bedroom window, where the once-grassy meadow was now covered with a thick white blanket, was too pretty to permit gloomy thoughts. Besides, she had nowhere she needed to be, and plenty to keep her occupied inside. She pulled on comfortable sweats and descended to the kitchen.

She was surprised to hear a vehicle pull into her driveway. Peering out the kitchen window, she saw an unfamiliar truck with a snowplow in the front. Seth climbed down from the cab.

She beat him to the back door. "You're up early."

He smiled. "Good, you're awake. Thought you could use a little help with the driveway."

"What are you, psychic? I just realized I know nothing about shoveling snow."

"Not a problem—I can have you cleared out in a couple of minutes."

"Bless you. Can I give you a cup of coffee? Heck, I seem to spend all my time pouring coffee down you and everyone else. How about this: can I offer you a bowl of hot oatmeal?"

"If you've got brown sugar." Seth stamped his feet on the stoop, then stepped into the kitchen, suddenly taking up a lot of the free space in his bulky sweater and down vest.

"Sit," Meg commanded, and started assembling oatmeal,

sugar, milk, and utensils. "How did you know I'd need rescuing? I didn't even think about it myself until I woke up this morning," she said, filling a pot with water and setting it on the stove.

Seth dropped into one of the kitchen chairs. He hesitated before answering. "Lucky guess. But there was something else ... Listen, I thought we should talk. About me and Detective Marcus."

Something in his tone made Meg stop foraging and study him more closely. He looked uncertain, which was unlike him. "Do I need to sit down?"

"No, it's nothing like that."

Meg sat anyway. "All right, talk. Is there a problem?"

"There's no pretty way of putting this. Look, Meg, you and I, we're both suspects in Chandler Hale's murder. I hope not the only ones, but we're going to be under some suspicion, just because of how and where he was found. And that may affect how people treat you. Doesn't seem fair, but that's the reality. Me, I've lived here all my life, and people know me. May not like me, but they know who I am, and they'll give me some leeway."

Meg couldn't see where he was going. "Seth, I think I understand what you're trying to say, but why do you think you need to say it at all? I'm not naïve, and I'm not about to feel hurt if local people would rather blame an outsider than one of their own. I'm an outsider, period. What is it you're worried about?" She paused, searching his face, and then was struck with an awful thought. "You don't think I actually killed him, do you?"

"No, of course not. For one thing, you couldn't have hoisted him into that hole by yourself."

"Gee, thanks for the vote of confidence. So I'm off the hook because I couldn't have lifted a body?"

Seth shook his head. "No, that didn't come out right. I don't believe that you had any reason to kill Hale *or* any desire to. I can't see you killing anybody. But ... there's something you have to know, about me, my history here."

Meg was becoming more and more mystified. "What? You have a criminal record?"

"Sort of. I need to explain ..." Seth stopped again, searching for words.

Meg decided it might be easier if she wasn't staring at him

while he tried to find his way. "Go on. But I'm going to start that oatmeal." She stood up, found a measuring cup, poured oatmeal into it, then stirred it slowly into the boiling water. None of that instant stuff, nope, not her. Her mother had brought her up right.

What the hell could Seth want to tell her, and why was it so difficult for him?

"So. Detective Marcus and I have, uh, sort of a history."

"So you *do* have a criminal record." Meg strove for a light tone as she concentrated hard on mashing lumps in the oatmeal.

"When I was a senior in high school, I got into a fight with another guy on the football team and did a pretty good job of beating him to a pulp. First and only time, honest."

"And you were arrested?"

"Yeah. It probably wouldn't have gone that far, except that the other guy was Marcus's son. He wasn't detective then, but he was in law enforcement, and he has a long memory."

"What happened?" Meg watched the roiling surface of the oatmeal as large bubbles rose to the surface.

"The charges were dropped, finally."

"Why?"

"Why were they dropped? Or why did I get into the fight in the first place?"

"Both, I guess. Are they related?" Meg turned off the heat under the pan. It wouldn't hurt it to sit for a few minutes. She turned to face Seth, leaning against the counter.

Seth was silent for several beats. "Let's just say that there was good reason for the fight, and leave it at that. All parties agreed, in the end."

"Why are you telling me this, Seth?"

"Because the story's going to come out again. Oh, yeah, Seth Chapin—didn't he beat some guy up once? So maybe he does have a violent streak. Or—how do they put it these days?—he has problems with anger management. Maybe last time the mess got covered up, or somebody got bought off. Which is a joke, because Dad never had that kind of money *or* clout. Or, maybe Seth got really pissed off at Chandler Hale about losing his land and whacked him one. That's the problem with a small town: people remember, and it's usually the bad things they remember. I didn't want you to get tarred by association with me."

Meg reached into an overhead cupboard for some bowls, all the while trying to frame a response to what Seth had said. "Seth," she began slowly, "do you have an alibi for the night Chandler died?"

"Huh? Heck, we don't even know exactly when he died—we just know he had dinner with you in Amherst, he brought you home, and he was dead the next evening sometime, after he got back from Boston."

"You heard about that? Where he was that day, I mean?"

"Sure, Art filled me in. He had to have died after six o'clock. And that night I did what I would normally do: had dinner with Mom till about seven, took care of some billing for the business, went home and went to bed with a good book, fell asleep after about ten pages. Alone. So, no alibi, past dinner. I had plenty of time to do the deed, if I had wanted to."

Meg carried the bowls to the table. "I never said I suspected you. And I can't imagine that people around here would—after all, they elected you to the board of selectmen, didn't they?"

"I suppose. I just didn't want you to get dragged into this mess, or make things any worse. Although you're in it anyway, aren't you?"

"Obviously. I knew him, and he was found in my septic tank." She sat down opposite Seth. "You sure you aren't worried that people think I killed him, and that your reputation is going to suffer? Let's see. The detective believes either Chandler came here to seduce me and I fought back to protect my virtue, or he came here to rub my nose in the fact that I couldn't have him, and I got so mad that I killed him. And then there's the crowd-pleaser: you and I did it together. The detective likes that one."

Seth looked at her and began to laugh. Meg responded with mock wrath. "What, you don't think I'm capable of murder? Beware the wrath of a woman scorned. Or trifled with. Or something."

"Sorry. It's just that I have trouble visualizing you bashing him over the head and stuffing him into the tank. It can't have been easy. He must have weighed close to two hundred."

"One ninety-five—he was very proud of maintaining that," Meg responded absently, spooning a liberal amount of brown sugar onto her oatmeal and stirring it in. "All right. We've agreed you didn't kill him, and I didn't kill him. So who did?"

Seth's attention had wandered to his own hot cereal. "This smells great. Oh, what? Who killed him … Frankly, I have no idea."

"Great. You know, your police buddy made a good point—who else knew about the open tank? Or was that just dumb luck, to have a place to dispose of him sitting there, ready-made?"

"Who else knew? Heck, anybody who drove by and saw the backhoe from the road would have known what was going on. Your neighbors. Total strangers. I think the better question is, who wanted Chandler dead?"

"I've been thinking about that, but I haven't come up with anyone yet. But you have to remember I hadn't seen him lately. He might have made a whole new crop of enemies."

She was surprised by Seth's next question. "Did you care about him?"

Meg met his look. "Chandler? Once, maybe, I thought I did, or could. He was charming and smart and … powerful, I suppose. He was going to go places, make things happen, and it was kind of fun to be a part of that. Am I upset by his death? Not personally—but that doesn't mean he deserved to die. And I'm pissed that whoever did it, did so here, whether or not that person wanted to point a finger at me. I didn't do anything to earn that."

"I think you've got a right to feel that way. I didn't mean to pry—I just didn't want you to think that I was taking his death too lightly, if he was someone who meant something to you."

"That's nice of you, but don't worry about it."

Seth's worries had not blunted his appetite, and he finished his oatmeal quickly. But as he chased a last lump of sugar around his bowl, Seth ventured, "You know, there's no reason for you to believe me. You're taking a risk here, you know. I could be a serial killer sizing you up for my next victim."

"Seth," Meg said, "you've been a good friend to me, and I appreciate it. Besides, if you hid someone, I'll bet no one would find him. Anyway, I wouldn't want to lose a good plumber—they're even harder to find than good friends."

Seth smiled at her, and then his cell phone rang.

He answered quickly. "Seth Chapin. Right. Now? I guess. I'll have to swing by the shop first and pick up what I need. Half an hour? No, make it an hour—I don't know what the roads'll be like. Say, ten?" He signed off, and sighed. "Sorry. Another emergency. I should have been a doctor—although I probably would have made less money. But I'll clear your drive first."

"Thanks."

He bounded up, energy and good cheer apparently restored by their conversation and food. As he headed toward the door, he turned to her. "Meg, I'm glad you trust me." And then he was gone.

Meg continued to sit, watching her oatmeal congeal, lost in thought. She had always been a numbers person, good with math, and good at seeing patterns and connections. She had never been a good "people" person. People were not logical, and they were a lot harder to read than a balance sheet. Looking back, she could see now that her instinctive reaction to Chandler had been right: he had never really cared about her. She had gone along with his halfhearted pursuit because she was flattered by his attention, and because she didn't really trust her own instincts. Now she had made a quick decision about trusting Seth, but was she right or wrong this time?

21

True to his word, Seth cleared the end of her driveway nearest the road in three or four quick passes with the plow, then chugged off down the road. It was sweet of him to have taken care of it for her, but she was in no hurry to go anywhere. In Boston she had seldom used her car, and she had never spent much time learning to drive in snow. It was not a skill she'd thought she needed, and she was usually content to wait until the snow had melted. Unless, she added to herself, it took weeks to melt. Ah well, one day at a time.

The cell phone rang, and when she picked up the phone she didn't recognize the number. "Hello?"

"Meg," Cinda's voice gushed in her ear. "I'm so glad I caught you. I can really use your help. Could you meet me here in Northampton for, say, lunch?"

How clueless was Cinda? Meg wondered. But she relented: Cinda was a city girl, just as she had been. "Uh, Cinda, have you looked out your window this morning?"

"What?" Meg heard a sound of clattering curtain rings. "Oh, how pretty—it snowed. But the road is perfectly clear."

Meg sighed. Maybe in Northampton, the bustling county seat, the roads were clear, but in idyllic rural Granford they most definitely were not. "Sorry, Cinda, I'm out in the country, and I have no idea if or when the roads here will be plowed. Why don't we do this tomorrow? Things should be pretty well cleared up by then."

Meg could almost hear the pout in her voice, but Cinda rallied. "I'm sorry—I didn't think. Of course it can wait. But," she added with calculated self-deprecation, "I'm just so worried about the special meeting coming up, and I want to make sure I have all my bases covered. I'd really appreciate your help here, Meg."

Cinda was quick on her feet, Meg reflected. "Fine. Tomorrow, then. Is there anything in particular you want me to think about?" Given the state of the roads, Meg didn't think she'd be traveling around trying to talk to people today.

"Well, you're in place, so to speak. I'm still playing catch-up, after Chandler ... If you could give me a sense of who the players in town are, who's really going to make the decisions. You know what I mean."

Meg did. But she also knew that she hadn't been around long enough to have forged the kind of connections that Cinda could use. If she really wanted to help Cinda succeed, she would have to ask ... someone like Seth. As in fact she had. Was that what underlay Cinda's question? Had Cinda made assumptions about Meg's relationship with Seth and assumed she would go to him first? The detective had made that same leap of logic. Or was Cinda just testing her? "Yes, I do. I'll see what I can find out. Lunch tomorrow, then? I'll meet you at the hotel around noon."

"Wonderful. Thank you so much, Meg. I'm really looking forward to working with you." Cinda hung up. Meg stared at the phone, confused. Now she was working with Cinda? Not likely. But if Cinda had been close to Chandler, she might have a better idea about who killed him. If Cinda wanted to use her, she could just as well use Cinda. She gave a fleeting thought to Cinda as murderer, and almost laughed out loud. Cinda, of the designer suits and French manicures? Cinda, who might weigh 110 pounds soaking wet? And why would Cinda want to kill her meal ticket? Chandler had brought her onto the project; Chandler had been her mentor. Among other things.

And yet now Cinda headed the project. For a newbie at Puritan Bank, she'd ascended the ranks extraordinarily fast, an ascent Chandler had no doubt facilitated. But murder? Not Cinda. No way.

Okay, Meg, admit it: you don't like Cinda. That was a no-brainer. Cinda was smart, attractive, young, and aggressive. Meg was ... smart. Cinda was Chandler's type, and Meg had always known that she wasn't. Was this about jealousy? She hoped not, but she had to consider it. Cinda had snared Chandler's attention and affections, even while Chandler was still involved with her. Had Cinda known about her then? Had it made any difference? Somehow Meg doubted it. Cinda knew what she wanted, and knew what to do to get it. Meg would've been a minor inconvenience at best.

But although she might not be a brilliant blonde, Meg had a brain and connections of her own, and she was not going to let Cinda take advantage of her.

Meg wandered into the parlor, blazingly bright from the light bouncing off the snow—which highlighted the patchy job she had done scraping the walls. Maybe she was overreacting to Cinda's request for help. Maybe it was completely innocent, and Meg was seeing duplicity where there was none. Her primary concern was not to make Cinda's life easier but to determine what would be most advantageous to her when she sold this property.

When? Or if?

Meg, what are you thinking? She crossed the room to the window overlooking the fields, snow sculpted by the wind into improbable billows. *You came here to fix up the house for sale and to figure out your next career move. You've got a business degree and a good track record; your last supervisor would give you a glowing recommendation. You're unencumbered and can go anywhere you want. But where is that?*

She had no idea. She had been here a month, and she had maybe another three months to make up her mind, apply for jobs, plan a life. Maybe she owed herself some downtime. Maybe she had been too focused on her career, and a break would do her good. Meg laid her hand on the window frame, rubbing the time-worn wood. *I want to know who built this house, over two hundred years ago; I want to put a name to the man who planed this wood. I could find out who lived here, men and women.* Frances had said that a dash of history might enhance the sales appeal of the place.

As if conjured up by Meg's thoughts, Frances's car surged into the driveway, undeterred by snow. Meg went to greet her at the door.

"Hi, Frances. What brings you out in this mess?"

Frances looked a bit disheveled, and she held something behind her back. "This? This is nothing. Wait until we get some *real* snow. But I was shoveling my walk this morning and it hit me that you might not be prepared, so I brought you this." With a flourish she pulled out a shiny new snow shovel with a big red bow.

Meg laughed. "You're right! Seth already figured I would need help with the driveway, but then he got a call and left."

"I wondered how you got that done so fast. Well, I won't keep you ..."

"You don't have to run off, do you, Frances? You have time for coffee or something?"

Frances wavered a moment. "If it's no bother."

"Of course not. Come on in." Meg stepped back to let Frances in. Frances stomped her feet on the grubby mat in front of the door, and once inside, she slipped her boots off. "Gotta remember, Meg, these old floors don't have polyurethane on them, so you've got to watch out for water stains."

One more thing she hadn't thought of. When would she ever get a handle on this house? "I didn't know that. I've almost always lived in the city, and in a rental. Seems I have a lot to learn about owning a home. Come on back to the kitchen."

Frances padded behind her in brightly patterned socks. "Hey, you've made some real progress here," she said as they passed through the parlor and the dining room.

"I hope so! Sometimes it's hard to tell. Sit down, please. Coffee okay?"

"Sure." Frances sat.

Meg set two mugs on the table. "Do you know, I was just thinking about talking to you. I went to the historical society meeting last week." *The night that Chandler died*, she added to herself.

"I was sorry I had to miss that meeting. Christopher always has something interesting to say."

Frances attended historical society meetings? And knew Christopher? "Are you a member?"

"Sure. It's good to know the history of a place if you're trying to sell houses here, you know? And they need all the help they can get. Membership's cheap."

"And Christopher goes often?"

"Now and then. What, you know him?"

"He's been working in the orchard for years, he tells me. He introduced himself one day. He really loves the orchard. I'm worried about what will happen to his research if the development deal goes through."

"Yeah, that's a problem."

Frances leaned back in the kitchen chair and contemplated Meg. "Ah, Meg, Meg, Meg ... what have you gotten yourself into?"

"I keep asking myself that," Meg said, with some asperity. "But what do you mean? Is there something I need to know?"

"Hey, you're smart. Bet you've figured out a lot of things. Like Chandler and me."

"I guessed. So he, uh ..."

"Sweet-talked me into his bed? Yup. Honey, don't look at me like that. I know I'm no prize, and I never thought it was true love."

Meg said cautiously, "Chandler could be very charming when he wanted to."

"And he was great in bed. Oh, never mind. I knew what I was getting into. But then he turned around and shut me out."

Meg was getting confused. "What do you mean? He dumped you?"

Frances shook her head. "I expected that. What I didn't see coming was that he was going to suck me dry about all the property in town—who owned what, who would be likely to sell. He was a smooth one, all right. And I'm no dummy. I figured, sure, I'd tell him what he wanted to know, but I figured he'd give me a piece of the deal. I mean, that is how I make my living around here. But, nooooo. After I feed him all the good info, he leaves me high and dry, cuts his own deals—him and his high-price banker buddies."

That certainly sounded like the Chandler Meg knew: always looking at the bottom line, at getting the best possible deal on the properties he wanted, not toward maintaining good relations within the community. That would give Frances a good motive for murder—dumped and betrayed, in more ways than one—Meg reflected.

As if reading her thoughts, Frances burst into laughter. "Now you're wondering if I murdered him, and if you're sitting here with a crazy killer, right? Relax, sweetie. Sure, I killed him—in my fantasies. The way I would have done it, I would have stuffed him in that tank alive and kicking and let him sit and whine in shit until he froze or drowned or whatever. Serve him right. But I didn't do the deed, much as I might have wanted to. I'd be happy to send a thank-you card to whoever did."

Lost in processing what Frances had said, and trying to visualize them together, Meg was startled when Frances drained her coffee and stood up. "Well, I'd better run. I've got more shoveling to do. Keep up the good work, Meg. I know it's slow, but it'll be worth it in the end, you'll see."

Meg escorted her to the door and watched as Frances pulled on her boots. "I hope so. Thanks for the shovel, Frances. Now I just need to figure out how it works."

Frances laughed. "City girl, huh? You'll learn. But better clear the front path before it freezes, or you'll be slipping and sliding all winter. I'll be in touch!"

Meg watched as Frances waded through the snow in front. She was right: Seth had cleared the front end of the driveway, but the front walk was still covered. As Frances pulled away, Meg hunted down her coat and gloves and boots and prepared to do battle with the snow. She had forgotten how heavy snow could be. Bend, lift, toss; repeat. Her shoulder muscles started complaining almost immediately. By the time she was halfway to the driveway, her back muscles had chimed in. She had thought she was in pretty good shape, after all her renovation efforts, but apparently shoveling snow used a whole different group of muscles. Still, Frances had said she had shoveled out her own place, so Meg should be able to handle it, right?

She reached the driveway and leaned on her shovel, panting. How often was it going to snow in Granford? She had a newfound respect for Frances: she was stronger than she looked. Strong enough to handle a body? That thought came out of nowhere. *Meg, you're getting paranoid*. Did Frances have a motive? Maybe. But if Frances had spent a morning shoveling and then come bounding over to her house bearing a snow shovel, then Meg had to believe she had the physical strength to do the deed.

In the meantime, she had better clear off her car so that didn't freeze into a block of ice. She'd hate to miss her rendezvous with Cinda tomorrow. And if she was going to be out anyway, she could check back with Gail and see if she had located anything relevant. Or go to the library. Or talk with the town clerk about local records. Tomorrow, when the roads were clear, after her lunch with Cinda.

Once she had finished shoveling, she went back inside, grateful for the relative warmth. What next? If she was going to meet with Cinda, she had to do her homework. Surely there would have been news reports about the development project in the Boston financial pages. Maybe she didn't want to drive anywhere today, but she could easily do an online search. And familiarize herself with the terms and legalities for eminent domain. And look up the details of Town Meeting procedures. That was more than enough to keep her busy—and if it wasn't, there was always more wallpaper to scrape.

She retrieved her laptop, plugged in the phone line, and booted up. No wireless access here; dial-up was slow, but it was better than nothing.

Three hours later her head was spinning. She had begun by reviewing the Boston financial articles announcing Puritan Bank's new initiative to invest in community development; Chandler's picture had appeared consistently. Chandler photographed well and he knew it. Buried somewhere among the articles had been a mention that Granford was among the communities selected. No surprise there.

From there Meg had segued to local news coverage, starting with the major papers in the western part of the state. The articles were cautiously optimistic, highlighting the decades-long decline in manufacturing and other industry in the region—although there was a hint of scepticism about the intrusion of a Boston bank. Sour grapes, perhaps? But it didn't surprise Meg. Start-up projects required deep pockets, and the local banks might not have had the resources.

Then Meg had turned to the comments in local papers and blogs. It had taken a while for the citizens of Granford to recognize what was going on, but when they had, there had ensued a firestorm of articles. And these were only the ones online; Meg guessed there would be plenty more that hadn't been posted on the Internet. But the individual responses were widely varied, from one pole to the other. Some people wanted things to stay the same forever; others applauded growth—probably foreseeing lower property taxes.

Meg sat back in her chair and stretched, rubbing her eyes. Reading between the lines in this case made an interesting exercise: the public statements made in Boston had been careful and discreet, but as the story trickled down to the local level, voices were louder and less polished. But sincere, undeniably. Meg could sympathize with that. Bankers made decisions based on numbers, but the residents of Granford were going to have to live with the reality of the project in their front yard. They had every right to be concerned, and vocal about their opinions.

What had she learned that Cinda and her legions of junior associates couldn't have dug up? Not a lot. In the local papers and a few blogs, several names cropped up regularly; Seth's name was conspicuously absent, but Meg guessed that he had made a point of staying out of the fray because of his elected position. It couldn't have been easy for him, caught in the middle—landowner and public official. When it came down to it, would he speak for himself or for the town?

So what could she tell Cinda? She must know that there were ruffled feathers in town, but which ones should she worry about smoothing? And where did Meg's own loyalties lie—with the bank or with the town?

She stood up to get her blood moving. Whatever her personal feelings, she owed it to the town to evaluate the facts objectively and to make a reasoned and informed recommendation to Cinda. She had no reason to believe that Cinda would even listen to her, but at least she would have done her duty, and anything she learned would be useful for her own ends.

22

By the next day, the weather had turned again. The snow from the quick storm was melting rapidly, and when Meg set out, she found the roads no more than wet and the heaps of plowed snow alongside dwindling fast. She arrived in Northampton shortly before noon and made her way over to the old hotel, whose squat profile dominated a block of downtown. Meg had never been inside and had to admit she was curious. The lobby was much as she had expected: high-ceilinged, with acres of polished wood and pseudo-oriental carpeting, massive bouquets of fresh flowers on marble-topped tables. She knew from its reputation that the place was expensive, and was not in the least surprised that Chandler had opted to stay there. He had liked his creature comforts. She was a little more surprised that his underling Cinda had been allowed to stay in such an upscale place—unless she had shared a room with Chandler?

Meg pushed that unappealing image out of her head and approached the reception desk.

"Cinda Patterson?" she said to the dapper young man.

"Your name, ma'am?" he responded promptly.

Ma'am? How old did she look to this stripling? "Meg Corey. She's expecting me."

"Just a moment, please." He turned away, picked up a phone, and after a few moments murmured something. When he hung up, he turned back to Meg with a bright smile. "Just go right up, ma'am. Room 302."

"Thank you," Meg answered, repressing an urge to add "sonny."

The farther Meg penetrated into the innards of the hotel, the more she felt as though she had walked into a time warp. She had to admit that retaining the slightly faded splendors of the venerable old hotel was preferable to ripping everything out and replacing it with shiny granite and track lighting, but there was a peculiar ageless quality to the place, as though it had been preserved in amber. As she headed down the silent, damask-clad hall on her way to Cinda's room, she made mental notes about the wallpaper and the wainscoting.

She rapped on the door to 302, and Cinda opened the door quickly. "Hi, Meg, right on time. I'm sorry, I'm running a little late. I got caught up in a conference call—you know how that goes." Cinda laughed prettily.

"I do." Meg discreetly studied the room. Not a suite, but more than comfortable. And very neat. Clearly Cinda kept everything hung in her closet or put away in a drawer. Nothing was out of place. "This is a lovely hotel. How long have you been here?"

"The last couple of weeks. Chandler thought it was a good idea to be available on short notice, rather than trying to go back and forth to Boston. Especially with the uncertainties of the weather this time of year."

Meg was impressed and vaguely annoyed. After two weeks, her room was still this tidy? Much like Chandler, as she recalled: he had always filed his cuff links by material, then by color. And he had never omitted putting them away, even in the heat of passion . . . He and Cinda must have made a good pair. She swallowed a sigh. She had to admit it was nice to be somewhere clean and orderly after her month living in renovation chaos.

Cinda was stacking the already neat piles of documents and slipping them into her briefcase. Meg prowled around the room, checking out the view. On a table near the window there was an old clothbound book, looking curiously out of place in the elegant room. Meg picked it up and opened it: Easton's *History of Granford*. Hadn't she had a copy of that? She turned to the flyleaf, and went still.

Yes, she had owned a copy. In fact, she had owned *this* copy—she recognized the author's inscription to Lula and Nettie. And she had loaned it to Chandler last week. What was it doing in Cinda's room?

"Almost ready. Just give me a minute, will you?" Cinda

chirped. "I want to freshen my makeup. I thought we could eat downstairs, if you don't mind."

"That's fine." Meg suppressed a small pang of disappointment. There were so many interesting restaurants in Northampton that she hadn't had a chance to try. But at least Cinda should pick up the tab for this one, since it was a professional consultation of sorts. "No hurry." Cinda retreated into the bathroom and turned on the water, ending conversation.

Meg stared at the book in her hands, then noticed a slip of paper lodged between the pages inside the book. A bookmark? Meg opened to the page. It was a credit card receipt from some place with a Northampton address.

And it was Chandler's credit card number. She had seen it often enough in the past, and her mathematical mind had filed away the last four digits. The slip had a date and time stamp. For the night *after* she had had dinner with Chandler, the night he had been killed. And at the time Chandler had been putting charges on his credit card in Northampton, Meg had been watching Christopher talk to the members of the Granford Historical Society. So how could she have killed him?

She inhaled sharply, her mind spinning as she worked through the implications. Chandler had had the book that night and stuck in the receipt when he returned to the hotel. Someone at this place should have seen Chandler, would remember him there.

Then she looked more closely. It appeared to be a bar tab, for multiple drinks. Meg knew that Chandler would not have consumed so many, alone. Therefore, he had had a companion. But who? As far as Meg knew, no one else had come forward to admit having seen Chandler that night. Although, she had to admit, it was unlikely that Detective Marcus would have shared such information with her. The detective said he had talked to Cinda last Friday: what had she told him?

Cinda emerged from the bathroom, looking even crisper than before, which Meg would not have believed possible. "Ready?"

Meg held up the book. "Is this yours?"

Cinda peered across the room as she pulled on her suit jacket. "What ... oh, that old thing. Chandler gave it to me—said he thought I might find something useful in it. You know, bone up on the history of Granford, use it to impress the locals. I haven't had time to look at it. It's not really my kind of thing, you know."

Meg wavered. Should she mention it was her book? Cinda would probably be glad to return it to her, since she obviously had no interest in it.

Meg closed it with a snap—with the receipt still inside. "Do you think I could borrow this? Since I'm selling the house, it might be a good idea if I knew more about the history of the town. My Realtor says buyers like that kind of information."

Cinda waved a careless hand. "Please, take it. I simply don't have the time to look at it."

"Thanks." Meg slipped it into her tote bag. "Are you ready to go?"

"I am. Meg, I'm so glad you're on board with this. I'm just so excited about this project ..." Cinda burbled on as she followed Meg out into the hall, carefully locking the door behind her.

Meg made appropriately noncommittal answers, while in the back of her mind she was puzzling over what to do next. Chandler had had the book, and now Cinda had the book. When did the credit card receipt go in? Cinda didn't seem concerned about it, but did she know the slip was there?

There was someone else in the elevator when she and Cinda boarded, sparing Meg the need to make further conversation, which gave her more time to gnaw on her problem. She wished there was someone she could consult with. She had a feeling the right thing to do would be to take the book and the slip directly to the detective's office. After all, she was already in Northampton, wasn't she? And this was evidence in an open murder investigation, wasn't it? She certainly hoped so. If someone else had been with Chandler that night, that could let her off the hook. And she was curious to know what story Cinda had given him.

The downstairs restaurant, its tall windows facing the main intersection in Northampton, was bustling, filled with older, prosperous-looking people. Once Meg had looked at the menu, she realized why there were no younger people in the place: no way they could afford it. Nor could she.

Cinda was speaking, and Meg fought to focus on her. "It seems a shame to lose any momentum, just because of a single unfortunate incident."

So Chandler's murder was now no more than an unfortunate incident. "If you have a viable project, you shouldn't have any trouble moving forward," Meg said, more tartly than she had intended.

Cinda looked startled. "You're right, of course. And the numbers are sound, believe me." She went on, stopping only to give her order to the harried waitress. An iced tea, despite the frigid weather—no alcohol for Cinda, who no doubt wanted to keep her head clear for business.

"You're awfully quiet, Meg," Cinda said as she ran out of steam. "I was hoping that you could help me shape my presentation to the town."

"Haven't you spoken to them before?"

"Yes, but Chandler always took the lead. This is my first presentation as project manager, and I want to be sure to make the right impression. Our bank has put a lot of work into this, and I'd hate to be the one who dropped the ball."

I'll bet. Might be a blot on your sterling record. "I'm sure you have nothing to worry about. The project stands on its own merits."

"Of course. But, Meg, as I'm sure you know, there is such a thing as a herd mentality. And a town meeting like this, it draws a small group of citizens, mostly the ones who feel strongly about the issue, pro *and* con, and they may well react emotionally rather than logically when it comes time to vote. Which can work for us or against us. Do you see what I mean? This vote will be binding, and I want to be sure it goes the right way."

And how far would you go to assure that? Meg wondered. "You seem to have an excellent grasp of the process. I admit I had to do some homework to be sure I understood it."

"As have I, Meg." Was there a flash of steel in her eye?

"I don't doubt that. So, what can I tell you?"

"You've gotten to know Seth Chapin fairly well, haven't you?"

Meg's hackles went up. "What's your point?"

Cinda was shrewd enough to read Meg's reaction. "Please, I don't mean to imply anything. But from what I've seen, Seth is something of a ... bellwether, I suppose you could say. He's a community leader, and people respect him. And he has a personal stake in this project. If he's in favor, that will carry a lot of weight. Has he said anything to you?"

Meg sorted through her possible answers, discarding most of them. "I think it's safe to say that he has mixed feelings about it. But from everything I've seen, he's been as fair and evenhanded as anyone could hope for, publicly. It's a decision for the community to make, and he's not about to throw his weight around."

Cinda gave her a long look, then shrugged. "He seems to be an honest man. I've been hoping we have him on our side, but he's been noncommittal when I've talked with him. But at least he's not against us." And then she deftly changed the subject.

The rest of lunch passed uneventfully, and talk drifted to safe topics. Meg was relieved when Cinda grabbed the check quickly, scribbling her room number on it. Meg accompanied her to the lobby.

"Thanks for the lunch, Cinda. I don't know if I helped much, but I warned you that I hadn't been here very long."

"Meg, I appreciate your candor. And sometimes an outsider, a newcomer, can see things more clearly than someone in the thick of things. May I call you if I have any more questions? And you will be at the meeting, won't you?"

"I wouldn't miss it," Meg said drily. "Good luck. I'm sure you'll do fine."

"Thank you. Oops, I've got to run. Another conference call, you know. Bye."

Cinda turned and boarded a waiting elevator. Meg hesitated in the middle of the lobby, conscious of the solid weight of the old book in her bag.

This was evidence in a murder. The detective needed to see it. Detective it was, then.

Meg walked the short block to the courthouse and entered the building, stopping, as required, at the front desk. "I'd like to see Detective Marcus, please."

The young officer behind the desk looked at her critically. "He expecting you?"

"No. But this is about the Hale murder investigation."

The officer picked up the phone and pushed a button on the

console, then turned slightly away so that Meg could not over-hear him. When he was done, he pointed toward the cluster of plastic chairs in the waiting room. "Wait there."

Meg sat and watched various people come and go. Mostly women—visiting inmates? It was fifteen minutes before Detective Marcus appeared, stopping for a word at the desk before he approached her. He didn't look happy to see her.

"What is it?" He said without preamble.

Meg stood up. "I found something I think you should see."

He studied her for a long moment before saying, "Okay. Follow me."

She followed him silently back to his office and took the chair he pointed to. He sat behind his desk and stared at her. "What did you want to show me?"

Meg pulled the book out of her bag and laid it on the desk between them. "This is a book, a history of Granford, that came from my house. I know it's the same book because of the inscription inside. Chandler saw it there last Monday, when he came to the house, and asked if he could borrow it. I said yes, and he took it with him."

The detective made no move to look at it. Unnerved by his silence, as no doubt he intended, Meg pressed on. "Today I had lunch with Cinda Patterson at the Hotel Northampton, where she and Chandler were staying, and I saw the book in her room. I asked if I could borrow it."

"What's your point? Hale probably gave it to her."

"I know, and that's what she said. But when I looked inside, I found a receipt from a bar or restaurant in Northampton, from Tuesday night. And it's for multiple drinks, more than Chandler would have had on his own. That means someone must have been with him."

"So?" The detective was not about to concede anything, and Meg was beginning to wonder why she had bothered to come.

"Look, Detective, this means that someone was with him that night, the night he died. When I was clearly somewhere else. Do you know who it was? Was it Cinda Patterson?"

Detective Marcus looked at her, but his expression gave away nothing. "Ms. Corey, I appreciate your coming forward with this, but as I've told you before, I'm not under any obligation to give you details of an ongoing investigation."

Meg's anger simmered. "Has anyone come forward? Why don't you go ask at that restaurant, see if anyone remembers seeing Chandler and who was with him? And why don't you ask Cinda how she came by the book? She says Chandler gave it to her, but she didn't say when."

"Ms. Corey, that's none of your business. Was there anything else?"

For a long moment Meg wrestled with the thought of telling the stone-faced detective that Cinda had been sleeping with Chandler. In the end she decided she needed time to think it through: the fact gave her a good reason to be angry with Chandler, or at least the detective might think so.

Meg smiled sweetly at him. "No, Detective. I just wanted to be sure you had all available information." *Especially information that could clear me.* "But you will agree, won't you, that if there was someone who was with Chandler that night, then it could have been the killer?"

"I'm not ruling anything out, Ms. Corey. Thank you for stopping by." Detective Marcus stood up, indicating that the meeting was over.

"You will keep me informed, won't you?"

Detective Marcus declined to answer. He escorted her to the front of the building, and then Meg found herself on the sidewalk, feeling deflated. He hadn't exactly jumped for joy at her precious piece of evidence. But of course, she had no idea what he knew at the moment. Maybe he had already identified the other person and it had turned out to be a respectable contractor who had gone straight home to a hot dinner with his wife and six children. Meg could only hope that the server at the bar had not left for Alaska to seek his fortune and that he had a good memory. But she had no confidence that the detective would tell her what he did—or did not—find out.

As she drove back to Granford, she wondered just what role Cinda had played in all this. The innocent interpretation would be: Chandler met someone for drinks, after he had returned to Northampton from Boston; later, Chandler came back to the hotel and, seeing the book, had the brainstorm that Cinda should do a little light reading and delivered it to her door. Which would be credible if it weren't for the receipt carefully tucked inside, which meant it had been late in the evening. Why would he have given the book to Cinda so late—surely it could have waited until morning? Unless, of course, Cinda was right there in the room with him. That was altogether possible, but it didn't make Cinda a murderer.

A second alternative: an unknown stranger, who had accompanied Chandler back to the hotel. Someone who hadn't come forward and admitted to being with him. If the detective was doing his job, he could find out who had been at the bar with Chandler. Did he already know about Chandler and Cinda's personal relationship? Would Cinda have told him? No one else around here knew about it, as far as Meg was aware. But there was no way she could tell Detective Marcus, especially since she wasn't sure how he would view that information coming from her. Still, the fact remained: Cinda had the book; the book had the receipt. Cinda had to be involved. And whether or not it was Cinda in the bar with Chandler, at least there was some evidence to point to someone other than Meg.

As Meg let herself in the back door, she saw that the message light was flashing on her phone. When she retrieved the message, she found it was from Lauren.

"Hey, girl, where are you? I thought you never got out of that money-pit of yours. Anyway, quick news flash about the late Mr. Hale and the lovely Cinda. Word has it that they split up more than a month ago. Must've been sticky, working with him—but I'll bet she would've slapped a gender discrimination suit on him in a minute if he tried to remove her from his pet project. Interesting, no? Anyway, gotta go. Talk soon."

Yes, Lauren—very interesting. It would be really satisfying to go back to the detective and rub his nose in the fact that Cinda had as much—or more—reason to be pissed at Chandler as the detective thought Meg did. But the detective would accuse her of grasping at straws and trying to throw the blame anywhere else.

As Meg digested Lauren's news, another thought hit her. If Chandler and Cinda were no longer together, why would she have gone to his room, or he to hers, that night? And if that hadn't happened, how would she have gotten the book? It looked more and more credible to Meg that Cinda could've been the one sharing drinks with Chandler. In fact, maybe he or she had decided that it would be preferable to meet in a public place, rather than in one of their rooms, under the circumstances. Meg wished she knew where the place was, but she wasn't up to speed on Northampton bars. Most likely it was close to the hotel. Maybe Chandler had had enough of the stodgy hotel bar and had wanted a change of scene.

But why hadn't Cinda mentioned it to anyone?

23

A night's sleep didn't bring Meg any brilliant insights. She had a gut feeling that Cinda was involved in Chandler's death, but she didn't see how, and she couldn't prove it anyway. She knew that Detective Marcus preferred either Meg or Seth as Chief Suspect. No way she was going to take that lying down, but what could she do about it? The Special Town Meeting was drawing closer minute by minute, and there the people of Granford would make a decision that would irrevocably change the face of their town. To do that, they deserved facts—all the facts. Such as why their lead banker had been found dead, and who had killed him, and if his death had had anything to do with the project or was purely personal. Suspecting what she did, could Meg let Cinda move forward? That felt wrong. But how could she stop her?

She had finished breakfast and was doing the last of her laundry when her phone rang. When she answered she was surprised to hear Rachel's voice.

"Hey, Meg. How's it going?"

"Not bad," Meg said, wondering if she meant it. "What's up?"

Rachel hesitated briefly. "Listen, do you mind if I stop by for a minute? There's something I'd like to talk to you about."

"Sure," Meg replied, mystified. "How soon?"

"Give me fifteen."

Meg went back to stuffing sheets in the dryer and turned it on. Miracle of miracles, Rachel had actually called first instead of just appearing, the way everyone else seemed to.

Rachel arrived in thirteen minutes, bearing a bag that turned out to contain homemade apple muffins. Meg recognized the aroma before Rachel had even opened the bag. "Coffee?"

"Always." Rachel plopped down at the kitchen table. "Nothing like some good carbs and caffeine to pick you up, I always say. You seem to be surviving all right."

Meg sat down gratefully. "At least the detective hasn't arrested me yet. I don't think he likes me much."

Meg saw Rachel stiffen slightly. "You've talked to him again?" Rachel asked.

"More than once. Yes, I knew Chandler. No, I hadn't seen him in months before he showed up here. No, I didn't kill him. I don't think the detective wants to believe that."

Rachel bit off a large chunk of muffin and said around it, "I know he's talked to Seth."

"Rachel, Detective Marcus can't think that Seth killed him."

Rachel chewed pensively, avoiding Meg's eyes. "The detective isn't too fond of Seth."

"I know. Seth told me."

Rachel stopped chewing and stared at Meg with surprise. "He told you?"

"He said he had been arrested once, for beating up the detective's son. Why? Am I missing something?"

"Well, that's not the whole story." Rachel chewed some more, then sighed. "That's why I wanted to talk to you. Look, I don't want you to get the idea that Seth has a mean streak or a violent temper or anything. I guess he told you as much as he did because he didn't want you to be surprised by anything the detective said or hinted at. But he probably didn't tell you the rest of it ... because it involved me."

"Oh." Meg didn't know what to say. "Listen, you don't owe me any explanations. It's your business, not mine."

Rachel snorted. "Well, since you and my brother are now the prime suspects in a murder that the detective would be only too happy to pin on one or both of you, I'd say that makes it your business. When Seth lit into Bobby—that's Marcus's son—it was because Bobby was trying to get into my pants, and he didn't seem to understand the meaning of 'no.' Bobby and Seth were both on the football team in high school. Seniors when I was a lowly junior. I thought Bobby was really hot, and I followed him around like a puppy dog at football practice, while I was waiting for Seth to give me a ride home. And then after a game one weekend, things got a little out of hand. Bobby had been drinking. I guess he knew how I felt, not that it was hard to tell, and he decided to give me a treat—him. Right there under the bleachers. I discovered real fast that I wasn't interested, but by then there was no stopping him, at least until Seth came looking for me and found Bobby on top of me."

Rachel studied her muffin, avoiding Meg's eyes. "Well, he really lit into Bobby. I'd never seen him like that—and I haven't since. He and Bobby were pretty well matched, but Seth hadn't been drinking, so he did some damage. And he told Bobby that if he ever spread any nasty stories about me, he'd finish what he'd started. I guess it worked, because I never heard anybody talk about it, after. But Bobby's dad was a cop then, and he was real pissed about what Seth had done to Bobby—messed him up enough, he couldn't play football for the rest of the season. So he arrested Seth for assault. Didn't stick. I don't know who told what story, but in the end it all went away. Last I heard, Bobby went into the army after graduation."

Oh my, Meg thought. She hadn't been expecting anything like this. "Rachel," Meg began carefully, "I never thought Seth was violent. And I assume that he didn't tell me any more about what happened because he didn't think it was his story to tell. So thank you for filling me in, but it doesn't change what I think anyway." She sighed, and took another bite of her muffin. "What a mess! I thought I was coming to a nice, safe, quiet town, and look what happens! Bodies in the backyard."

"Guess this wasn't quite what you expected, huh? You haven't found any more, have you?" Rachel grinned at her, relieved.

"No, thank goodness, but the ground is still frozen. Who knows what will pop up next? By the way, have you met Chandler's successor?"

"No, but then, I don't live here in Granford anymore, so there's no reason why I would have. Why?"

"Just wondered if you'd heard anything, or if anyone had said anything, about Cinda."

"It's a her? You've met her?"

"Recently. I didn't know her in Boston."

"You don't like her, do you?"

Rachel didn't miss much, Meg thought. "No, honestly, I don't. I just found out that she was Chandler's next"—Meg fumbled for an appropriate word—"diversion, after me. But I don't trust her, and not because she was carrying on with Chandler."

"Why? You think she had something to do with his death?" Rachel asked, sweeping her crumbs into a neat pile.

"I'd like to think so, but I can't prove it." *Except for the receipt,* but Meg decided not to bring that up.

"Well, look at it this way: if she ends up dead, you'll know it's related to the deal and not to Chandler, right?" Rachel said cheerfully.

"Gee, that makes me feel a lot better." Meg paused before adding, "Thanks, Rachel, for giving me the rest of the story. Not that I had any suspicions about Seth, but it does help explain why the detective seemed so set against me from the start. Sort of guilt by association." Meg wavered before tossing out her next question. "Rachel, can I ask you something?"

"Sure, ask away."

"Seth was married once, wasn't he?"

Rachel's expression registered surprise. "Yeah, years ago. It's ancient history, and he doesn't talk about it much. Why?"

Why indeed? As she shaped her next words, Meg realized that it might be another piece in the murder puzzle. "The person who told me about it said that the ex was carrying a torch for Seth. I wondered if she might have a stake in the success of the Granford Grange project."

"I never thought of that. You've been talking to Gail, right?"

"Well . . ."

Rachel laughed. "It's okay. Gail knows everybody, and she's not a mean gossip. She probably thought you might want to know. Anyway, Nancy doesn't stand to benefit financially, if this deal happens. The whole divorce thing was settled years ago, and she has no claims on anything of Seth's. But I wonder . . ."

"Yes?" Meg prompted.

"Maybe she thinks that if Seth lost the land, and the shop, he might rethink this whole plumbing business. I mean, he got into it for a lot of reasons, mostly because of Dad, but if we lost the land, this might be a good opportunity to get out. I hadn't considered that. Heck, I don't know if *he* has. He gets so wrapped up in what's good for the town, and for everybody else, that he doesn't even think about what's good for him."

"What about you? Or Stephen? What do you think?"

"Dad left Mom a life interest in the place, but the property reverts to us kids equally. Or did. The guys, mainly Seth, bought me out years ago—that was the seed money for the B and B. Stephen still owns a share, and he'd probably be thrilled to cut and run. Although he'd blow the money in no time." Rachel shook her head. Then she looked at her watch. "Shoot, I've got guests coming. Sorry to dump this on you and run, but I just thought you should know."

"Thanks, Rachel. I'm glad you did."

After Rachel pulled out of her driveway, Meg went back to folding laundry. The association amused her: Rachel had been talking about dirty laundry. Although whose dirt it was wasn't quite clear.

Rachel's story had left Meg unsettled, and also drove home the fact that there were far too many undercurrents in Granford that Meg didn't understand. She puzzled about them as she did her errands: groceries, the inevitable trip to the hardware store. High on the list was a new ice scraper for her car windshield, and a bag of salt or deicer or whatever was politically correct for clearing walks. The last thing she wanted at the moment was a lawsuit from one of her steady stream of visitors if one slipped and fell on her property.

She was driving back to the center of town when she noticed Gail walking quickly toward the historical society building. Meg turned onto the side road and pulled up in front of it. Gail had noticed her approach and was waiting for her on the stoop, hands tucked under her arms. When Meg climbed out of her car, Gail said, "Hi! I was just thinking about you. I've found some stuff you might be interested in. Come on in and I'll get it for you."

"Terrific!" Something to work on that didn't involve murder. If she was lucky, the only bodies involved would be those who had lived long, full lives and died peacefully in some other century. Meg followed Gail into the building. It was, if possible, colder inside than the last time she had been there.

"I put the stuff back here by the desk," Gail said over her shoulder as she wended her way through the jumbled collections. "The boxes were actually in my attic, which is the only reason I could find them so quickly. Ah, here we go." She reached down behind the rolltop desk and hoisted out a dusty banker's box. "You want me to carry it out to your car?"

"I can manage. Is that it?"

"One more box. You're lucky. The Warrens were good record keepers, and I guess Lula and Nettie never threw anything away, and whoever found this stuff gave it to us rather than just dumping it, thank goodness. You should have plenty to keep you busy." Gail hesitated a fraction of a second. "How's the murder investigation going?"

Meg was surprised to find Gail eyeing her speculatively. "I'm still on the suspect list, if that's what you want to know. You worried about being here alone with me?"

"You're no killer. Just dumb enough to get involved with Chandler Hale." As Meg watched, Gail appeared to come to some sort of decision. "You might as well sit down."

Meg sat, confused.

"You know, Chandler was ... an opportunist, shall we say?" Gail began.

"I'm not sure what you mean."

Gail leaned back in her chair, which creaked in protest, and studied the ceiling. "He used all the means at his disposal to get what he wanted. And he was a charming and attractive man."

For a moment Meg was puzzled. And then, as she put the pieces together, she was horrified. "Gail, did he make a play for you?"

"In a word, yes. When he first started sniffing around Granford, last year, he got in touch with a lot of people in town. Funny thing, most of them were women. Of course, women run a lot of the local organizations—the town clerk, the library, this place. Anyway, he'd invite a woman to dinner, purely for business, of course. Then he'd turn on the charm and pump them for information. When it was my turn, he wanted to know what I could tell him about any restrictions on historic properties that might get in the way of his project. I looked him in the eye and told him that if he wanted that information, he could submit a formal request through proper channels. He took it fairly well, and he didn't bother me again. But I'm pretty sure he tried it out on some other people who were more, uh, compliant." Gail looked at Meg to see how she was taking it. "Can't say I wasn't tempted, though. I love my husband, but Chandler was ... well, sort of glamorous, at least by local standards. And he could make you feel special. Heck, I don't have to tell you that, do I? He was a piece of work, though."

Meg was getting angrier and angrier at dead Chandler. First Frances, and now Gail? How could she have been so blind to what a rat he was? A self-serving, egocentric, arrogant ... "Believe me, I know what you mean. But I guess I had never realized how manipulative he could be. Maybe I should be happy he dumped me when he did."

"Yeah, I'd say you got lucky. So it really was a coincidence, you two ending up in Granford?"

"Cross my heart. But he did pull the same stunt on me—asking me to nose around town and see what I could find out—and I told him to forget it. He wasn't happy about that. He was used to me saying 'yes' to him."

"Good for you! Anyway, I don't know if this has anything to do with his murder, but there could be a lot of women around here who fell for his line. Maybe there's a local husband who wasn't too happy about it."

"Great. Maybe I should fill the detective in and see if I can get him to pay attention to anyone beyond me. Or me and Seth."

"He's still playing that tune? He's a stiff-necked idiot." Gail glanced at her watch and stood up quickly. "Hey, I've got to pick up my daughter at basketball practice. Why don't I take one box and you take the other one?"

Meg grabbed the handles on one box to lift it and was surprised by its heft. "What the heck is in here? It weighs a ton."

Gail lifted hers much more easily. "Old paper, mostly. A few books, diaries or ledgers, most likely. All a lot denser than the modern stuff. Go ahead—I'll follow you out."

Meg concentrated on carrying the bulky box without tripping

over anything, and sighed with relief when she made it to her car.
She popped the trunk open and settled her box in it; Gail slid the
second one alongside it.

"Good luck with the papers. I hope you find something useful. I'll see you at the meeting Monday?"

"I'll be there. Thanks, Gail."

Driving the short distance back to her house, Meg noted that
living around here seemed to spawn hearty women: Frances
shoveling her own walks, Gail slinging loaded file boxes around
as though they were empty. Meg had a lot of catching up to do.
But as she pulled into her driveway, another thought crept in: a
strong woman could move a body. She had trouble visualizing
Cinda hauling a body around, but it was far easier to picture Gail
or Frances, or even Rachel, doing it. It was a disturbing thought.

24

Back inside, Meg decided to use the remaining daylight hours to tackle the front room across the hall from the parlor, a space she had managed to avoid so far. Its windows faced the street and the orchard, although the orchard wasn't visible from the lower floor. In fact, not much at all was visible, since years of dirt covered the wavy antique panes. If she hoped to do anything in the room, she would have to clean the glass first.

It was when she was scrubbing the side windows that she noticed activity at the top of the ridge. She stopped to watch the group: a woman and three men—no, four. Unlikely though it seemed, the woman appeared to be Cinda, elegantly clad in a long tailored coat and high leather boots with heels. Not the ideal choice for standing out in the open on a cold February day, and although most of the snow had melted, it had left behind mud. Cinda had apparently opted for form over function.

But what were they doing there? Meg felt a spurt of annoyance. Cinda could at least have asked her permission. After all, it was still her land. And who were her companions? The men were making sweeping gestures in all directions. Surveyors? Planners?

She damn well was going to find out. Meg went to the hall and pulled on her boots and her down jacket. No time for niceties like clean clothes and makeup. But she was in the right here, and she didn't appreciate visitors—aka trespassers—on her property.

By the time she approached the group at the top of the hill, Meg's anger had swelled. Cinda spotted her first.

"Why, Meg, we were just talking about you." She beamed, but her eyes were wary.

"Cinda," Meg said, without smiling, "what brings you here? And who are your, uh, friends?"

Before answering, Cinda turned to her companions. "This is Meg Corey, the current owner of this property. Meg, we were just looking at the lay of the land, so to speak, and I'm sure you'll be interested. Jack, could you give her the rough outlines of the project?"

"Glad to. Ms. Corey, good to meet you. Nice piece of ground you've got here." Jack shook Meg's hand with enthusiasm. "We're looking to clear from the corner of County Line Road and Route 202, back to about here, following the ridge line. Sure, there's a bit of a slope, but we can do some terracing in the parking lot. Actually, that might help our drainage situation—don't want the lot to ice over in winter, do we?"

How dare he? That was Meg's first thought, her anger blossoming. The town hadn't even approved the deal, and this jerk was already laying asphalt over her orchard. She struggled to speak calmly. "Excuse me, Jack, but the project hasn't been approved yet. Aren't you being a little premature?"

A flicker of doubt appeared in Jack's eyes, and he looked briefly at Cinda. "Way I understood it, it's pretty much a done deal. All over but the paperwork."

Cinda looked nervous. "Well, Jack, that might be overstating it a little, but things look pretty good. Right, Meg?"

Meg declined to answer Cinda's question. "Jack, what's your interest here? And these other men? Do they work for you?"

"Tri-County Asphalt and Paving—that's my company. Biggest paving contractor in this end of the state." He fished in his jacket pocket and pulled out a business card. "I could give you a good deal on your driveway down there—looks like you could use some help with it. We're bidding on the job, just wanted to get a look at what we'd be dealing with. It's not the same, looking at a map."

Cinda was still looking at Meg with concern. "Meg, this is still preliminary. But I'm just thinking ahead. It's important to get in touch with local suppliers, let them know what's in the pipeline, so they can plan ahead. That way, everybody benefits, and we can get the project rolling quickly. Right, Jack?"

"Yes, ma'am. I guarantee we'll do a good job for you." Jack smiled down at Cinda, clearly besotted. And his verb tense didn't escape Meg: he was talking as if he knew he had a lock on the contract. Who else had Cinda been talking to? She was making it plain that this project was a sure thing, wasn't she?

"You didn't introduce me to these other gentlemen, Cinda," Meg said, her voice level.

"Oh, sorry—where are my manners? This is Al Kozinski— he's a general contractor, does a lot of work on commercial projects around here."

A second man stepped forward to shake Meg's hand. "Pleased to meet you, ma'am. We did that pretty little strip this side of Hadley—maybe you've seen it?"

Cinda pressed on. "And this is Irv Janssen—he supplies building materials. And he's promised us a very good price. Right, Irv?"

"Sure thing. Good to meet you, ma'am," he said to Meg, taking her hand in turn. "Guess we'll be seeing a lot of you over the next year or two."

Meg managed to produce an insincere smile. "Perhaps. Cinda, may I have a word with you?"

"Of course. Excuse me, gentlemen?" She looped her arm through Meg's and walked a few paces away. "Problem?"

Meg extricated her arm. "Yes, I do have a problem. I don't appreciate that you're already dragging a construction crew around and that you didn't even ask my permission to come onto my property. As far as I know, there is no guarantee that this proposal of yours is going to pass, and I'd prefer if you waited until it does to start rolling asphalt."

Cinda's gaze was cool, and Meg wondered if she saw lurking hostility in it. "I'm sorry, Meg. Perhaps I overstepped my bounds. And you are certainly within your rights. But I thought you were in favor of this going forward?"

Meg looked her squarely in the eye. "Cinda, I haven't decided. There are a lot of factors I have to consider, and I don't intend to be rushed into a decision."

When she responded, Cinda's voice was edged with contempt. "Frankly, Meg, I don't think your one vote is going to make a lot of difference. I believe we have the votes we need. Chandler and I laid the groundwork carefully for this, believe me. But we're almost done here. And let me tell you—we *will* be back next week." Cinda turned away from Meg and rejoined the group of men. They were clustered awkwardly, stamping their feet to keep warm, and they avoided looking at Meg. "Gentlemen, you said something about access roads?" Cinda said brightly.

The men wavered, unsure of what was happening. But apparently they answered to Cinda, not Meg, and after nodding silently to Meg, they turned back to Cinda and began pointing toward the distant highway.

Meg's anger continued to simmer. Cinda had just insulted her in front of her cadre of builders. Unfortunately, Cinda was right: if the town approved the project, they'd be back with their backhoes and dump trucks as soon as the paperwork cleared. Spring was coming, and they'd want to start construction as soon as possible. And the apple trees would never bloom again.

Depression washed over her. Meg turned abruptly and went back down the hill. When she reached the front of her house, she was surprised to find a Chapin Plumbing truck in the driveway, but it was Stephen who was leaning against it, waiting for her, rather than Seth.

"Hi, Stephen. What's up?"

Stephen took a bite of the apple he was eating, chewed, and swallowed it before answering. "Seth said he left a sink in your barn—he thinks he's got a buyer for it. Asked me to pick it up."

"Oh, right, I'd forgotten. Sure, but I'll have to get the key to the barn padlock. It's inside."

Stephen didn't move from his slouch against the van. He nodded toward the direction from which she had arrived: Cinda and her pals were still visible. "What's that all about?"

Meg laughed bitterly. "Oh, just the new head banker and her construction cronies, carving up my land."

Stephen continued watching them, a half smile on his face. "Things're really moving right along, aren't they?"

"I'm not sure I'm happy about that," Meg replied tartly. "And it's not guaranteed that the town will vote for the project, you know."

"Maybe not. But I think she's doing a good job. Good deal for the town, too."

Meg had her doubts about Stephen's affection for Granford. On the other hand, maybe he thought there was something in it for him. There was, of course, the money that the land sale would generate, some of which would flow to him. Would he take it and leave town?

After a few more moments of watching, he turned back to Meg. "Hey, how about that sink?"

"Sure. Hang on a sec." Meg fled eagerly through the back door. The padlock key hung on a nail next to the door. She grabbed it and went back outside, leading the way to the rickety barn. She opened the padlock, then let Stephen pull open the sagging door. He'd pitched his apple core at the edge of her driveway, which annoyed her.

"That's gotta be the one," Stephen said, pointing to a Victorian pedestal sink lurking in a dim corner. He lifted it easily and carried it to the van, slamming the door shut. "I'll get the barn door for you. Thanks for letting Seth use the space." He swung the creaking wooden door back into place and waited while Meg threaded the lock through the hasps again and closed it.

"So you don't have room at your place?" Meg asked, struggling for something safe to say.

"Nah, Seth just keeps collecting more and more. Don't know why he bothers with this old stuff, but some people like it. No accounting for taste."

"You don't like historic restorations?"

Stephen made a noise that sounded like a horse's sneeze. "Pfah! Penny-ante stuff. You want to make any money in this business, you've gotta go for volume. Housing developments, office buildings, that kind of thing. Not this one-house-at-a-time crap that Seth's into."

"There hasn't been a lot of that kind of construction around here for quite a while, has there?"

"But that's going to change, right? Granford Grange first and then maybe some housing complexes. Things are gonna be different soon, and I aim to be part of it." He pulled back his sleeve and looked at his watch. "Shoot, gotta go. Thanks again for storing this stuff."

"No problem. Oh, Stephen, is Seth around?"

"He's on a job over toward Belchertown—new construction, probably take all day. That's why he wants the sink, to show to the owners before he goes any further. Want me to give him a message?"

"No, thanks. I just had a question. It'll keep." She forced herself to smile.

"Right. Bye, then." Stephen slammed the van door and pulled out, leaving Meg staring after him, her mind racing. She leaned against the barn door and watched the van disappear toward the highway, then walked slowly back toward the house.

Stephen had answered a question she hadn't even known she had. He clearly hated the family plumbing business—and working for Seth?—and had visions of bigger, better things. And he had offered one more reason for Seth to recuse himself from the town's vote: not only did he stand to profit from the sale, but it could boost his business substantially. Funny, Seth hadn't mentioned it. So why wasn't Seth more enthusiastic?

Meg picked up Stephen's discarded apple core and took it inside to throw away. Her brain kept churning. She had too many bits and pieces that didn't fit together, and new ones kept popping up. Like Chandler coming on to half the women of Granford: who knew how many had fallen for his charm? And she had no way of knowing which ones might be capable of murder, although the list kept growing. And what about Cinda? Cinda had been with Chandler on the night that he'd died, after he had had drinks with someone. Was she that someone? If not, had Chandler told her who it was? Had she told the detective?

On the other hand, why would she have killed him? Based on what Meg had learned about her, Cinda was too smart to act out of anger over Chandler splitting with her. Unless, of course, he had planned to dismiss her from the Granford project and send her back to Boston. Cinda wanted to run this project—that much was obvious. How much control would Chandler have given her? And was managing Granford Grange enough of a motive to kill?

At the end of the day, edgy and frustrated, Meg made herself a cup of tea and, leaning on the countertop in the kitchen, contemplated the Great Meadow outside her window. Fancy name for a swamp. How appropriate: she felt as though she were wading through a swamp, trying to find a path, and she kept sinking deeper into it. Still, the view was soothing even at this bleak time of year. She shut her eyes and willed herself to relax, to think clearly. An occasional car passed on the road. One slowed, then pulled into her driveway with a crunch of gravel. She opened her eyes and saw Seth emerging from a car. He rapped at the back door, and she opened it.

"Hi, there," Seth said with his usual good cheer. "Stephen said you had a question? I was on my way home and thought I'd swing by. And I've got some information to pass on, although you'll have to tell me what it means." Then he took a harder look at her. "You all right?"

Meg sighed. "Just tired. Come on in."

Seth shut the door behind him and shucked off his coat, hanging it over the back of a kitchen chair. He stopped again, eyeing Meg curiously.

Meg realized he was waiting for her to do something. "Oh, sorry. Sit, please."

He sat down at the table, still watching her.

Meg poured two mugs of tea and sat across from him. "Why don't you go first?"

"Okay. I had a little chat earlier today with Art."

"And?"

"Detective Marcus is keeping him in the loop on the investigation, as a professional courtesy. He said you'd given something to the detective, something about a book?"

That's right, she hadn't had a chance to mention that to Seth. "Sorry—I haven't talked to you since, have I? When I had lunch with Cinda yesterday, I found a book that I had loaned to Chandler the day he was here. I'd forgotten all about it, but I recognized it when I saw it in Cinda's room. She said Chandler had given it to her."

"So?"

"It wasn't the book that was important, it was the bookmark. There was a receipt inside, a credit card slip with a time stamp for the night Chandler died. And it was for a lot of drinks, more than Chandler would have had alone, so I figured there was someone with him. I took it to the detective as soon as I left Cinda's, and he said he'd look into it. I'm glad to see that maybe he did. So what did he tell Art?"

"Okay, now what Art said makes more sense. He told me that the detective had the place checked out and found the server, who remembered Chandler. And he said Chandler did have a companion, and it was a woman."

"Could he identify her?" Meg said.

Seth shook his head. "The server was a guy, but ... to be blunt, he was more into men than women. So he remembered Chandler very well, down to his cuff links, but he couldn't remember much of anything about the woman, except that she was maybe thirtyish and had dark hair, kind of shoulder length. The description was too vague to be much use. It was late, and the place was dark, and he was coming off a long shift ... You get the picture."

"Too bad," Meg said glumly. One more dead end. Cinda in a wig? Not likely.

They drank their tea in silence for a few moments. Finally Meg said, "Seth, is there anyone else you can think of who wants to stop this project?"

He shook his head. "You think I haven't been over this in my head? Sure, there are lots of people who care a lot, but nobody I can think of who would be willing to kill someone. Is that how they do business in Boston—eliminate the opposition?"

Meg ignored his jibe. "What about someone that Chandler had promised something to and reneged on, or hadn't been willing to promise anything to?"

"Meg, you're not making a lot of sense."

She was beginning to feel desperate. "Seth, Chandler was a user. He used people, women in particular, to get information, and to do that he flattered them and wooed them and made them feel special, maybe even slept with them—and then dropped them when he had what he wanted."

"Are you talking about anyone in particular? Like, you, for instance?"

Meg shook her head hard. "No, not me. But we didn't last, as you know. Maybe that was part of the problem with us—I wasn't much use to him."

Seth's expression hardened. "Cinda?"

"Yes, Cinda. I talked to a friend of mine in Boston, and she said they were a couple. That surprised me, because Chandler liked to keep his private life and his professional life separate."

"That does put things in a different light," Seth said slowly.

"There's more. He dropped her, not too long ago. But she wasn't the only one he was fooling around with. And now there's this mystery woman he was with the night he died."

He help up a hand. "Meg, I don't want to hear what amounts to gossip. Maybe you don't like Cinda, but she's got a lot riding on this project professionally. I can't believe she would think that killing her boss was the best way to get what she wanted."

"Why not? Maybe she thought she could get away with it," Meg replied bitterly. "It sure gave her a great motive, especially if Chandler was about to send her back to Boston." But even to her own ears her argument sounded weak. Cinda resorting to murder? Improbable, as Seth had pointed out. Maybe it was time to give up: she couldn't prove anything to anyone, and her suspicions kept falling on deaf ears. Maybe she should just pack up and get out of Granford before she lost what was left of her sanity. Or dignity.

"Seth, why didn't you tell me you'd been married?" The words were out of her mouth before her brain caught up.

Seth looked startled at her abrupt change of subject, and as she watched, his expression changed. She wanted to crawl into a hole. He'd been a friend, nothing more, and now she was poking into his private life. She had no right to ask him anything personal—even though her personal life seemed to be common knowledge in Granford. She didn't belong here; she just kept getting it wrong.

"I didn't think it mattered," he said quietly after a long pause. "It was over a long time ago."

"Does she think so?" Meg parried. And hated herself for doing it. He'd as much as said it wasn't her business. What did she hope to gain?

"Meg, I don't know what you're getting at. Yes, I was married once. It ended. So what?"

"Rachel and Gail believe that Nancy thinks she still has a chance with you. If the plumbing business goes under."

Seth stood up, so abruptly that the mugs rattled on the table. "You've talked to Rachel and Gail about this? Jesus, Meg, what do you want?"

She stood up, too, and faced him. "I want to know who killed Chandler! I want to know why everybody around here knows things I don't. But this is Granford, where everybody has lived in their neighbors' hip pockets for the last two hundred years and can tell you what their crazy great-uncle ate for breakfast. I'm not part of this place, and I'm the one being accused of killing Chandler. It's not fair!"

As Meg fought back tears, she thought she saw pity on Seth's face. "Meg, I think you need to cool down. I'm sorry that you're a suspect, and I don't believe you killed him. But I think you're grasping at straws. I don't see that my ex-wife has anything to do with this, and I think you're throwing mud at Cinda because on some level you're jealous of her, whether or not you admit it. She took Chandler from you, and she's the one with the hot job."

"I never *had* Chandler! Not in any way that mattered. She was welcome to him. Tell me, Seth, did Cinda come on to you?"

"What? Try to seduce me, to get me to go along? You're suggesting she used Chandler's tactics? You really are losing it, Meg."

"I'm asking. Yes or no?" Meg said stubbornly.

Seth leaned back against the kitchen counter and crossed his arms. "No. Maybe I should take that as a compliment. Maybe she figured I wouldn't be easy to manipulate." He paused before adding, "Unlike the way Chandler manipulated some of the women around here. If what you say is true." His doubt was clear.

"Seth, I'm sorry I even had to bring this up. I know how it must sound." *Desperate.*

"Do you?" But his expression was still closed to her, and Seth chose his words carefully. "I can see how it looks to you. Cinda's smart, ambitious. Knows her business. Uses her charm when she has to. But last time I checked, that's not a crime. So, what are you proposing to do with your suspicions? Go to the detective? He already figures you're a jealous woman. Maybe he's not far off."

"Seth!" But even as she protested, she had to acknowledge that he had a point. Was she being irrational? Meg stood up and stalked across the kitchen, looking out at the gathering darkness. "Listen, I know you don't know me very well, but I really don't feel that way. I didn't know the woman before I came to Granford; I didn't know she was involved with Chandler. Chandler and I were over, period. So, for the record, no, I'm not trying to attack Cinda for my own personal reasons." She paused to gather her thoughts. "Seth, my own issues aside, if somebody doesn't get to the bottom of this, what if the town passes the article? It'll be too late to turn back."

"Probably. I hope it passes, for the sake of the town."

"And you want Cinda running the show in that case? Is the project really worth overlooking Chandler's murder?"

"Meg, you can't prove that Cinda had anything to do with this."

"Believe me, I know that. Look, I'm sorry about this whole mess, but I didn't ask for it."

Seth stood up. "I hate to leave things like this, but I've got to get going. Listen ... be careful, will you? This is a dangerous game you're playing, throwing accusations around." With a last look, he headed for the door.

"Seth, wait!"

He hesitated at the door. "What?"

"Can you postpone the Town Meeting?" Her last desperate shot.

He looked disgusted. "Meg, you have no idea what goes into planning a meeting. There are legal requirements, announcements, time limits, all that kind of thing. We just can't turn off the process because you have some vague suspicions. I'm sorry, I've got to go."

Meg didn't move, staring blindly into space as the door shut behind him.

She felt more miserable than she could ever remember feeling. How had things gone so horribly wrong? She had come to Granford to accomplish something simple: fix up the house and sell it. Somehow that had evolved into a murky soap opera slash murder, with her as a prime suspect. As far as she could tell, nobody was going to end up happy. Except possibly Cinda, assuming she managed to smooth everything over with her combination of charm and brains, and the project went ahead as scheduled. Cinda would get everything she wanted, and Meg would get … squat.

So why did it hurt so much? She could walk away from Granford once the house was sold and forget the whole mess. She could go someplace and start rebuilding her life, find a new job, new friends. Chandler would still be dead, but was it really any of her business?

The answer that popped into her head surprised her. She liked it here. She liked the house: it was tough, and it had withstood years of neglect and mistreatment. She admired the sense of community she had found in Granford. She liked the people she had met. She wanted to see the town prosper, yet retain its own character.

Was that what this was about? The place had gotten under her skin while she wasn't looking? And if that was true, maybe what she couldn't stomach was that Cinda held the power to twist things around to serve her own selfish ends. She couldn't stand by and watch while good and decent people got hurt for someone else's impersonal financial gain. She didn't want to see her orchard turned into a parking lot, putting Christopher out of a job, eradicating a piece of history. Maybe she had no control over how the town voted, but at least she could do her best to see that the citizens had all the facts before they made a decision.

Seth didn't believe her, and that hurt. If she was wrong, she had probably alienated him. And then she thought, *Damn, I'm going to have to find another plumber.*

But she wasn't done yet. She had one last option. If no one

was going to listen to her, she was going to have to make a lot more noise; if she had already destroyed her reputation in this town, she might as well go out in a blaze of glory. She had the perfect venue: the Special Town Meeting. As a registered voter and a local property owner, she had every right to speak at the meeting. And she was going to.

25

Meg chafed at the delay, but there was nothing she could do until the meeting Monday night. She spent the next few days holed up in her house—there was certainly plenty to keep her busy—but she couldn't shut up the nagging voices in her head. Somehow she was not surprised to see Frances's car pull into her driveway Sunday afternoon, but she was definitely relieved at the distraction. She opened the door before Frances had a chance to knock.

"Hi, Frances. What brings you here?"

"I wanted to talk to you about how we're handling the sale of your place. Can I come in?"

"Sure." Meg wasn't sure she was in any mood to talk business, but it beat her noisy thoughts. Frances walked into the hallway while Meg struggled with the door. When Meg had managed to close it, she turned to find Frances in the parlor.

"Nice," Frances said approvingly. "You're doing a great job."

"Thanks," Meg replied with mixed feelings. She was beginning to resent putting this much work into something she might not get to enjoy.

"Hey, did you get a chance to talk to Gail?" Frances rubbed an almost-affectionate hand over the now-bare plaster.

"I did, on Thursday. I told her what I was looking for and she said she'd dig around and see what she could come up with."

"Then she will. She's good about following through, when she can find the time."

"She said something about a job in town. And she has a family, doesn't she?"

"Sure does. Husband, two daughters, high school and middle

school, I think. Good kids. And she still finds time for volunteer stuff. I don't know how she does it."

"Do you know everybody in town?"

"Pretty much." Frances smiled. "Hard not to, when I've lived here all my life. And selling real estate means I've been inside most of the places here, at one time or another. And in case you're wondering, no spouse, no kiddies. Just didn't happen for me."

Meg couldn't think of a good answer for that. Her state wasn't very different: no spouse, no long-term relationships, no children even on the distant horizon. But at least Frances had a place where she belonged, which was more than Meg could say for herself.

"Can we sit?" Frances asked hesitantly.

"Sure. Is there something we need to talk about?" *Please let it not be bad news.* Meg wasn't sure she could handle any more.

"We've kept things pretty loose up to now, about me selling this place, right?"

Meg nodded, mystified.

"Well, business is tight, and after Chandler shut me out … I just thought we should get some things clear up front. It's customary to sign a contract with a Realtor, setting out terms and stuff, but in your case, your mother is co-owner?"

"Yes, but I can act on her behalf. Listen, Frances, before we go any further—"

Frances interrupted. "You aren't going to welch on me, are you? Sell out to the developers, cutting me out?"

Like Chandler? "No, I wouldn't do that. The thing is, I'm not sure I want to sell at all. If the project goes through, I may not have a choice about the orchard, but I'm beginning to think I might want to keep the house, or at least think about it awhile longer. But when and if I do sell, you're my Realtor, I promise."

"Fair enough. But I've been burned once, so I'm trying to protect myself. Nothing personal."

"Understood. Listen, Frances, can I pick your brain?"

"Sure. You still chewing on Chandler's murder?"

Meg nodded. "Who had the most to gain or lose, from a real estate perspective?"

"All the folks along the highway," Frances said promptly.

"You, for a start. Then the Chapins, next door. Theirs is probably the biggest single piece. The plumbing business sits right on the road there. They'd have to relocate, and that'd be a hassle. A bunch of other small lots, some already zoned commercial. About twenty people in all."

"Were most of them willing?"

Frances shrugged. "More or less. Like I said, the Chapins might suffer, but if the deal is fair they'll have enough cash to set up someplace else. Of course, it means that Mom's house will have a strip mall in the front yard."

"Is the money being offered fair?" Meg asked.

"To be honest, yeah, it is. Nobody is getting ripped off. Chandler wasn't a complete sleaze. At least, not *that* way." Frances made a sour face. "So most people will get a good deal, if the project happens."

"You think this is going to be approved?"

"At the meeting? Shoot, I really don't know. It's pretty close, you know? I think the town at large is pretty split between the 'keep it rural' bunch and the 'bring new life to Granford' crowd. So, the place is getting to you, eh?"

"I guess it is," Meg answered slowly. "I never thought much about putting down roots anywhere. I've been on my own since I went to college, and I figured I'd keep my options open, go wherever the job took me. And that worked fine for a while. But I come here, and I talk to people, and they have a very different perspective on where they belong. They have history, connections here. And I wonder if that's something I want." She laughed shortly. "If I even have that choice. After all, half the town thinks I killed Chandler."

"Maybe the detective, but the police chief doesn't," Frances replied. "I don't. Hey, give folks a chance—they don't even know you. I don't think they've all jumped to the conclusion that you're a murderer."

"But someone out there is. Damn it, Frances, who killed Chandler? Maybe he exploited people, but he didn't deserve to die."

"He sure was one busy boy around here, wasn't he? I get the feeling I wasn't the only one. You two didn't, uh, reconnect?"

"No, we did not!"

"What about his pretty little, um, colleague?"

Meg stared. "You knew they were involved? I didn't even know."

Frances laughed. "They tried to keep it professional in public, but you could tell, if you were looking. Am I wrong?"

"No, you got it right. Although a friend in Boston told me that Chandler and Cinda were over, too, about a month ago."

"Oh-ho!" Frances said. "The plot thickens! That must have been sticky for both of 'em."

"No doubt. Especially if he was tomcatting his way through the local female population, and Cinda knew about it. Even if it was for business, it must have stung."

Frances was watching her with a gleam in her eye. "Sure." Suddenly she snapped her fingers. "Damn, I almost forgot! There's someone else who has a stake here: Nancy Chapin."

"What? Seth's ex-wife?"

Frances nodded. "You know about her?"

"A little. But how is she involved? Did she know Chandler?"

"She owns a piece of land next to Seth's—bought it right after they got married. Near as I can tell, when they first got married she thought the plumbing business was going to expand and become something bigger and better. Besides, it was cheap when she bought it. I think her parents put up the money, right after the wedding. Not a big piece, but prime footage along the highway. So of course she would have known Chandler."

"Ah." Meg sat back in her chair and tried to process that information. Her mind was working slowly. "But that gives her a reason for wanting the deal to succeed, but not a reason for killing Chandler. Just the opposite, in fact." There went one more nice theory. Maybe Nancy could have been the woman with Chandler that night, but she made a lousy murder suspect: no motive. Unless maybe Chandler made a pass at her, too. Since she didn't know Nancy, it was hard to say how she would have reacted. Or maybe he had, and she had told Seth, and Seth had felt compelled to defend her honor ... No, this was getting far too convoluted. Still, it would be nice to know if Nancy was the mystery woman. Or if the detective even knew about her.

It was all too much. Her thinking was muddled. "Well, thanks for the information, Frances. And for the vote of confidence. I seem to keep alienating people around here."

"No, you don't. This is New England, remember? Bunch of stiff-necked Yankees, and they don't take kindly to strangers. But if you tough it out, you'll be fine. This murder stuff will all blow over."

"Amen to that."

"Look, Meg, I'm glad we had this little chat. We're good people here in Granford—except for one bad apple, I guess, whoever it is—and if you want to stick around, I think you'd like it. And we'd be happy to have you. Just let me know what you decide about the house, okay?"

"I guess I'll have to see what happens at the meeting before I make up my mind. But thanks, Frances, I appreciate the vote of confidence."

She watched from her doorstep as Frances pulled out. The air outside smelled of wet earth, and maybe a hint of spring, even though it had barely turned into February. Meg suddenly felt restless. She wanted to get out of the house. She certainly didn't want to be here when somebody else dropped by, which happened with alarming frequency.

Maybe it was time to pay her respects to the sisters who had gotten her into this mess, and to all the Warrens who had come before them. Even if she had no previous interest in the whole genealogy thing, the oldest Granford graveyard lay no more than a mile or two away, and she would have plenty of time to say hello to all the past Warrens before whatever warmth the February sun provided faded. Before she could talk herself out of it, she grabbed her coat and her keys and headed for her car.

She drove slowly toward town, turned at the stoplight on the highway, but then quickly made a left onto a local road, which her map told her led to the old cemetery. She knew roughly where it was, but she took a few wrong turns through residential neighborhoods before she spotted it. She pulled off the road and parked under a low-hanging pine tree, avoiding muddy patches. Out of the car, she surveyed the scene: on one side of the road, the cemetery spread over several acres, with the oldest stones close to the road where she stood. On the opposite side of the street was a row of generic ranch houses that looked as though they dated from the 1950s. There were few people around—probably all inside, watching TV and staying warm. Meg turned to the cemetery and found a gate through the chain-link fence.

For a time she wandered aimlessly, getting a feel for the place. The sinking sun blazed on the west-facing old stones. The grass beneath her feet was brown and muddy, and her footsteps made no sound. She noted a number of familiar names, including a few Chapins, but she wanted Warrens. At last she found a row of them, parallel to the road, and she hunkered down to study the stones. She could see several generations, side by side. The earliest was Stephen, who had built her house, according to Gail. He had died in 1796, and Meg noted the verse at the bottom of the stone: "Death is a Debt / To Nature due. / I paid my Debt / And so must you." Cheerful sentiment.

Then Deborah Warren, wife of Eli Warren, died 1823. Eli had died later, and his name had been added below hers on the stone in 1843. Meg reached out to push away the dead grass at the base so she could read the final inscription. She ran her finger carefully over the deeply etched letters.

THEIR GLASS WAS RUN THEIR WORK WAS DONE
FOR THEM GOD THOT IT BEST,
TO TAKE THEIR RANSOM'D SPIRITS HOME
TO HIS ETERNAL REST.

Meg's knees were stiffening, and the wind had picked up, teasing the edges of her coat. She stood up: time to check in on the rest of the Warrens. She spied Eli Junior, the carpenter, next in line, and his wife, Speedwell, had her own stone next to his. And then Eugene and Olive—offspring of Eli and Speedwell? Quickly Meg moved down the wavering line of stones, and finally located Lula and Nettie, tucked next to their parents—the maiden ladies who had held on for so long, who had somehow managed to maintain the nineteenth century in their home while the twentieth century passed them by. Here they all were, side by side, only a mile or two from where they had begun.

What was she doing here, freezing her toes? What did she

hope to find? Nettie and Lula were dead, and their line had died with them.

Or had it? After all, here she was. They had touched her life, even though they could not have foreseen it. Which meant that their memory lived on, in her, and even among other people in the town where they had been born and died. Maybe there was something to be said for the old New England tradition of keeping your dead nearby, where you couldn't forget them. Would anyone remember her when she was gone?

Not if she didn't stay long enough in one place—that much was clear. Maybe this wasn't the place, but it was time to think about where she really wanted to be. But first she needed to know how Chandler had died, and lay him to rest. Then she could figure out her own life.

She found a dry spot scattered with pine needles, sat down cross-legged, and wrapped her coat more snugly around her, her back against a tree, staring at the late Warrens. She was going to think this through or freeze to death trying. The thought made her smile: at least she'd be in the right place. *Okay, all you dead citizens of Granford, help me out here.* Who killed Chandler? Who had wanted Chandler dead, and who was capable of doing it? *Let's start with the old standbys: motive, means, opportunities.* She believed Cinda was involved in Chandler's murder, but she still couldn't figure out how. Cinda clearly had motive: control of the project, professional advancement, and a dash of revenge thrown in. But not means. Cinda could not have hauled Chandler's body to Granford and stuffed him in the septic tank.

Who else was on the short list? Frances, whom Chandler had toyed with and then dismissed? Motive, yes, but would she have had the opportunity? Christopher, who had devoted decades of his life to the orchard, only to see its existence—and his position at the university—threatened? No, Christopher had an alibi: he had been at the historical society meeting with her, until nearly ten. Although maybe Frances had brained Chandler and then called Christopher to help her dispose of the body later? But that would have been late at night, and Meg was sure she would have heard the killer and/or accomplice barging around her driveway with a body at that hour.

What about Gail, who might have succumbed to Chandler's

wiles and then lied about turning him away? She might've over-
heard Meg telling Christopher about the new septic tank. Gail
had been at the meeting early but had ducked out after a phone
call. If there had been a family crisis, surely someone could give
her an alibi.

The unknown brown-haired woman at the bar with Chandler?
Had the detective even looked for her, much less found her yet?

And then there was Seth, who might love his land more than
the town, whatever he said. Mister Good Guy, looking out for
everyone's best interests, even at his own expense. Maybe he'd
gotten tired of putting them first; maybe he'd just snapped. He
had the physical strength to do the deed, and he certainly knew
about the septic tank. The problem was, Meg couldn't visualize
Seth killing anyone. What's more, she didn't want to. There had
to be some nice guys left in the world.

Meg's mind spun off, shuffling the cast of characters: Chandler seducing Rachel, bringing down the wrath of her husband or
brothers? Seth had defended Rachel before, hadn't he? Or some
local developer or vendor who thought he was not getting due
consideration for the job? Or any combination of these? Maybe
this was like that old Agatha Christie story where it turned out that
everyone had done it. By the time Meg had worked through the
ever more absurd litany, she actually felt better.

She also realized she was shivering. The sun had fallen below
the horizon and it was cold; Meg didn't want to go back to her
empty house and put together a pathetic meal for one. A hot,
greasy pizza sounded appealing. There weren't a lot of other
choices for dining in Granford. Meg went back to her car and
headed for the highway.

She stopped at the first pizza place she came to, pulled into
the parking lot, and hurried into the relative warmth of the interior. The windows were steamed up, and she didn't see Stephen
Chapin until she was standing in line to order. For once he looked
almost cheerful, and after she had placed her order, he waved her
over with a grin. Meg hesitated about joining him: she didn't like
him much, but it would be rude to ignore him. She wove her way
through the tables, and it was only when she neared him that she
realized he already had a companion.

"Hey, hi, Meg. Pull up a chair. This is Nancy...Chapin.

Nancy, this is Meg Corey." He looked at Meg with a wicked gleam in his eye, pleased with his own little surprise. Was he trying to make mischief?

Meg sat. "Hi, Nancy. You're Seth's ex, right?" She rather enjoyed deflating Stephen's little bubble. If he'd hoped to catch her off guard, he'd failed.

Nancy managed a tight smile. "Oh, right—Stephen said you're at the Warren place. Too bad about the orchard. It used to be pretty in the spring."

"The deal's not settled yet," Meg replied. "What brings you this way?"

"Stephen and I get together now and then." She flinched as Stephen grinned, scooted his chair closer to her, and nudged her with his elbow.

Meg wondered what their relationship really was, but she didn't feel any need to explore further. Maybe Nancy was using Stephen to keep tabs on Seth, and on the Granford land deal. She studied Nancy: nicely dressed, trim, and with sleek dark hair. On an impulse, she said, "You must have known Chandler Hale."

Nancy nodded, her surprise clear. "Yes, I did. He approached me about selling my property. He wanted to get all his ducks in a row before this went to a vote in Granford."

"By any chance, did you see him the night he died?"

Stephen stiffened but said nothing, watching with wary eyes. Nancy looked down at the napkin she was shredding. "How do you know that?"

"Lucky guess. Have you told the police?"

"I did today. I would have sooner, but I was attending a business conference and didn't hear the news right away."

"What were you and Chandler talking about that night?"

Nancy looked up at her. "Why is that any of your business?"

Stephen bristled. "Jesus, Meg, you're way out of line! Nancy's right. What's it to you?"

Meg wondered why Stephen was defending Nancy. "Stephen, I'm suspected of killing Chandler, and I don't particularly like it. Nancy, I'm sorry if I'm being rude, but this *is* a murder investigation, you know."

Nancy glanced briefly at Stephen, then finally shrugged. "I'm not hiding anything. Yes, I wanted this Granford Grange project to go forward, and I wanted to unload that useless piece of land I own. Whatever possessed me . . . But Chandler was the one who got in touch with *me* and asked me to meet him for drinks in Northampton. Turns out he just wanted to know if I still had any pull with Seth, or if I knew what he was thinking. I told him no on both counts. I don't see Seth at all these days."

"Was that all?" Meg said carefully, avoiding looking at Stephen.

"Was that . . . ?" To Meg's surprise, Nancy blushed. "He hinted that . . ." She stopped.

Meg didn't press her. "I get it. I knew Chandler."

"So I've heard," Nancy said.

Stephen had watched this exchange with confusion. "Chandler was a jerk, all right. But just because he's dead doesn't mean that the project won't happen. Right, ladies?"

"So it seems," Meg said glumly.

Nancy ignored him and said to Meg, "Anyway, as I told the police, I left him at the bar around eight and went straight home. I was online for a couple of hours after that. I suppose, if it came down to it, someone could trace what sites I looked at. But I don't think anyone is going to bother. I left town the next morning."

Did she believe Nancy? Unfortunately, yes. Meg felt vaguely depressed. The police now knew who the mystery woman was, and she'd have to take Nancy off her suspect list. Not that she had ever ranked very high, but Meg was running out of candidates.

Stephen fidgeted in his seat. "Hey, Nancy, we better get going and let the lady eat in peace. Good to see you, Meg."

Stephen stood up, and Nancy followed suit more slowly. She looked as though she wanted to say something, but at that moment the guy behind the counter announced that Meg's order was ready. Meg stood up to retrieve it, and Nancy followed a few hesitant steps behind as Stephen waited by the door, shifting from one foot to the other.

"Meg . . ." Nancy began. "Seth, he . . . Oh, never mind. Nice to meet you." Nancy turned and fled toward Stephen, then followed him out the door, leaving Meg staring after her in confusion.

What had that been about? Meg collected her pizza, paid for it, then went back to the table, looking out through the misted windows, thinking hard. Frances and Rachel thought Nancy was still hung up on Seth. Nancy had been with Chandler on the fatal night. Stephen and Nancy knew each other and had kept in touch. The last was the only new piece for the puzzle, and it didn't fit. Neither did any of the others.

The pizza was mediocre. *Granford can use some new restaurants*, Meg reflected as she chewed the rubbery cheese. *Wonder if it'll get them.*

26

Monday. The scheduled date for the Special Town Meeting. Meg had done her homework, had reviewed the rules, and had figured out her right to speak: as long as she addressed her comments to the moderator, rather than any individual, she'd be fine. Theoretically. The reality might be something else. She drove to the high school, which she had never seen, with some trepidation.

Even though she had arrived early, the parking lot was nearly full, and the only spot Meg could find was at the far end. That didn't surprise her, though, given what she knew about opinions in the town—every voter had a right to attend and to have their say, and nobody was going to miss this piece of local theater. Once inside, Meg queued up behind a line of people and waited until her name was checked off the voter list, then followed the herd to the school's gymnasium. Local police flanked the doorway, and more were stationed inside. Were they expecting trouble?

Meg had heard that meetings like this one were generally held in the school's auditorium, which had room for perhaps four hundred people. The shift to the larger gymnasium signaled higher expectations. Tables were set up at one end, and behind them, a large projection screen had been jerry-rigged, awkwardly dangling from the rafters above. Meg made her way down one of the aisles, choosing a seat not far from a microphone, feeling peculiarly isolated. Everyone else seemed to have come with friends, and there was much calling back and forth and joking among groups. Was she the only stranger here? She looked around for a familiar face and spotted Frances sitting on the bleachers on the other side of the room.

Frances waved and gave her a thumbs-up but stayed where she was.

Meg searched the voluble crowd for any more familiar faces. She spotted Gail across the room and nodded to her. Gail waved, then plunged back into conversation with the person sitting next to her. Christopher had already told her he wasn't planning to come, and she understood why. Who would want to witness the official eradication of a large part of his life? She didn't see Rachel either, but Rachel didn't live in Granford anymore, and she wasn't as invested in the future of what had been her family's land as her brother Seth was.

The seats filled rapidly, both the bleachers and the folding chairs set up on the polished wood floor, the crowd swelling to several hundred people, by Meg's rough count. The din grew, bouncing off the cinder block walls. People kept pouring in, until they were lined up two deep along the back wall. The person Meg assumed was the moderator stepped to the microphone at the podium and made a garbled announcement about keeping the aisles clear for fire safety reasons, and people shuffled to redistribute themselves. As the clock clicked past the designated seven o'clock starting time, Meg saw the selectmen gathered in a clump behind the tables at the front. And then Cinda walked in, flanked by a pair of younger colleagues—assistants already? Cinda pointed them toward the projector already set up, and they scurried toward it.

Meg scanned the name tags set up on the tables at the front: selectmen on one side, members of the town's finance committee on the other. The town manager merited his own small table between the two. The moderator's podium with its own microphone stood front and center. Meg found Seth's nameplate among the selectmen, but there was no sign of him. There were two microphones set up in the aisles for the use of the attendees.

Having dispatched her minions, Cinda looked around at the crowd, then approached the selectmen. Meg watched her in action: what she did wasn't exactly flirting, but she made a point of laying a hand on the arm of one and looking up at him from under her artfully enhanced lashes. Meg noted that she didn't speak to the two women members, no doubt saving her ammunition for where it would do the most good.

Seth finally came in, looking distracted. Meg didn't know whether she wanted to try to catch his eye, or if she'd rather duck down in her seat and hide. In the end, she did nothing, watching. If he saw her, he could make the first move.

Out of the corner of her eye, Meg was surprised to see Stephen Chapin also slide in through one of the side doors—she wouldn't have pegged him as particularly civic minded, although of course he did have something at stake here. He found himself a space along the wall near the door and leaned back against the wall, crossing his arms. His eyes were on the group at the front, and he looked ... smug?

The moderator called the meeting to order. "Welcome to the Granford Special Town Meeting. I hope this one will go a little more smoothly than the last few." There was a smattering of laughter from the audience. The moderator scanned the audience. "I think we have a quorum." Another laugh rippled through the crowd. "We will begin by reciting the Pledge of Allegiance."

The crowd struggled unevenly to their feet and mumbled through the Pledge of Allegiance. The moderator resumed. "This meeting is called to order. There is a single article on the warrant for this evening: a vote to approve the development project known as Granford Grange and to empower the board of selectmen to represent the town's interests in this project. Mr. Chairman, will you read the article?"

The chair of the board of selectmen, whom Meg recognized from the bank meeting as Tom Moody, read the brief text into the record. He then went on. "I'm sure most of you know Cinda Patterson, who recently took over management of the project"—Meg noted that he carefully avoided mentioning why Cinda was now in charge—"and I think we will all agree she's done an admirable job. She has asked if she could make a final summary presentation to the group tonight, with updated plans and figures, and she will be available to answer any questions you have."

Seth interrupted at that moment. "Mr. Moderator, point of order, please? I will not be voting on this article, since I have a direct interest in the outcome. I'm here as an observer, although I'll be happy to respond to any technical questions relating to the project, as they apply to the town's role."

"Duly noted, Mr. Chapin. Now, let me refresh your memories about how this meeting will be conducted …" The moderator launched into a recital of the rules, and requested that members of the audience confine their comments to him and refrain from name-calling and other outbursts. His last request met with a round of scattered boos. After staring down the culprits, he gestured to Cinda. "Ms. Patterson, would you like to begin?"

Cinda, who had taken a seat in the front row of chairs, rose quickly. She nodded at the young man running the projector, and an artist's rendering of a glossy commercial complex sprang up on the suspended screens. Cinda equipped herself with a handheld microphone, smiled at the audience, and launched into her speech.

"Good evening, residents of Granford, and thank you all for coming out on this cold night. It's my pleasure to have the chance to speak with you tonight, and share Puritan Bank's vision for this project and what it can do for Granford. Before I begin, I'd like to say that Chandler Hale's death was tragic, and he will be missed, but I can assure you that his absence in no way impacts the project. The bank is committed to working with your community leaders to make this happen.

"I'd like first to review the project and give you a quick outline of the plans …" Cinda proceeded to expound on square footage, anticipated foot and auto traffic, secondary access, and other related issues. Meg tuned out, concentrating instead on watching rather than listening to Cinda's performance. She was good, no question. She was well armed with numbers and details, yet managed to avoid boring the townspeople. Her slides were limited in number, professional in execution; her pacing was fluid and unforced. If Meg hadn't known what Cinda had done, she would have been impressed. She would have been happy to vote to move forward. Everything sounded wonderful. Too bad she was sure that Cinda was involved in a murder.

Ten minutes later Cinda was winding down, without a hair out of place. She had the audience eating out of her hand. Finally she smiled and said, "Thank you for your attention. I'm sure you all have some questions, and I'll be happy to answer them. Mr. Moderator? Do you have to do something official for that?"

The moderator smiled approvingly. "Yes, Ms. Patterson." He turned to the audience. "For those of you not familiar with the process, this is the time for discussion. The floor is now open for questions. Please use the microphones set up for that purpose. Identify yourself and where you live. And don't push—we'll give you time to ask everything you want."

A short line had formed at each of the audience microphones, and the moderator called on each speaker in turn, alternating between the sides. One man complained that he wouldn't be able to get in and out of his driveway if the access roads were located as planned; a woman worried about noise and litter. A half hour passed, then an hour. As Frances had hinted, opinions were evenly divided, and questions ranged from thoughtful to silly. Cinda answered them all with patience and intelligence. When Meg sneaked a look at Stephen, he was smiling.

When there were only a couple of people left in the line on her side, Meg stood up, her heart pounding. Seth saw her for the first time and looked startled. He stared at her as she joined the end of the line, and she returned his look with as much calm as she could muster. His expression gave nothing away.

One person, then another spoke. The man ahead of her wrapped up his statement, reading from a sheaf of three-by-five note cards. Mouth dry, Meg stepped up to the microphone, and the moderator looked at her expectantly.

Meg swallowed, once, twice. "Mr. Moderator, my name is Meg Corey. I've just moved to Granford, and I live on County Line Road. I've never participated in a meeting like this, but I understand I have the right to comment?"

"Yes, that's right. Limit your comments to the article under discussion, and address your question to me. Go ahead."

"I have a question for Ms. Patterson. Mr. Moderator, I understand that Ms. Patterson is the project manager for this building project, representing Puritan Bank? And that she will be responsible for continuing oversight of the financial aspects of the project?"

"Yes, that's correct. Is that your question?"

"No." Meg took a deep breath. "I want to know what would happen if Ms. Patterson was unable to continue in that role, especially in light of the death of her predecessor, Mr. Hale." She sneaked a glance at Cinda, who was watching her with barely concealed hostility.

The moderator turned to Cinda. "Ms. Patterson, would you like to respond to that?"

Cinda smiled sweetly. "Of course. Ms. Corey, I'm glad you raised that issue, because I'm sure we are all concerned about Chandler's death and the continuity of oversight. I worked closely with him on this, and I am fully up to speed on the details. I expect to continue to be an active part of this project, and I can assure you that I will brief the members of Puritan Bank's commercial development department so that Granford will have the full advantage of the bank's expertise. Does that answer your question?"

Meg looked her in the eye. "Yes, thank you. I was concerned that the project, and the town, might suffer if you were found to be involved in Chandler Hale's murder."

27

There was a moment of startled silence, followed by a roar of voices as everyone started talking at once. Meg stayed at the microphone, but she realized she was trembling, and she was strongly tempted to grab the microphone stand for support. The moderator was pounding on the podium, trying to restore order.

"Quiet, please!" He waited a moment for the storm to subside. "Ms., uh, Corey, is it? That is an extraordinary statement. And as far as I know, this is not the appropriate time or place to raise such an issue. We are here to discuss a community project, not fling unfounded personal accusations."

Meg found her voice. "Excuse me, but this does have an immediate bearing on the future of that project. And it is not unfounded. There is evidence that suggests that Cinda Patterson was involved in Chandler Hale's death." Meg fought a childish desire to cross her fingers, because she knew just how flimsy her evidence was. But her goal now was to delay the vote, to allow time to find out if Cinda had been involved; proof could come later.

The uproar surged, louder than before; the moderator's pounding did little to quell it. He looked helplessly at the police officers posted at the doors and they began to move, slowly and deliberately, toward Meg. As she watched their advance, she leaned again toward the microphone. "I will be happy to share that evidence with the proper authorities."

Conscious of the looming presence of the officers, Meg looked at the cluster of people at the front, first at Seth, then at Cinda. Meg couldn't read Seth's expression, but he didn't look surprised. Cinda, on the other hand, appeared headed for an explosion. Unlovely red blotches mottled her china-pale complexion; her teeth were clenched, her nostrils pinched as she tried to control her rising rage. Very unattractive. Meg decided to take another poke at her, while she had the chance—before the police officers dragged her away. "Ms. Patterson, would you care to respond?"

Cinda's knuckles were white on the microphone she gripped. When she finally managed to speak, her voice was shrill. "Of course I do! How dare you say something like that? I ... I ... I'll sue you, for defamation of character, libel, whatever! Chandler was a friend and colleague."

"He was more than that, wasn't he, Ms. Patterson?" Meg kept her eyes on Cinda, ignoring the hubbub around her.

The moderator had resumed his frantic pounding on the podium, until the head of his wooden gavel broke off and went flying. Then he started yelling into his microphone. "Ms. Corey, I must ask you to leave immediately. This line of discussion is not appropriate for this meeting." He nodded to the police officers.

Seth stood up, holding the table microphone. "Oh, let her talk. I think we can pretty well assume that the business part of this meeting is over, and I believe a lot of people here want to hear what she has to say." Several members of the audience yelled out encouragement, while others booed. The officers halted, confused. The moderator threw up his hands. "Hell, go ahead. This is a disaster anyway."

Seth nodded toward Meg. "Go on."

Meg wasn't sure who she was supposed to be addressing at this point, so she kept her eyes fixed on Seth. "You all know who I am, mostly because Chandler Hale's body was found on my property in Granford. It's no secret that I had a prior relationship with him, but what you don't know is that Cinda Patterson also had a romantic relationship with Chandler Hale. That in itself is not an issue—what people do in private is their own business—but when it ended, she was afraid that she would be forced off this project, maybe even lose her job with Puritan Bank. She wasn't going to sit back and take that, so Chandler had to be ... removed."

"Have you gone to the police?"

"Why hasn't she been arrested?"

"How'd she do it?"

A jumble of voices threw out questions. Meg grabbed at the only one for which she had an answer. "The state police think I'm a suspect in his death. But so is Cinda Patterson, or she should be. Her motives were a lot better than mine. Cinda was with Chandler the night he died, and the police have proof of that. Before you endorse the Granford Grange project tonight, with her as its manager, I'd like to know what she's hiding."

And then the eyes in the room shifted to Cinda, who had regained control of her emotions. She spoke with an unsettling icy calm. "Ms. Corey, I feel sorry for you. You didn't mention to this crowd that it was Chandler Hale who ended your relationship with him. And as for my relationship with Chandler—which as you rightly point out is none of your business—we were professional colleagues first and foremost, and we both wanted this project to work. I think everyone here should look closely at your own motives."

Meg regarded her levelly. "No, Cinda, that's not the whole story. You and Chandler were involved, and then Chandler got tired of you, just like he got tired of me. It was over, and you couldn't accept that. You don't like to lose, do you? And you saw the chance to take over the whole development deal, make a name for yourself at the bank, and take your revenge on Chandler, all at once. Great package, huh? No one said you weren't smart."

The room had fallen silent as everyone focused on the interchange, fascinated by the soap opera unfolding before them. Finally Seth abandoned his place at the table, strode to the moderator's central podium, and spoke into the microphone. "I think we will all agree that the article on the warrant is not going to come to a vote tonight. If there's any shred of legal structure left to this meeting, I move that we indefinitely postpone the article until the selectmen can determine a date for a continuation of this meeting. Do I have a second?"

Several people shouted out "second" at the same time. The moderator nodded at Seth and leaned toward the microphone. "Voice vote. Yeas?"

A surge of voices shouted "yea." It was clear that no vote for the nays would be needed.

"The motion for postponement passes. The selectmen will determine when we will reconvene. Please, all of you, go home now and let us sort this out."

Seth glanced toward the police officers flanking Meg as she stood forlornly in the middle of the aisle. Meg wondered briefly if what Seth had just done carried any legal weight. But what did it matter? People would be sorting out tonight's events for years to come. Right or wrong, she'd given them a new piece of local mythology.

And at the same time, shocked herself. Never in her safe and tidy life had she stood up and spoken out in public like this, especially with such flimsy grounds. Of course, how often did anyone have the opportunity to accuse someone of murder, much less publicly? If she hadn't been so horrified, the whole thing might have seemed funny to her: she had certainly found a way to introduce herself to a lot more people of the town. Although right now they might be more inclined to tar and feather her than to welcome her with open arms.

The crowd rose uncertainly, grumbling among themselves, then began to trickle out. Several people slid by Meg, avoiding looking at her; others stared openly as they passed. As Meg watched, Seth approached Cinda and leaned close to say something to her. For once, Cinda didn't turn on the charm. She said something, and Seth responded calmly, gesturing toward the waiting police. She looked their way, then back at Seth, and nodded once, her neck stiff. She summoned her assistants to gather up her computer and the projector, and Seth escorted her up the aisle until they were standing close to Meg.

"I think we should take this out of here, don't you?" Seth said.

Meg met Cinda's eyes. "By all means. I'm happy to talk with the police."

Art Preston finally pushed his way against the tide of the departing crowd. "Ladies, why don't you come with me? Oh, not together. Collins, why don't you take Ms. Corey here, and Ms. Patterson can ride with me."

"Are you taking us into custody?" Meg demanded.

"No, Ms. Corey, nothing like that. I just thought the station would be an appropriate place to sit down and talk this through. You have a problem with that?"

Cinda had her temper under control, but her flushed skin betrayed her. "This is outrageous! You can't do this to me, based on nothing but the wild accusations of this ... woman."

"I'm afraid we can, ma'am. In fact, we have to. An accusation has been made, and there's enough credibility that we need to follow up. The sooner you talk with us, the sooner we can get it all cleared up. Right?"

Meg squared her shoulders. "No problem, Chief."

"Well, then, let's go, before it gets any later."

"Art, I'm coming with you." Seth's interruption startled Meg.

"No need, Seth," Art answered.

"I think I'd better."

"If that's what you want." Art shrugged. "Ms. Patterson?" Cinda gave Meg one last hostile glare, then stalked toward the door, with Preston following in her wake. Officer Collins hovered, unsure of his next move: Meg wasn't exactly a prisoner, but the police chief had said to take charge of her.

Seth stepped up. "It's okay, Gus. I just want a word with Ms. Corey. She's not going to cut and run. Are you, Meg?"

"Of course not. I want this cleared up as much as anybody."

After another confused look, Collins turned and took a few deliberate paces toward the nearest exit door, then stopped and turned to watch them.

"Meg, do you have any idea what you're doing?" Seth demanded.

No, not really. "Yes. I've derailed the development project until we can figure out who killed Chandler."

"Well, this isn't the best way of doing it. Do you have anything more than you did a few days ago?"

Meg looked at him for several seconds. He was right: she didn't have a leg to stand on, just a lot of vague suspicions, even if they all pointed in one direction. But at least she had bought some time. "No," she admitted.

He shook his head. "Look, we'd better get going. It may be a long night."

Meg nodded and turned to leave, Seth close behind. She had no idea what Seth was thinking. She had come waltzing in out of nowhere and made a flogging mess of things, on his home turf. Well, time to go lay out what she knew to the police and let them laugh at her. She knew how full of holes her theory was, but she had to follow through. She knew in her gut that Cinda had been involved, and she wasn't about to let her get away with it, not without a fight. Granford deserved better. But how could she get Cinda to implicate herself? She'd been pretty damn careful so far.

Officer Collins waited silently until Meg climbed into his police cruiser. She had to give the police credit; they weren't taking any chances until they had heard both of their stories and could make a guess who the good guys or bad guys were. Gals. Whatever. She sat silently in the rear seat as they drove the short blocks to the police station. She felt powerless, dragged along by the process she had started without any idea where it was going to end up. *Damn it, Meg, what's wrong with you? Chandler died, and you want to see that avenged. Fine. You think Cinda did it. Less fine, but that's what you believe. Now you're about to go head-to-head with the lovely Cinda—smart, sophisticated, determined Cinda.* Who would stop at nothing to get her own way. And, she had to admit, Cinda could point to plenty of evidence that Meg had as much reason to kill Chandler as she did. The same reasons, in fact: Chandler had toyed with her and dumped her. And that had driven her to the wilds of Granford—or so Cinda would claim. Maybe she should admire Cinda: Cinda had stood up for herself and sought revenge, had acted instead of running away. Maybe murder was a little extreme, but at least Cinda didn't lack self-esteem.

Meg reviewed the facts in her mind. *Keep it simple. Tell them what you know, and what you think happened.* And Meg knew she was right, and hoped in her heart of hearts that when faced with the truth, Cinda would crumble.

So why didn't she believe that was going to happen?

It was probably too much to hope that Seth would support her, even though his word would carry a lot more weight with the police than hers would. But at least the chief of police was willing to listen—and the Town Meeting had been postponed.

They had arrived at the police station. As Officer Collins helped her politely out of the backseat, Meg stole a look at her watch. Was it really only nine? How long were they going to be here? Would they put them all together or interview them separately, like on television? Did the Granford station even have more than one interrogation room? Maybe they'd have to go someplace else, like the church or town hall or even the historical society. Meg suppressed a hysterical giggle at the mental image of giving a statement under the glassy stares of all those long-dead animals. *Get a grip, Meg!*

Officer Collins led her to a small room with a table and two chairs. She sat down and listened to Cinda's voice raised in obvious displeasure, out in the hall; she couldn't hear any words, but her tone was clear. Chief Preston came in and shut the door behind him.

"Well, Meg, you've certainly started something here."

"I didn't do it just to make trouble, you know," she protested. "Chandler was murdered and dumped on my property, so I'm involved. I'm just trying to clear myself. What happens now?"

Art sighed. "Meg, you know I don't have any jurisdiction over the murder. The state police are handling that."

"I know that! I've talked to them, and they don't believe me. And if you can't do anything, why am I here? And Cinda?"

"I just wanted to get you out of that meeting before I had a riot on my hands, and bringing you and Ms. Patterson here seemed to be the easiest solution. Look, I'll give you the benefit of the doubt. Tell me what you've got, and I'll decide whether it's worth calling Marcus." He pulled out a small notepad and opened it. "Why do you think Cinda Patterson was part of Chandler's murder, in any way, shape, or form?"

Meg inhaled, then let her breath out slowly, buying time. Finally she launched into her recital of the sequence of events, starting with her defunct relationship with Chandler, her flight to Granford, and her interactions with Cinda, and ending with the discovery of the book and the receipt and the conclusions she had drawn from it.

Preston nodded. "Meg, you haven't told me anything I don't know. Marcus has kept me filled in on the investigation. He told me about that receipt, and what he found when he followed up on it. But the waiter at the restaurant wasn't much use, and his description was pretty vague—a woman with dark hair. Could've been almost anybody."

Meg shook her head impatiently. "I know. In fact, I know who the woman at the bar was, and so does the detective now—Seth's ex, Nancy. But let me finish. When Chandler died, Cinda stepped into his shoes on the project, right? When I met her, I didn't trust Cinda, so I asked a friend in Boston to ask around a little. I wanted her to find out how Cinda came to take over this project. What she found was that Cinda arrived at the bank and shot straight up the ladder, with Chandler as her mentor. But my friend also said that Cinda and Chandler had been involved in a personal relationship."

"Like you used to be." His voice was not unkind.

Meg looked at Art Preston's face, trying to find any encouragement. "Yes. Look, I'm not stupid. What I've told you, you can take in more than one way. My history with Chandler gives me a motive to kill him and to lay the blame on Cinda. But my friend also said that Chandler had broken up with Cinda not long before he died. Which means not only was she jilted by him but she also might have been worried about losing her job, or at least this project—although I'm sure she would have sued him up one side and down the other for sexual harassment if that had happened. So she had stronger motives than I did, overall."

Chief Preston sighed. "Meg, this is all very interesting, but I haven't heard anything new, and certainly nothing the state police could act on. You don't like the woman, but so what? It's a big jump to accusing her of murder."

"I'm getting to that. Let me break it down: I saw Chandler on Monday afternoon, and gave him that book. The detective found out that Chandler was in his Boston office the next day, Tuesday, but he came back that evening. He went out again to some bar in Northampton and had drinks with Nancy Chapin. He paid for the drinks by credit card, which tells us that he was still alive at eight fifteen. After that, he walked back to the hotel, to his room. Maybe he picked up the book to read it, but for whatever reason, he stuck in the credit card slip, maybe as a bookmark. So when did Cinda get the book? Did he deliver the book to her? Or did she come to his room? Maybe she had seen him with Nancy and went a little nuts. Or maybe she made one last play for him and he rejected her or threatened her job, and she lost control. All we know for sure is that he died that night and ended up in my septic tank, before I got home at ten."

Preston didn't look convinced. "There's another piece you don't have. Cinda and Chandler were together in his room at eight thirty, to take a conference call. It lasted until nine or so. They were talking to somebody in their Boston office, and there's a record of it—Marcus checked it out. Chandler was still alive at nine."

"And with Cinda! Doesn't that look suspicious to you?"

"She says she left after the call and went back to her room. And doesn't that make it even more unlikely that she did the deed? Say she hit him over the head, in a fit of whatever—without leaving any evidence in the room, mind you. What did she do about the body? Can you see her dragging him out of the building and driving him to your backyard? And the timing's pretty tight. You were home by ten, right? So she had to kill him and get him to your place and hide the body before that, all in an hour. Assuming she even knew the hole was there, and what it was. Would you believe this story if you heard it?"

The combination of fatigue and desperation was catching up with Meg. "I know it sounds silly if you put it like that, but she could have had help. And she did know about the hole—she'd seen it."

"Say she did have help. You have any candidates in mind?"

Meg felt a stab of despair. This interview was going as badly as she had feared. "No, but from what I've seen, she's pretty good at getting men to do whatever she wants. Somebody out there was an easy target. Look, add up all the pieces. Cinda is smart, ambitious, determined. She wanted Chandler, and she wanted this project. She lost Chandler, but she wasn't about to lose the rest of it. So she got rid of him."

Preston stood up. "Meg, I'm sorry, but I think we're done here. You've disrupted a Town Meeting for your own ends, whatever they are. You've fed me a line of BS that's straight out of a bad movie. I think you're a good person, but maybe you've been under a little too much stress lately. Ending a relationship, losing your job, moving to a new place—they're all hard, and you've been hit by all of them in a short time. I'll see if I can persuade Ms. Patterson not to take legal action against you, and I don't know if the town can hit you with anything, but I have to say, you haven't given me a thing that I can do anything about. I'm sorry, really I am."

Why had she expected anything else? And he was right: given a choice, why should he believe her? "I'm sorry you feel that way, but I can understand how it looks to you. Am I free to leave?"

"Sure. I don't even have jurisdiction on this, you know."

"I know. But, can I ask one last thing? Try to make sure Detective Marcus keeps looking, will you?"

"I'll do what I can, Meg. I don't want to see someone get away with this any more than you do. Anyway, I guess your car's still over at the school. I'll find an officer to take you back there."

Meg stood up wearily and followed him to the waiting area. Cinda and Seth were seated side by side; Cinda had her hand on Seth's arm and was leaning close to him, talking earnestly. But when the door opened, she stood quickly. She eyed Meg with icy contempt, then turned to Chief Preston with a practiced smile.

"Are you ready for me now? I do hope we can get this resolved quickly. I have no idea what this woman has been telling you, but I'm more than happy to give you my story."

"Come right in. Meg, you wait here till I track down Collins for that ride. Seth, you mind hanging around awhile longer?" Meg sank into the chair Cinda had vacated.

Meg stared at the worn pattern on the floor, wondering how long she was going to have to sit here. How long before Seth would speak to her again, if ever. She felt numb. How had everything gone so horribly wrong? She had just stood up in a public meeting and accused someone of murder. And—surprise— nobody believed her. But she'd tried to go through the right channels, and no one had paid attention to her. Maybe she was desperate, but she hadn't seen any other way to get this out into the open, or to stop the juggernaut that would change the face of the town.

"You want coffee?" Seth's voice startled her from her thoughts.

"What? Oh, sure. Sugar, please." She watched him stride off toward a small room near the reception area. Obviously he knew where the coffee was; obviously he'd been here before, and not as a suspect. Obviously he belonged here, and she didn't. She wondered how long it would take to sell her house so she could leave for good.

"Here." Seth was back with the coffee. Meg took the cup and stirred it idly with the plastic straw. She had no idea what to say, so she just waited.

"She explained about the book," Seth said quietly.

"Oh?" Meg found she didn't really care anymore.

"She says Chandler called her when he got back to the hotel, about eight thirty, and she went to his room so they could take a conference call. Some guy from the bank in Boston, following up on something Chandler had asked for earlier that day. Anyway, there's a phone record, and the guy remembers talking to both of them. Cinda claims that was when Chandler fobbed that book on her, and then she went back to her room for the night. End of story. So Chandler was still alive at nine."

"Convenient, isn't it? Probably some junior number cruncher who had to work late to run the latest numbers for the deal." It would have saved her a lot of useless worrying if the detective had told her about Cinda's alibi, and now she'd made a fool of herself publicly. But there was still that hour after the phone call ended. Plenty of time to drive Chandler's body from Northampton to Granford, if she'd had some help.

"I still don't like it," Meg said stubbornly. "She's hiding something. And she still could have done it, with help. The timing might be tight, but it's possible. She wants us to believe that she tucked herself in with that book while some unknown killer showed up at Chandler's door at 9:02 and killed him, and then disposed of the body in a convenient hole several towns away?"

"Maybe." Seth seemed unconcerned—or maybe he was just humoring her. "But, Meg, there's no evidence to connect her to his death, no matter what you want to believe."

He was right, and Meg knew it. She lapsed into silence. After no more than fifteen minutes, the door to the interview room opened, and Chief Preston escorted Cinda out. She was laughing at something he had said, and looked completely at ease. Meg's heart sank: Cinda had won over yet another male? How did some women manage to have that effect on men? How could men be so willfully oblivious? Meg stood up, as did Seth.

The chief nodded to Meg, with a notable lack of warmth. "You're both free to go. Oh, Ms. Corey, I believe Collins is out on a call, but if you can wait a bit—"

Seth broke in. "Listen, I can give Meg a ride, if you're tied up."

Meg turned to him in surprise, just as Preston said, "Thanks, if you don't mind."

"No problem. You ready, Meg?" Seth asked.

"Yes. Just take me back to my car, will you? Then you can go on your merry way." A wave of exhaustion washed over her.

Seth led the way to the parking lot. They drove in silence back to the school, and Seth pulled up by her car. "Meg, I know you acted with the best of intentions. And this isn't over yet."

Meg nodded, more to herself than to Seth. What choice had she, anyway? "Oh, don't be nice to me. You think I'm crazy, too. Don't worry, I haven't got anything more to add." Meg opened the door and got out. The parking lot was dark and empty, and a cold wind swept across the asphalt. She climbed quickly into her car and watched Seth pull away, then started her engine. She was in no rush to get back to her house, but she had nowhere else to go. At least she had bought some time for the town.

Damn! Cinda was going to get away with it. And so was her shadowy accomplice, whoever that was. Meg was running out of answers.

Time to go home and face the silence.

28

Meg drove the short distance home on autopilot. *What now, Meg? You've managed to alienate just about everyone in Granford, from your few almost friends to total strangers. Worse, now you look like a fool, someone to be pitied.* Time to go back to Plan A: sell the house as fast as possible and get out of town. And find a life somewhere else, because she doubted she would be welcome here.

As she approached the old house, she looked at it dispassionately. In the winter dark, it was still lovely, strong and square. The few lights that she had left on were glowing gold. Meg pulled around to the side near the barn, turned off the engine, and slumped in her seat, unable to move. She was tired. No, worse, she was tired and depressed. She had tried to do the right thing, had talked to the state police, told the truth, but no one had wanted to listen. So she had stood up in public and made her case, but it still looked like no one wanted to believe her. She was the outsider, and the community would close ranks against her. Of course, Cinda was an outsider, too, but she came equipped with charm and with the promise of a venture that would bring money and new life to the town. How could she compete with that? *All right, Meg. You can't sit here all night.* She smiled wryly at the image of someone coming by and finding her frozen corpse still sitting in the car.

She hauled herself out of the car and walked toward the back door, jiggling her keys in her hand. Then she stopped: even in the dim light, it was clear that the storm door hung askew, the lock splintered in the jamb. Someone had broken into her house; someone might still be there. She fumbled in her bag for her cell phone and punched in 911. When the operator answered, she said in a low voice, "This is Meg Corey at 81 County Line Road in Granford. There's an intruder in the house. Send somebody— now!" She waited while the operator repeated the information.

"Please stay on the line, ma'am," the operator's tinny voice instructed.

"Okay," Meg answered, and then looked up to see Stephen Chapin looming in her doorway. He must have stopped somewhere between the meeting at the high school and her house, because he was obviously drunk—swaying, pig-eyed drunk. And angry. Why was he here? Her heart started racing, and she looked down at the phone still in her hand.

"'Bout time you got here. We need to talk," he slurred. He lurched down the steps, and only then did he see the phone in her hand. "Dammit!" he swore, and swatted it out of her hand. She heard it skitter into the foliage next to the house. He grabbed her arm and dragged her toward the door, and she didn't resist.

Maybe if she started talking to him, she could calm him down. "Stephen," she said, striving for a normal tone, "how did you get here? I didn't see your car."

He shoved her into the kitchen, and she hit the counter hard. "Left it back at the office. Had to stop there for . . . for . . ."

He appeared to have lost his train of thought, but Meg was willing to bet he had kept a bottle of something stashed there. And then he had walked over? Well, why not? It was less than a mile across the fields, and in his condition he probably hadn't even noticed the cold.

But she did, and now she was shivering. She straightened up and moved toward the sink, catching a waft of alcohol on his breath. "Can I get you some coffee?" How silly did that sound?

"Forget it." He slammed the door shut, then grabbed her arm. "Come on." He hauled her into the dining room and thrust her into a chair. He stayed on his feet, pacing back and forth. "You talked to the cops," he said belligerently. "You just couldn't let it go, could you? Sticking your nose in it, and nagging, nagging. What'd she ever do to you?"

Should she apologize, try to placate him? He was swaying on his feet, sorrow and anger battling on his face. Would he even listen to anything she had to say? "Stephen, what are you talking about?" she said with a calm she didn't feel.

"At the meeting. You said Lucy killed Chandler, or near enough to it."

Lucy?

Stephen shook his head like a bull. "But she didn't. She didn't. I did."

Cinda. Lucinda. Lucy. *Oh damn.* Stephen was Cinda's accomplice. "I don't understand," Meg said, stalling. The police were on their way. Weren't they?

She shrank back into the chair as Stephen roared, "Bitch! You don't think I got the balls to do it? Nobody thinks I can do anything around here, starting with that big brother of mine. Always telling me what to do. Make an effort, Stephen. Get your act together. This is a good business, Stephen, if you'll just work at it. Goddamn plumbing! Like I want to spend my life diggin' through other people's shit." He approached her chair, leaned over her, bracing himself on the arms of the chair, his breath hot and sour in her face. "Well, I showed 'em. I killed Hale—me. Lucy didn't even know about it, till after."

Meg almost forgot Stephen's bulk hanging over her as she tried to digest what he had said. She'd been wrong; she'd been stupid. She'd been so focused on bringing Cinda down that she hadn't looked any further. Or maybe she hadn't wanted to. But by standing up and making her declaration in public, she'd brought this confrontation on herself. Stephen could quite easily kill her, just as he claimed to have killed Chandler. One blow was all it would take, and he looked all too ready to do it.

No. She was not going to let him kill her, not in her own house. He was hurt and angry, but he was sloppy drunk, and she knew the police were on their way. She had to stall, buy some time, just a few minutes ...

"Tell me what happened, Stephen," Meg said quietly.

Stephen lurched away from her, across the room, then turned again to face her. "Oh-ho, now you believe me? That's just swell, now that you've told the cops, and she's pretending she doesn't know anything. She knew, all right."

"You mean Cinda?" Meg prompted.

He shook his head. "No. Not Cinda. Lucy. She thinks Cinda sounds classier for business, but when it's just the two of us,

she's Lucy. She's the best thing that's happened to me in years
We got plans—I was gonna get my part of the money when the
town bought the land the business sits on, and then she was
gonna make sure I was one of the contractors for the construction. I'd have people working for me. Me! No more Seth bossing
me around."

What was she supposed to say? But apparently Stephen didn't
expect an answer, because he was still talking.

"It woulda been fine if you'da kept your damn mouth shut.
But no, you had to waltz in here and screw it all up. Why'ja have
to do that?" He looked ready to cry.

She had to keep him talking. What was taking the police so
long? "How did Chandler die?"

He ignored her question. "Ha! Damn good thing he's dead.
Don't know how he could have treated Lucy like he did—first he
keeps her on a string just so she could do his work for him, and
then he dumps her when he doesn't need her anymore. Mr. High
and Mighty. I was the one she came cryin' to. So I told him to
his face, he couldn't treat people like that. Bastard laughed
at me, told me to go home and sleep it off. I got the last laugh,
didn't I?"

"You talked to him, Stephen?" Meg said.

"I was at this Noho bar I go to, and I got to thinking about
how he'd treated Lucy bad, and I decided to tell him off."

After quite a few drinks, no doubt. "But, Stephen, how'd you
get into the hotel?"

"Worked a job there a couple of years back—I know where
the back doors are. I found his room, and I saw Lucy come out,
but she didn't see me. After she left, I banged on his door, told
him I needed to talk to him. He tried to shut the door on me, but I
was stronger. I told him he had to let Lucy work the project. Hell,
what did he need with this penny-ante job? He was the Boston
hotshot, right? But Lucy was gonna do a good job for Granford.
He wanted to ship her back to Boston, now that he was done with
her. After she'd done all the work. That wasn't right. So I kind of
threatened him." Stephen looked at her, as if begging her to understand.

Meg nodded her encouragement. "Go on. Then what?"

"He laughed at me. And I guess I kind of lost it then, 'cause the next thing I know, he's lying on the floor and he's not breathing."

Well, now she had a confession, even if it wasn't the one she had expected. Too bad no one else had been around to hear it. Where the hell were the police? "Stephen, that sounds like an accident. You didn't mean to hurt him."

He shook his head again, as if trying to clear it. He didn't pay any attention to what she had said. "All I wanted was a job that doesn't mean wallowing in shit. Enough money to make a new life. I want to be with Lucy. And now I can't, because of you. Why'd you do it? You coulda kept your mouth shut and nobody woulda known."

No way Cinda had planned a future with this sodden plumber, Meg thought. Not that she was about to tell him that. But Meg was willing to bet that Cinda had used him, fed him a line about how Chandler was mistreating her, about how handy it would be if Chandler was out of the way. And then Stephen had decided to play hero and had nearly blown everything for Cinda, when he confronted Chandler and Chandler ended up dead. No doubt Cinda had masterminded the cleanup—which meant that she'd been concealing evidence, interfering with an investigation, whatever. Or maybe Stephen was lying; maybe Cinda had witnessed the scene when drunken Stephen barged in and hit Chandler. That might explain her silence. She had wanted to deflect attention from the fact that she had been there at all.

But none of that mattered much at the moment. As Meg watched, horrified, she could almost see Stephen laboriously processing information in his liquor-fogged brain. All his dreams, crumbling—no land deal, no Lucy. And he blamed it all on her.

The anger flared again in his eyes. "You . . . you had to go and mess it up, didn't you? You couldn't take it that your boyfriend liked Lucy better than you. And then maybe she could be happy with me, while you still didn't have anybody. So you had to go blowing your mouth off, just to get back at her. But it didn't work, did it? Betcha the police didn't believe you. Nobody believes you. It's time you shut up. 'Poor Meg Corey, fell down her own cellar stairs.' Gotta watch them dark basements—bad lighting and all. I should know—I see plenty of 'em. With you gone, who's gonna point the finger at Lucy?"

The cellar door was only a few feet away. Meg stood up from the chair where Stephen had shoved her and backed away slowly, trying to keep the table between her and Stephen as he stumbled toward her. He was large, he was drunk, and he was mad as hell. Maybe he wasn't thinking clearly; maybe he had no plan. But it made no difference. He'd already killed once, so he didn't have much to lose. No way could she wrestle with him. Could she outrun him? *God, Meg, you're going to die here just because you wanted to clear your name and get to the bottom of this.* She took another step back and bumped into the wall.

Stephen kept coming.

29

"Stephen." The sound of Seth's voice halted Stephen in his tracks. Meg had been so focused on Stephen that she hadn't heard Seth come in, but by God, he was here now, big as life, standing in the kitchen doorway, with Art Preston behind him. "What are you doing?"

Stephen swung around to face him. "Well, if it ain't my big brother. Mr. Perfect. Hey, I'm just takin' care of business. Meg here's been spreadin' lies, and I had to set her straight."

"Back off, Stephen. We need to talk." Seth stepped into the room. For a moment the two brothers faced off, and Meg was struck by their similarities—and their differences. Stephen was like a blurry photocopy of Seth, both larger and softer than his older brother. Stephen was the first to back down, in the face of Seth's implacable stare, and he took a step back, then another, and his hands fell to his sides. Seth spared a quick glance for Meg. "You okay?"

Meg nodded, not trusting her voice. Seth turned back to his brother.

"Stephen, you've got to tell me straight: did you kill Hale?"

Meg watched expressions shift across Stephen's face. His defiance turned to fear, and then he morphed into a sulky little boy. "He was scum. He deserved to die, for what he wanted to do to Lucy."

Meg, leaning against the wall, saw Seth's face age ten years as he heard his brother admit to murder, and her heart ached for him. Preston raised an eyebrow at her, and she mouthed, "Cinda. Lucinda." She looked at Seth. "How'd you get here?"

"Went back to talk to Art, after I dropped you off. I heard the call come in and figured maybe I should tag along."

Preston was still focused on Stephen. "Stephen, let's take this down to the station."

"You arrestin' me?" Stephen seemed to swell, even as he swayed on his feet.

"Looks like it. Didn't we just hear you admitting to murder? Right, Meg?"

"Yes, Chief, Stephen told me that he killed Chandler Hale. But it sounded as though it might have been unintentional."

Preston nodded briefly. "I think we'll let Stephen sleep off whatever he's been drinking in a nice, cozy cell. We can sort out the details in the morning."

Preston put his hand under Stephen's elbow. "Come on, Stephen. Do I need to cuff you?"

Stephen rocked, confused, his gaze shifting from one person to another, and finally his shoulders slumped. "Nah. I'll come." He looked plaintively at Seth as the officer led him out, but Seth said nothing, his face stony.

As Preston turned to follow, he said, "Sorry, Seth. You better get him a lawyer."

Seth roused himself. "Thanks, Art. I'll do that. You going to have another talk with Cinda?"

"Guess I'll have to. I'll be talking with you in the morning, Meg. Seth, you coming?"

Seth didn't move. "No."

Preston gave Seth a long look, then escorted his prisoner out the back door, leaving Meg and Seth alone.

Meg remained frozen in place. It was over. She had been right about Cinda, but she'd also been wrong. She never would have pegged Stephen as Cinda's accomplice.

"I'm sorry," she whispered, aware of Seth watching her. She started shaking, and tears came from nowhere. And then Seth's arms were around her.

She had no idea how long she stood in the circle of Seth's arms, sobbing against his chest. She wasn't even sure who was comforting whom—he had to be hurting even more than she was. But she didn't want to move, and it was a long time before she could. Finally she disentangled a hand to wipe the tears off her face.

"Sorry."

"Meg, don't say that. You didn't do anything. Stephen did, the damn idiot."

"But you have to hate me. If I'd just kept my mouth shut . . ."

"No." His breath was warm against her hair. "If you hadn't said anything, Stephen would still be guilty. Or you would have ended up in jail. It wouldn't have fixed anything." He drew back slightly. "We could sit down, you know. You look like you're ready to fall over."

"I guess." He was right, she was exhausted. Stephen's invasion had been the last straw, and now she felt boneless, unable to think or to act. She let Seth lead her to the only remaining piece of furniture in the front parlor, a lumpy couch, and she fell onto it, leaning back against the cushions.

"I'm going to make you some tea," he said as he headed for the kitchen.

Meg watched him go. She should be the one doing that, in her own kitchen, but it was nice to be taken care of. Despite what Seth had said, she still felt horribly guilty. *Guilty about what, Meg? Well, it's quite a list.* About her long-ago decision to get involved with Chandler, when her heart really wasn't in it? About the way she had dealt with the split, or avoided dealing with it? About her poorly planned move to Granford? About trying to solve a murder? About hurting a man she cared about?

Whoa. Where had that come from?

Seth appeared in the doorway juggling a mug, a sugar bowl, and a cream pitcher, which he set down quickly on the floor by the couch. "Watch it—that's hot," he cautioned as he handed her the mug.

Meg grasped the mug and focused on adding sugar, happy to have an excuse not to speak for a few moments. But she couldn't stall forever. "Seth, I'm so sorry about this whole mess. I didn't think it through, I guess. I knew Cinda had to have had help if she killed Chandler, at least to get rid of the body, but I didn't really look too hard for a candidate. I still can't believe it."

"Believe it. I think Stephen's been looking for trouble for a long time. He doesn't pull his own weight at work, and he's got a huge chip on his shoulder—thinks I've had every advantage and he's gotten the short end of the stick. I let him get away with it. And I've known about his drinking problem for a while, and so has Art. But it's never gone past a couple of barroom brawls before this."

"It sounds as though he just wanted to threaten Chandler, not kill him. Maybe he did the deed, but I can't imagine that Cinda didn't encourage him somehow, and now he's convinced himself he did it for love. I can't believe she really cares for him, but she's good at getting what she wants from people. Let's hope this is the end of it. Although the project is probably going to suffer. Damn!" Meg sat back and drank some more tea, fighting another wave of tears.

"Meg, I know how hard the past couple of months have been for you, what with losing your job, and the house, even before ... Chandler's death. You put yourself in a difficult position, moving here, with nobody to lean on."

Meg nodded. "Maybe you're right. Heck, Art said the same thing, more or less. I didn't plan things very well, did I?"

"I've got to say it took guts to stand up in front of a room full of strangers and do what you did."

"Even if I was wrong?"

"You got some pieces right. Look, a lot of people would have said, 'It's not my business,' and walked away. But that would have been wrong."

"That's what I thought," Meg answered. "I just wanted to buy some time, to find out why Chandler died. I never meant ..." She set down the mug and laid her head back against the couch. She was tired to her very bones ...

30

Meg woke with a start to find light pouring into the room. What was she doing sleeping on the parlor couch? She shifted, then amended that thought: what was she doing here on the couch with Seth Chapin? He lay sprawled, half sitting, half reclining, and here she was, with her head on his chest, his arm around her. She lay still, trying to reassemble what had happened the night before. Pieces filtered back slowly: the Town Meeting, the police station, her return, and finding a belligerent Stephen in her home. And Seth's arrival, and the police, and...that's right, Seth had stayed on, after the chief had left. And he'd made her a cup of tea. He had every right to be angry at her, since she'd tossed a bomb into his life, but instead he had worried about her. Just like he worried about everyone else—his sister, the people of the town. Didn't anyone ever worry about Seth?

What would today hold? Obviously they were going to have to sort out the legalities with the police. Meg couldn't wait to hear Cinda's version of the story. No doubt she would pretend to be shocked and surprised—and would find a way to weasel out of any responsibility. Meg sat up cautiously, dislodging a crocheted afghan that Seth must have draped around her when she fell asleep. She had no idea where he had found it.

"Seth?" She gave his shoulder a gentle nudge.

Seth's eyes opened, and she watched him struggle to wake up. What would he remember first—Stephen's arrest or what had come after? She was rewarded with a smile. It didn't last, as the rest of yesterday's events caught up, but she had seen it. Then he, too, sat up quickly, as if unsure of his welcome. She almost laughed.

"It's okay, Seth. You didn't take advantage of me. In fact, I think I fell asleep on you. But I'm sure there will be a lot going on today. Can I make you breakfast?"

"Sounds good. Let me wash up."

"You know where the bathroom is."

Meg had done a hasty job of brushing her teeth and was sticking a pan of muffins in the oven when she was startled by a knock at the kitchen door. She opened it, and Rachel strode in.

"Do you know where Seth is? Somebody calls and tells me Stephen's in jail, and then Seth disappears, and his van's nowhere to be seen. Damn him, everything's falling apart," she said without preamble. Her hair was uncombed, and there were dark circles under her eyes.

"Sit down and have some coffee, Rachel," Meg said. "Seth's here. And I know about Stephen, because Art Preston picked him up here last night."

Rachel remained standing, tense. "Seth's here?" Her voice was shrill.

Seth chose that moment to appear. "Hey, Rachel. What're you doing here?"

"Playing catch-up, apparently. What the hell is going on?"

"Sit down. Have you had breakfast?"

"No, damn it! Will you just tell me what happened?"

Meg set a mug of coffee on the table near her, then retreated to lean on the stove as Seth said, "Rachel, I'm not going to talk to you until you sit down." Seth stared at his sister until she plopped into a chair like a sulky child, then resumed. "Stephen admitted to killing Chandler Hale. At the Town Meeting last night Meg stood up and more or less accused Cinda Patterson of murder, and then the meeting fell apart, and Art took Cinda and Meg back to the station to talk with them. Cinda stonewalled, and Art had nothing to hold her on, so he had to let her go. But when Meg came back here last night, Stephen was waiting for her. Luckily Art and I got here before he did anything stupid. But, Rachel, you've got to know, we all heard him confess. He was seeing Cinda, and he confronted Hale, and things went wrong."

Rachel was staring at her brother with shock. "Stephen and Cinda? And murder? No way. What the hell was he thinking?"

Seth shook his head. "That's the problem—he wasn't thinking. I don't think he meant to kill Hale. It sounds like it might have been an accident. Anyway, Art took him off to the jail to sober up, and I stayed with Meg, because she's had a hell of a time, and I wanted to be sure she was all right. And that's all I know. I assume we'll be talking to Art and Marcus this morning."

As Seth fell silent, Meg felt a pang. Where did Rachel's loyalties lie? With Seth or with Stephen? And where would Meg come out in the equation? She held her tongue and stayed put, watching Rachel.

Rachel stared into her coffee. She nodded once. "Damn. He really did it?" She looked at Seth, pain in her eyes.

He nodded. "Looks like it. But I'd be willing to bet he had some help with the aftermath, like getting rid of the body and getting the stories straight. He said he'd been drinking, and he's not very good at details under the best of circumstances. So I find it hard to believe that he managed to conceal all evidence of Chandler's death ..."

Meg finished the sentence for him. "Without help. Cinda. She's got the brains to handle it, and she was right there in the hotel. At least we've got her for something, like lying to the police or concealing evidence." Meg felt obscurely cheered by her own reasoning. "I'll bet he hoped she would thank him for eliminating Chandler."

"Did Seth and I get the only brains in the family? That idiot," Rachel burst out. "I'm sorry, Meg. You shouldn't have gotten dragged into our little drama. I love Stephen, but I'm not surprised. He's always thought he deserved more than he got, and he was always looking for a shortcut. I just never thought he could do anything like this. Poor Stephen."

Relief surged through Meg. Rachel didn't hate her. Maybe she could salvage something from the wreckage. She took her own coffee and sat at the table. "Rachel, I'd give anything if all this hadn't happened."

"I know. Just give me time to get used to it, all right? So, Seth, is there anything we need to do? Should I go see Stephen?"

"First things first. Eat breakfast. I'm going to get him a lawyer, and I'm sure they'll want Meg and me at the station sometime today. Other than that, there's not much to be done."

Rachel stood up. "Okay. In the meantime, I've got full bookings for tonight, so I guess I'd better go take care of business. Call me as soon as you know anything, Seth." She hugged him briefly, then she was gone, leaving Seth and Meg alone.

Seth spoke first. "She'll be okay with it. She knows it's nothing you did."

"I hope so. I can't afford to lose any friends right now."

"Don't worry, Meg. Rachel's good people."

"I know. But I'm worried about the rest of the town. So far they know me as 'the lady with the body' or 'the crazy lady who blew up the Town Meeting' or maybe 'the lady who shot down Granford Grange.' And now it's going to be 'the lady who sent Stephen Chapin to jail.'"

"Meg, it's Stephen's own fault that he's in jail. No one will think of you that way, at least, not if you stay around long enough for them to get to know you."

Meg wondered how to answer that, or if it was even a question. The silence swelled. Finally she said, "The muffins are about done. I'd better see about that breakfast I offered you."

31

After breakfast, Seth went home to change clothes, walking back over the hill to his place to clear his head, or so he said. Meg took a fast shower. She was downstairs wandering aimlessly from room to room while she waited, when Seth rapped at the front door.

"Art wants us. Can we take your car? The van's still at the police station."

"Sure. I'm ready." Meg found her purse and coat and joined Seth at the door, pulling it firmly closed behind her. She paused for a moment on the granite stoop.

Seth looked at her. "You up to this?"

"Hey, I'm looking forward to it. I can't wait to see how Cinda plays this out. Let's get it over with."

At the station, Art greeted them. "The detective's on his way to take custody of Stephen, and Cinda'll be here any minute." He led them together to the now-familiar interview room.

Meg smiled at him. "Can I take it I'm no longer a suspect?"

"What? Oh, no, sorry about that."

"What happens now?" Seth asked.

Art rubbed his hands over his face. His stubble suggested he hadn't gone home all night. "We should wait for Marcus—save time repeating everything. But I can tell you that Stephen has made a statement. He stuck to what he said to you last night, pretty much: he confronted Chandler, he didn't mean to kill him, and Cinda didn't know anything about it."

"Why am I not surprised?" Meg said.

"I've called a lawyer for him—old college buddy of mine," Seth added quickly.

"That's a good thing, Seth," Art answered. "I think Stephen

would say just about anything to make sure that Cinda stays out of it."

"And you don't believe him?" Meg asked.

Art shrugged. "Not for me to say. I probably shouldn't have said this much, and the detective'll have my head, but I thought you should know where we're at. Hell of a situation, isn't it?"

Cinda arrived promptly, but when she walked into the room, Meg thought that something had changed. She was still dressed in a power suit, but was it a bit wrinkled? Her hair was still sleek, but maybe a few strands had escaped her attention? And there was definitely a patch of skin on her chin that she had missed with her foundation. *Yes*, Meg thought, *Cinda is starting to fray around the edges.*

Cinda seemed surprised to find Meg and Seth in the room. "Why, Art, I thought you just wanted to talk with me?" She didn't greet Meg or Seth, acknowledging them only with a cool glance.

"Ms. Patterson." Art nodded her toward a chair. "We're waiting for the detective to arrive, so we might as well hold off on discussing anything until he gets here. We took Stephen Chapin into custody last night."

Cinda sat. "Really? Why?" she said cautiously.

"He killed Chandler Hale, or so he says."

To Meg's amusement, Cinda managed to look shocked. "That's terrible. Did he say what happened?"

"Ms. Patterson, it would be inappropriate of me to discuss any details at this time. Let's wait for Detective Marcus."

A charged silence fell. Meg and Seth exchanged glances, and Seth gave a small shrug. Meg had nothing to say. Maybe Art wanted to use the silence to make Cinda nervous. Or maybe he was just being careful.

Cinda kept checking her watch as they waited. Finally Meg couldn't stand it. "Do you have an appointment, Cinda?"

Meg's question appeared to startle her. "What? Oh, no. I just wish we could get this over with."

"Have you talked with your higher-ups at the bank yet?" Meg thought a question not related to the murder should be safe.

She was surprised by Cinda's reaction: she seemed to wilt. "I spoke with the division vice president before I left Northampton." She bit her lower lip, destroying her carefully applied lip gloss.

"And?" Meg prompted.

"He thinks that perhaps we should step back and reevaluate our options, due to the series of unfortunate incidents here in Granford." She sounded as though she was quoting.

So the bank was running scared, Meg thought, and might even withdraw from the whole Granford project. Not that she would blame them—there was too much negative publicity surrounding it now, and there were plenty of other small towns in this part of the state in need of economic stimulation. But what would happen to Cinda? Did Meg really care?

She looked up to see Detective Marcus striding into the room. He paused in the doorway, inventorying the people there. Art rose to greet him. "Marcus," he said.

The detective nodded. "Preston. You've got Chapin in custody?"

"I do. Picked him up last night, but he was three sheets to the wind at the time."

"Read him his rights?"

"I didn't arrest him—left that for you."

"He say anything?"

"He said plenty."

Meg, watching Cinda's face, noted that she had turned even paler behind her blotchy foundation.

"Then let's get this over with."

"Sure thing. I'll go get him." Art left the room. The detective turned and for the first time acknowledged that there were other people there. "Chapin, Ms. Corey, Ms. Patterson."

Cinda summoned up a smile. "Detective Marcus, I can't tell you how awful I feel about all this."

"And why would that be, ma'am?"

Cinda faltered. "Why, that Stephen killed Chandler, of course."

Meg could almost feel sorry for her. Clearly Cinda wasn't sure how much the detective knew or had been told, and she knew she was treading on thin ice.

Art reappeared with Stephen in tow. Stephen definitely looked the worse for wear this morning, his eyes bloodshot, his clothes rumpled. But his face brightened when he saw Cinda.

"Lucy! I told them the whole story. I told them it was me that did it, and you didn't have anything to do with it."

"Mr. Chapin," Cinda said, in an icy voice, "what else would you tell them? It's the truth. I had nothing to do with Chandler Hale's murder. Why would anyone think that?"

Stephen's face fell. He looked to the others for help and found none. Meg could almost see the gears turning in his head: Cinda was not going to acknowledge him. In fact, Cinda was going to put as much distance between them as possible. That had to hurt. Maybe Stephen had inherited some share of the Chapin intelligence, because his expression hardened. When he spoke again, he addressed the detective.

"Fine. Like hell, she had nothing to do with it. She was the one told me what to do with the body."

The detective swivelled toward Cinda. "Ms. Patterson, I think it might be a good idea if you came with me."

Cinda sputtered, "Can it wait, Detective? Because I really need to get back to my office in Boston, at least for a short while."

"No. This is a murder investigation, and I have some questions for you. And you might want to think about some of the answers you gave me the last time we talked." He nodded toward Art. "Preston, let's get this sorted out."

"Hang on a sec," Seth interrupted. "Stephen, you don't have to say anything. I've called a lawyer, and we'll meet you over at the county jail. Just keep your mouth shut until then, okay?"

Stephen looked dully at him. "Right. Sure."

The detective ignored Seth. He stared pointedly at Cinda until she realized he was waiting for her to leave the room first. When she stalked out, he followed, his hand on Stephen's arm, with Art bringing up the rear.

Meg turned to Seth. "What just happened here?" she asked.

"The district attorney will charge Stephen with the murder of Chandler Hale. It sticks in my mind that concealing evidence is some kind of felony, but I'm not sure what Marcus will want to do about Cinda. It's going to be pretty much Stephen's word against hers, unless someone saw them together hauling the body around. I'll make sure Stephen gets decent representation, for whatever good that will do."

Meg didn't know what to say. She was tired of saying, "I'm sorry," even though she was. Seth did not deserve this kind of trouble. Instead she asked, "What now?"

Seth sat back in his chair. "I want a word with Art when he's done. Did you want to go home now?"

"No, I'll wait. I'd like to hear what he has to say. Unless I'm not supposed to hear it?"

Seth shrugged. "I don't know. I'm not sure if you'll have to testify to anything." He lapsed into silence.

Fifteen minutes later Art returned, alone. He threw himself into a chair. "Damn, what a mess. Too bad it's Marcus handling it, but it can't be helped. Seth, if it's any consolation, I don't think Stephen meant to do any real harm."

Seth shook his head. "I doubt it. He just doesn't think, especially when he's been drinking. Did you get any more of the story?"

Art glanced briefly at Meg. "Some. He wasn't real coherent last night. We already knew that when Chandler went back to the hotel after that trip to the bar, Cinda joined him—purely for business purposes, or so she said. She came out sometime later, and Stephen was waiting the whole time, getting madder and madder. So when Cinda finally left—with that book—he barged in on Chandler. I'm guessing that Stephen pushed him or something, and Chandler hit his head and died—just plain bad luck. And make sure your lawyer friend knows that, Seth. That's gotta be involuntary manslaughter. But then he hid the body, which goes against him."

Seth nodded. "With Cinda's help, don't forget. I don't think Stephen can plan more than three minutes ahead."

Art rotated his neck to work out the kinks. "I'm pretty sure that if the detective checks his phone records, he'll find a call to Cinda's room just about then. Although Stephen probably came up with the idea of your septic tank."

"I wondered about that," Meg said. "I mean, why did he think that a body wouldn't clog up my plumbing?"

"Seth, you want to take that one?"

Seth laughed bitterly. "Told you he wasn't a very good plumber. He knew you were the only one using the system, so the volume would be pretty low. I'll bet he figured Chandler would rot, once the ground warmed up come spring, and nobody would be the wiser. As usual, he didn't think it through."

Meg shivered involuntarily at the image of Chandler rotting away outside her kitchen window. "Art, will Cinda be charged with anything?"

"That's up to the DA. But I'm guessing he'll find something. After all, she made him look like a fool, too."

Then Seth broke in. "Cinda and Stephen must have been seeing each other for a while, if Stephen was willing to go after Chandler for her."

"A few months, I gather. Not long after she arrived in town."

It took Meg a moment to do the math. "Wait a minute—you mean Cinda was sleeping with Stephen even before Chandler dropped her? What a . . ." Words failed her.

"Yeah, you have to admire her planning," Art said, with a barely suppressed smile.

At least Cinda was off the Granford Grange project—if there even was a project anymore. Whatever penalty Cinda faced, Granford faced a larger one. Meg couldn't think of anything else to say. She caught Seth's eye and raised an eyebrow, and he nodded. "I guess we should be going," he said.

Art stood up. "I'll let you know if I need anything from you, Seth. And, Meg? What you did at the meeting—that took guts. Maybe you didn't have all the facts right, but you certainly blew things wide-open. Sorry if we gave you a hard time." He extended his hand.

Meg stood up, too, and took it. "You were doing your job, Chief. I knew the evidence was shaky, so I can't blame you."

As they walked back to the lot, where Seth had left his van the night before, he was quiet. "You okay?" Meg asked.

He jerked out of his reverie. "Sorry. As good as can be expected. Just trying to sort through what jobs I've got lined up, what I can handle on my own. I'm going to need to find some help with the business, and fast."

"Oh. Right." The business was his livelihood, and his business partner was in jail. "I suppose I'd better get back to my to-do list." *After I take a long nap.*

"You've got a great house," Seth said, almost wistfully. "You know, it seems a shame for it to pass out of the family, after all this time."

"I'm not sure I am family."

"The sisters left the place to your mother, right? That makes you family. Fact is, most of the people in Granford are related, if you go back far enough. You and I are probably related somehow. Look, Meg . . ." He fumbled for words. "I don't know what your plans are, or were, or if they've changed. But I don't want you to judge Granford on what's happened in the last couple of weeks. If you give it a chance, you might like the place."

What was he saying? "Seth, with all that's happened lately, I haven't made up my mind about anything. And even you don't know what's going to happen with the town, now that it looks like the project may be dead. I'm sorry about that."

"We'll manage. We've survived for over two hundred years, right?"

Back at the house, after pushing the balky front door shut, Meg turned to survey her domain. The house was very quiet, a few dust motes dancing in the light from the windows. Her house. Her history—and now she had added an unexpected and unlikely new chapter. What would Lula and Nettie think about this turn of events?

What are you going to do, Meg?

The to-do list waited, and now she had to add getting her back-door lock replaced. But what was the point? She could pour more time and effort into the house, and increase the selling price by a few thousand dollars. But was it worth it?

"Yes."

The word echoed in the room, and Meg was surprised to realize she'd said it out loud. It was worth it, not because it made the house an easier sell, but because the house deserved it. It deserved someone who cared about it, and who would care for it. It had suffered neglect and abuse over the past few decades, waiting patiently for someone to recognize its worth. Waiting for her.

Meg sat down with a thump. How had that happened? When? Why?

She recognized now that she had retreated to Granford with her tail between her legs, and Granford had . . . well, not precisely welcomed her, but had let her be. Living in a small town was different than living in Boston—here everyone knew who you were and knew your history. How would they react, now that she had made a public fool of herself and trashed their economic prospects? Seth seemed to think that they'd forgive her.

And then there was Seth himself. He was no Chandler—thank heavens. Chandler had turned out to be the wrong choice, in so many ways. Maybe Seth wasn't even interested in a relationship. But he had offered friendship, had made her feel welcome, and then had stood by her when things had looked bad.

But what about her career? Or, if career was too grand a term, what the heck was she going to do to support herself? High school, college, MBA, one job, then another—she had always been focused, directed, determined. And look where that had landed her: no job, no relationships, no fixed home. Maybe it was time to reconsider her strategy.

Maybe what she had thought was a temporary diversion had become something more. Did she want to stay, in the house, in the town? She was surprised to find that she did, in spite of all that had happened. Now all she had to do was figure out how to make that possible.

She had a lot to think about.

32

In the end, the decision was easier than she had expected.

Meg spent the next few days scraping, sanding, painting, and thinking. She sought out no one's company, and, blessedly, nobody hounded her, as if they sensed she was in hibernation, something that required time and solitude.

Rachel was the first to break Meg's self-imposed exile. She showed up one afternoon at Meg's front door.

Meg pulled open the door—now planed into submission—with a smile. "Come on in. You want some coffee?"

"Sure." Rachel followed her, and in the kitchen held out a bag that smelled of cinnamon and apples. "Peace offering. More muffins."

Meg set a mug of coffee on the table in front of her. "Hey, you don't have anything to apologize for. I'm the one who should be apologizing. Rachel, I'm sorry about Stephen. If I had known he was involved, from the beginning ... well, I don't know what I would have done. I started out just to clear my own name, and things kind of happened from there."

Rachel stared into the depths of her coffee. "I know. I just needed some time to get my head around it all."

"I can imagine. Listen, can I ask you something?"

"Sure. What?"

"I think I want to stay in Granford."

"You mean, live here, in the Warren house?"

Meg nodded. "I think so. But I don't want to do that if the entire county is going to shun me. And I'm not sure I know the rules for small-town living. Do you think people are going to be willing to forgive and forget?" *Are you willing?*

Rachel was silent for a few moments. "Have you talked to Seth?"

"No. I figured he had enough to worry about."

"Ha." Rachel laughed shortly, but she didn't look as tense. "Sorry—that's not your fault. There's just a lot of stuff going on, with Stephen, and the plumbing business, and the town . . ."

Rachel was looking out the kitchen window, unseeing. She didn't speak for a while, but then she seemed to come to some sort of decision, and she turned to Meg. "I'm sorry, Meg. I know all this can't have been easy for you. It's been difficult for all of us."

Meg waited for Rachel to continue.

"We had one of those picture-perfect childhoods, you know? Mom and Dad, three kids, stable home life, supportive community. All the good stuff. But kids are different, and different kids react in different ways to the same environment. Seth—he's the big brother, the leader. The responsible one. Smart, funny, nice—all-around good guy, you know? And you've probably heard that he took over the business when Dad couldn't keep it up any longer, and he made it work, took on Stephen as a partner. Even though he had his doubts about Stephen, he did it. Family came first.

"Me, I was the middle kid, the only girl. I worshiped Seth. I wasn't as smart or as popular as he was, but he was always nice to me, looked out for me. We get along fine.

"Stephen came along a few years later—Mom lost a baby between me and him. And things were different then—Mom and Dad were older, they knew Stephen was the last baby, there was a little more money. Okay, they spoiled him, but not much. Thing is, Stephen . . . heck, I'm not sure how to describe it. At school he was always in Seth's shadow—you know how it goes, 'Oh, you're Seth Chapin's little brother, eh?' But he was never as good in classes or in sports or in anything else, really. And the folks never really pushed him, so he sort of drifted along. Somewhere along the way he developed this chip on his shoulder, like somebody owed him something, and it only got worse after Dad died and he had to work with Seth. Please, don't get me wrong. I love both my brothers. It's just, sometimes I have to work harder to *like* Stephen."

Meg nodded her encouragement, afraid to break the flow of Rachel's words.

Rachel went on. "I knew he was slacking off at the business, not that Seth complained. And I know he's had ... trouble with women. I don't pry, but he's been in and out of relationships most of his adult life. He tells us one story, and then I hear something different from somebody else. I guess if this smart, pretty woman from Boston showed up and came on to him, he might go along with just about anything. So Cinda used him. I buy that. But murder? I'm still having trouble with that idea, even though everything points that way."

Meg let go of a breath she hadn't known she was holding. "Rachel, I don't blame you. I wouldn't want to believe it either. To be fair, I don't think he planned it. I think it's just one of those awful, stupid things that happens. Stephen might not have gone to Northampton that night. Or he could have been too drunk to do anything, and Chandler would have called security at the hotel and had him thrown out. Any number of other possibilities. And I wish—I *so* wish—that I hadn't been the one to drag all this into the open, and hurt you, and Seth."

Rachel shook her head. "I know. It's not your fault. Hey, I'm just mad at the universe. It's a whole new world, having a brother who's been accused of murder." She summoned up a smile. "So, look, if you're staying around, how do you plan to support yourself? I mean, you're not independently wealthy, are you?"

"No way. Although my mother and I had agreed to share the proceeds on the house when it sold. Except if I don't sell it, there goes that. But, I've been thinking ... Rachel, what about the orchard?"

"What about it?"

"Well, if the development project isn't going to go ahead, then it's still mine, and I'm told it still produces a decent crop. Is that enough to live on?"

Rachel considered this. "I really don't know, but I won't say no right off. Maybe. You own the house, so no rent or mortgage. But you've still got to pay your expenses, taxes, that kind of thing. Isn't there someone at the university you could talk to?"

"There is, and I plan to. But am I crazy to even think about it? I mean, I have a degree in finance, not agriculture."

"But you're smart, and you can learn. If you want to. And you're the only one who can decide that."

"What about the rest of Granford?"

"Give them some credit, Meg—they aren't stupid. Stephen was one of their own, and Cinda managed to lead him around by his ding-dong. You had nothing to do with that. And there are other things ... No, I'll let Seth talk to you about that. So I say, if you really want to try, go ahead. Give it a couple of years and see how it goes. If it doesn't work out, you can always go back to Boston or go somewhere else."

"Rachel, I like the way you think."

Another knock on the door, this time the back one. Meg got up to let Seth in. "Come on in," she said. "Have some coffee. Have a muffin—Rachel brought them."

"Thanks." Seth carefully scraped the mud off his shoes before entering the kitchen. "Hi, Rachel."

"Were your ears burning, brother of mine? We were just talking about you. Oh, and the orchard. Meg's thinking of working it commercially."

Seth helped himself to a mug of coffee and sat down. "Great idea. Of course, maybe it's selfish of me to say so ..." He and his sister exchanged a conspiratorial glance.

"What?" Meg demanded.

"Looks like the development project's going to go forward, but on a more limited basis, without Puritan Bank. But their proposal got us thinking. In the long run, I'm not sure it would have passed a vote—the whole thing was too glitzy, too impersonal. Not a good fit for Granford. But it forced the town to take a hard look at some basic economic issues, and I think there's a consensus now that we need to do something to generate revenue. I've been talking to people, and I think we could put together a more modest project, using local funders and developers. Wouldn't pull in as much money, but it would help. And Puritan Bank's already done all the analysis and proved it could work."

"That's great! But, where would it go?"

"Don't worry—not on your orchard. But I'm willing to sell

my land, and I've talked to the other owners along the highway, so I think we could put together a good parcel."

"Your land? But what about your business? Where would you go?"

He shot another glance at Rachel. "That's another thing I've been thinking about, now that Stephen's pretty much out of the picture. You know it was my dad's business, and I joined him out of college, took over when he died?"

"Yes, Rachel told me. You don't want to keep it going?"

Seth smiled into his coffee cup. "To be honest, no. Not that plumbing isn't a good and honest profession, and it pays well. But over the past few years, I've found that I'm less interested in that and more interested in restoring old houses."

"Ah. So that's why you hang out at salvage places?"

"Yup. So I've been thinking, instead of relocating the plumbing business, maybe I could make a lateral move into renovation. I'd need to hire some people to cover the stuff I don't know, like finish carpentry, and I could still do the plumbing stuff, but the emphasis would be different."

"I think it's a great idea," Meg said firmly.

"I'm glad you think so, because I'll need a new space, if our land's gone. A place to work from and storage space for equipment, tools—and salvage. And you've got this barn, right?"

It took Meg a moment to figure out what he meant. "You want to use my barn? You'd probably have to shore it up, and put in lighting and heat, but I could cut you a good deal if you wanted to take it over."

"You'd have to put up with me in your backyard, and a lot of coming and going. Could you handle that?"

"I think so. And"—now that she'd started the ball rolling, ideas were popping into her head faster and faster—"I've been wondering how to support myself, if I'm really going to give this orchard thing a go. But if the town's putting together a local development project, I can help with the financial side. For a fee, of course." She grinned.

Seth smiled back. "That would be good. We could use the help. So you're okay with the barn thing?"

"Definitely." Meg raised her mug. "To a new and successful partnership."

*   *   *

Given the way her karma was working today, Meg was not surprised to see Christopher's van pass by not long after Seth had left. The very person she needed to talk to, to put her plan in motion. She grabbed her coat and headed up the hill to intercept him.

When she reached the ridge line, she waved to him. He turned and smiled, waiting for her to approach.

"You've heard that the project fell through?"

Christopher beamed. "I did. I must say I'm pleased, although I know the town may suffer for it."

Meg smiled. "Don't worry—there are other plans afoot. But I wanted to talk to you about the orchard."

"Yes?"

"Christopher, I've decided I don't want to sell this place." *Wow*, Meg thought, *I've gone from thinking about it to stating it as a fact, in the space of a day.* What would her mother say? "Which means, I think, that I'm going to need the income from the orchard. And I'm going to need some help running it, because I know next to nothing about orchard management."

"Dear lady, I think that's a wonderful idea—as long as the university may continue to use it for research purposes?"

"Of course—as long as what you do doesn't hurt my crop."

"Then we'll have no difficulty there. And, as for the management . . ."

"Yes?" Meg prompted.

"I think you would do well to hire an orchard manager."

"Christopher, I don't know if I can pay anyone to do anything right now."

"The person I have in mind . . . well, it's a complicated situation, but I think you might be able to work out some sort of arrangement with her—perhaps if you offered a living space, or a share of the profits. She's a student of mine, but she'll be graduating at the end of the school year, and she wants to stay in this area."

"Then let's talk to her. I trust your judgment."

"Grand! Well, then, I look forward to a fruitful collaboration."

"Christopher, that's a terrible pun, but I like the sentiment. So, where do we start?"

"Well, let me introduce you to the rest of your trees, shall I?"

As they walked the rows of still-bare trees, Meg felt a surge of hope. Maybe she could do her part to keep Warren's Grove—and Granford—alive. And then she tuned back in to Christopher's enthusiastic explanations.

"What we need to do next is ..."

The World of Apples

Apples have been part of this country's history from the beginning. The first European settlers found the native crab apples inedible and quickly sent for apple supplies: the earliest orchard in the colonies was planted in Boston in 1625. Apples were a part of everyday life, and almost every household had one or more trees on their property, using apples for eating, baking, and cider making. And cider vinegar was an essential preservative for our ancestors' food.

American school children grow up with the story of Massachusetts-born John Chapman, better known as Johnny Appleseed, but he was more than an eccentric wanderer scattering seeds. In fact, he was a shrewd businessman who acquired his seeds from the discards of commercial cider makers and established his own orchards to provide an ongoing source of new seeds and cuttings. He distributed apple varieties over a wide area for many years.

Apples have a funny habit of propagating themselves, constantly creating new varieties in the wild, even today. While modern commercial orchardists have focused their efforts on a very limited number of apple types, emphasizing yield and efficiency of production, many of the older varieties survive here and there, if you know where to look. The New York State Agricultural Experiment Station in Geneva, New York, is keeping the wealth of varieties alive, with over 2,500 examples.

Apple names recall their long history and even hold a touch of romance: Belle de Boskoop, Cornish Gilliflower, Hubbardston Nonesuch, Knobbed Russet, Pitmaston Pineapple, Sheepsnose, and Westfield Seek-No-Further—all link us to the long and diverse history of the apple.

There is no one perfect apple. Some make delightful eating (Baldwin, Fuji, Gala, HoneyCrisp, Braeburn), others work well for succulent pies (Cortland, Jonathan, Granny Smith, Winesap, Rome Beauty), and still others are bitter on the tongue but make great cider.

If you would like a charming glimpse into the diversity of apple varieties, please seek out Roger Yepsen's small illustrated book titled simply *Apples*. It is both delightful and useful reading.

Apple Recipes

Caneton aux Pommes et Poivre Vert
(Duck with Apples and Green Peppercorns)

One duck, fresh if possible, or four duck breasts or thigh pieces
Kosher salt
Pepper
1 tablespoon olive oil
1 large tart apple, such as Granny Smith, Cortland, or Braeburn
2 tablespoons preserved green peppercorns (You may substitute
    dried peppercorns, but soak them first to soften.)
2 medium shallots, thinly sliced
2 teaspoons finely chopped fresh rosemary leaves
1 cup hard cider (You may substitute fresh cider.)
2 teaspoons honey
1 teaspoon cider vinegar

Preheat the oven to 300°.

If you are using a whole duck, divide into quarters (removing the backbone). Score the skin and fat of the duck pieces without cutting into the flesh. Season with salt and pepper.

In a large ovenproof saute pan or skillet (into which you can fit a rack), heat the olive oil over medium-high heat, about 2 to 3 minutes. Sear the duck pieces, skin side down, for about 4 to 5 minutes, without moving.

Transfer the duck pieces to a plate and pour off the fat from the pan. Place a rack in the pan, and set the duck pieces on the rack, skin side up. Place in the oven and roast for approximately 45 minutes or until the duck is medium rare or registers 165° on an instant-read thermometer. Set the duck pieces aside to keep warm while you make the sauce.

Core but do not peel the apple and slice ⅛ inch thick. Pour off all but 1 tablespoon of the fat from the pan, then place the pan on the stove over medium heat. Add the apple slices and peppercorns and cook, turning occasionally, until the apples are golden, about 5 minutes. Add the shallots and rosemary and cook, stirring, until the shallots soften, about 2 minutes. Add the hard cider and increase the heat until the mixture comes to a simmer, and simmer for 4 to 5 minutes. Stir in the honey and cider vinegar, and simmer for another minute. Adjust seasoning to taste.

Serve the duck pieces topped with the apples and sauce.

Rachel's Apple Muffins

> 1¼ cups milk
> 1½ cups whole-bran cereal (You may substitute 3 cups corn flakes
>   or 2 cups instant oatmeal.)
> ¾ cup finely diced tart apples
> 2 tablespoons plus ⅓ cup sugar, divided
> ½ teaspoon cinnamon
> 1½ cups all-purpose flour
> 1 teaspoon salt
> 3 teaspoons baking powder
> 1 egg, beaten
> ¼ cup melted shortening or vegetable oil

Preheat the oven to 400°. Grease muffin tins for 12 muffins or line with baking cups.

Combine milk and cereal in a large mixing bowl.

Sprinkle the diced apples with 2 tablespoons sugar and the cinnamon and toss lightly.

Sift together ⅓ cup sugar, flour, salt, and baking powder.

Add egg and melted shortening to the milk and cereal, and stir in apples. Add the dry ingredients all at once. Mix only until the dry ingredients are moistened. Batter will be lumpy.

Fill greased/lined muffin tins two-thirds full. Bake for 20 to 25 minutes. If you like, you may dip the warm muffins in cinnamon sugar.

Aunt Nettie's Apple Goodie

¾ cup sugar
1 tablespoon flour
½ teaspoon cinnamon
Pinch salt
4 cups sliced apples

TOPPING
½ cup oatmeal
½ cup brown sugar
½ cup flour
¼ cup butter
⅛ teaspoon baking soda
½ teaspoon baking powder

Preheat oven to 375°.

Combine sugar, flour, cinnamon, salt, and sliced apples. Place in greased baking dish.

Mix together topping ingredients to make crumbs and sprinkle over apples.

Bake for 35 or 40 minutes until brown and bubbly.

Apple Pie á la Grace Paley
This recipe was inspired by the poem "The Poet's Occasional Alternative" by Grace Paley.

1 cup dried apricots
*2 cups apples, peeled and sliced (Choose a variety of apple that
    cooks well, such as Braeburn, Cortland, or Granny Smith.)*
1 cup dried cranberries
¼ cup sugar
2 tablespoons flour
*A double pie crust (top and bottom) of your choice, unbaked—
    homemade or purchased*
2 tablespoons butter

Preheat the oven to 400°.

Soak the apricots in boiling water to soften. Drain well and
pat dry.

Pare, core, and thinly slice the apples. Mix together the apple
slices, apricots, cranberries, sugar, and flour.

Line a 9-inch pie plate with one crust and fill with the apple
mixture. Dot with butter. Cover with the second crust and crimp
the edges. Cut vents on the top for the steam to escape.

Bake at 400° for 15 minutes. Reduce the temperature to 350°
and continue baking for another 45 minutes. If the crust appears
to be browning too quickly, cover loosely with foil.

**You may vary the filling by adding a peeled, sliced quince if
you can find one. This gives the filling a lovely silky quality.**

Fresh Apple Cake

1½ cups vegetable oil

2 cups sugar

3 eggs

3 cups all-purpose flour

1 teaspoon baking soda

2 teaspoons cinnamon

½ teaspoon nutmeg

½ teaspoon salt

3 cups shredded apples (Do not peel—the skin adds texture to the cake; the shredding disk of a food processor works very well.)

2 teaspoons vanilla extract

GLAZE

2 tablespoons butter

2 tablespoons brown sugar

2 tablespoons granulated sugar

2 tablespoons heavy cream

¼ teaspoon vanilla extract

Preheat the oven to 325°. Butter and flour a 9- or 10-inch tube pan (8-cup capacity).

Combine oil and sugar in a bowl. Blend very well. Add eggs, one at a time, beating well after each addition. Sift together the flour, baking soda, cinnamon, nutmeg, and salt. Sift these into the oil-egg mixture and combine thoroughly. Add the raw apples. Mix well with a spoon or spatula, then add the vanilla. Pour the batter into the pan.

Bake for 1¼ hours, or until the cake tests done (tester comes out clean). Remove from the oven and let rest while you prepare the glaze.

Glaze: Melt the butter, sugars, and heavy cream mixed with vanilla in a heavy pan. Boil for 1 minute without stirring, then remove from heat.

Let the cake cool for a few minutes before removing it from the pan. Spoon the glaze over the cake while it is still warm.

This is an excellent party cake, as it travels well and stays moist. You may also cut the recipe in half.